Cold Cases and Dark Secrets

J.M. Dabney

Hostile
WHISPERS PRESS

COLD CASES AND DARK SECRETS

J.M. DABNEY

HOSTILE WHISPERS PRESS, LLC

For my readers who make telling my stories worth it.

COLD CASES AND DARK SECRETS

COLD CASE UNIT BOOK 2

Time Didn't Heal All Wounds, and the Scars were About to be Ripped Open

Stevenson

When I'd moved from Homicide to the Cold Case Unit my friends headed, I'd thought it would be a new start. The minute my marriage fell apart, I'd lost my purpose. Years passed, and I hadn't found myself until I'd helped my friends catch a serial killer, but I'd also found friends and family. As I'd searched for a case among dusty boxes, a decades' old murder and missing person case caught my attention. The autopsy report sent me to the ME's office and the man I'd avoided for months.

Doc

Making death my job didn't allow for normal friends, but the dead needed an advocate, and it was the only purpose I'd known. Being a medical examiner was all I'd had for decades, and I didn't know what to do outside my job. I had a group of friends, all worked in law enforcement and forensics, but one thing was missing. Short, adorable middle-aged men weren't getting swept off their feet. When my secret crush needed my help with a case, to the detriment of my sanity, I said yes. All I had to do was not be my weird self and blurt out everything in my head.

When a missing person case turns out to be more than it appears, can Stevenson keep Doc safe from a twenty-year-old threat?

STEVENSON

COLD CASE
UNIT

This wasn't the life I'd chosen when I decided I wanted to be a homicide detective, and I gave all that up to move to the Cold Case Unit with my so-called friends. At forty-three years old, I was a slightly overweight divorced gay man living in a studio apartment with secondhand furniture and my belongings in two totes five years later, and my fridge was a biohazard zone I hadn't opened in months because I was never home.

I crossed and uncrossed my ankles where I had my boots propped on my desk as I randomly checked the inventory of cases. I heard a groan and leaned to the side to peer through the spaces in the shelves to find the faint outline of Detectives Remy and Robert Kauffman making out in their favorite corner. I hated them. Okay, maybe not hate—I was envious.

We'd worked together for years in Homicide until a shooting had put Robert on desk duty in Cold Case. Remy had decided to follow him. A long-ignored serial killer case brought them all back together. They'd decided to stay, and me and a pain in the ass Detective Graves had transferred. During the investigation into the serial killer, Fellows, we'd become friends—something I'd sorely lacked.

I straightened and closed my eyes, flipped the pages on the clipboard, and dropped my index finger. As I opened my eyes, I noted a homicide and missing persons case. I repeated the number as I tossed the board aside and got up. I checked the rows until I found the one I needed.

The case was from nineteen-ninety-seven. The file box hadn't looked like it had moved since it wound up in the dungeon as Cold Case was affectionately called. I carried it back to my desk, still ignoring the newlyweds. They had a kid at home, and who knew what that did to a parent's sex life.

I placed the box on my desk and removed the lid. I slipped out the too-thin file and groaned. Of course, I'd pick the case the detectives didn't bother to investigate. A lot of the evidence was marked as untested. A rape kit was performed during the post-mortem, but no notes on if it was run or not. Shit, Coleman, that bastard of a Lab Supervisor didn't do his job unless you threatened his life.

I scanned the autopsy report and groaned, seeing the name signed at the bottom. Doctor Morgan Warner. I'd known him well enough to ask questions until the serial killer case I worked on, and he'd been hands-on. He was an adorable little menace, and he put me on edge. I couldn't get a read on him. Yet he had a long memory, and if I wanted information on this case, I needed to visit the coroner's office.

"I'm headed to the ME's office."

"Say hi to Doc for us," Remy yelled. I took the file, grabbed my jacket, and left the dusty office and storage room.

The ME's office was over near the hospital with one of the old precincts before the city had turned the building into the new lab building. I walked out of the underground parking to my personal truck since it was close to the time for me to clock out. It was weird not to be on duty twenty-four-seven. Unless we were actively pursuing new evidence, we just did a lot of follow-ups.

When I moved to Cold Case, I was shocked to find a lot of the cases were familiar over my twenty years as a cop. I'd joined the academy a year after I'd graduated pre-law. A year of law school showed me it wasn't really my calling. My parents were disappointed, and I don't think they'd gotten over that failure yet. My sexuality was the next greatest failure as well. They really had a list they brought up every Sunday dinner until I'd stopped going altogether until my mother would guilt me into attending.

When I pulled into the parking lot, I didn't see Doc's cute little hybrid in his parking spot. The guy never missed work. I parked in his spot since it was the closest one open. I grabbed the file and hopped out of my truck. Visiting the medical examiner wasn't my favorite part of the job. Who the hell liked to watch the weird ghouls cut into people? Doc barely batted an eyelash, talking like he didn't have a body part in his hands.

The automatic sliding doors to the morgue opened, and I paused just inside. I rolled my lips between my teeth to hide my grin at finding Doc standing on a stepping stool. His lab coat hung down to his knees because he refused to wear a smaller size.

"What do I owe for the pleasure of one of my favorite Cold Case Detectives visiting my lair?"

I snorted at his impression of a mad scientist as he kept on working. I'd expect someone who dealt in death and tragedy all the time to have less of a sense of humor. Maybe it was a defense mechanism? I used sarcasm and jokes, occasionally some playful flirting, to manage my job stress.

"I chose a case at random, missing person and homicide. Your name was on the autopsy report."

"Name?"

"Angela Barnes, twenty-two, murdered. Aiden Maxwell, eight, Barnes's half-brother, missing."

"That was a particularly vicious one. Angela was disemboweled. Numerous defensive wounds. She fought like

3

hell. From the crime scene photos, it appeared she'd tried to save her brother even after the fatal wounds were inflicted."

"How do you remember that just from a name?"

"Eidetic memory aka photographic memory, but there's a controversy if photographic is real or not. Whatever. I remember almost everything I've seen or heard."

"You're a genius?"

"I hate that term even if it applies in the conventional sense. So, you've taken on the Barnes-Maxwell case?" He stepped down, and as he removed his gloves, he walked around the table to cross the room to his desk. He removed his paper cap to expose slightly matted thick silver hair that had recently gone from shaggy to framing his softly rounded face.

"I don't know. Like I said, I chose at random and wanted your opinion."

"Why didn't you ask the lovebirds?" He grinned up at me.

"No, those two were making out in a corner, and I wasn't interrupting that."

"Yeah, our poor Roo is starting school next fall. Well behind her classmates, and she's a bit out of sorts. Her nightmares are increasing in frequency."

"Do you know everything?"

"Vega and I babysat her the other night…full sleepover with all the sugar a five-year-old could want." He answered me as he took a swig off a too-large can of energy drink.

"You three on sugar terrifies me." Vega was a forensic genealogist who Remy and Doc had known forever.

"There definitely should've been spanking warnings for Vega and myself, but since Cash is Vega's Little and submissive, she took advantage of a free-for-all."

I shook my head thinking about the six-foot *butch* being the five-foot menace's submissive in anyway, but it took all kinds.

"So, what's your opinion on the case?"

"Swept under the rug. Barnes was her brother's guardian

while her mother was in prison. After three months of investigation, nothing panned out, and it was moved to the dungeon. From the toxicology run, she had no drugs or alcohol in her system. No signs of sexual assault, but I sent swabs to be tested anyway on the off-chance she'd had recent sexual activity, and we could match it to someone in the system."

"You're amazing."

"I know." His bratty smirk and attitude came out full force.

"None of the tests were run, and all the evidence in the case still had the original seals in place."

"Not shocking. Coleman runs that lab like an old-school boys' club. If you're not rich and white, you're not right."

"Wow, bitter there." But I didn't blame him. It wasn't a secret that Coleman was biased, and a lot of law enforcement wondered how he kept his job so long.

"You want to know bitter, talk to his now fourth ex-wife. The information ex-wives impart is a gold mine, I tell you. They have their own *we hate Coleman* club. They have weekly meetings."

"And how would you know that?"

"Now, now, Detective, some secrets are meant to be guarded until the time is appropriate for using them to get what someone wants."

"Devious."

"I know. It's one of my finer qualities." He winked and grinned. He kneeled in his chair with his ankles crossed beneath him as he rested his chin in his upraised hand.

"So, you think I should investigate?"

"The case is twenty-five years old, improper storage of evidence and forensics, probably extremely compromised."

"So is that a yes or a no?"

"Do it. I know the mother still called the old detective until he retired. He didn't return her calls and the only time he did speak with her was if he was at his desk when she made contact. The other detective on the case retired four years ago."

"Again, how do you know everything?"

"Listen, I'm the weird, adorable five-five ghoul in the basement. People talk around me like I don't exist, hence all the intel I get. There is something about the case that always set wrong with me. I chalked it up to a murder-kidnapping, the father of Aiden was interviewed and cleared, but I sensed he knew more than he wanted to admit. No buccal swabs were taken to compare DNA found at the scene."

I opened the file and scanned the reports, and made a mental note of the location. "That's in the middle of the strip."

"It is. So when Angela was found, they assumed what most cops would. Client attacked her for whatever reason. After further investigation and social services inquiries about Aiden's whereabouts, they did a half-assed job at best trying to locate him even though there were child-sized shoe prints in blood at the scene. If you talk to the mother, she may have more for you. Also, I think Roo's caseworker, Fran, may be able to help you, too."

"You want to talk to Coleman for me?"

"You're extremely handsome, Detective Stevenson, but what's in it for me to talk to our resident bigot?"

"You name it, and it's yours."

"What if I have extremely expensive tastes?"

"Within reason, it's yours."

"Deal, but I'm holding onto that favor until later. I currently have no needs that need to be filled."

I snorted at his bratty batting of his lashes and shook my head. What had I signed up for? I'd learned enough about Doc while working the serial case with him that there was more to the senior medical examiner than most people looked for. Figuring out what about him put me on edge had proved fruitless. He wasn't my type, and bratty men weren't exactly my thing either. I didn't know, but maybe I started to reevaluate my life when two of my closest friends hooked up and made it work. I'd dated my ex-husband for almost seven years, married for one before he'd told me he no longer found me attractive. That didn't hurt the old ego much.

"Thanks for the info. You think of anything else, will you let me know?"

"Of course, I have to finish this autopsy, and then Vega's coming to pick me up."

"Sleepover?"

"Sort of, my car was due for service. They said it would be ready tonight and I could pick it up in the morning. Vega's giving me a lift. She is *not* a morning person, so I'm spending the night to hopefully ease her normal murderous morning rage."

"Behave."

"Want to keep me in line, Detective?"

"I don't think I could handle you, Doctor."

"Shame." His heavy sigh was cute.

I said my goodbyes and made the decision to go back to the unit to check the rest of the information from the case file to take home to go over. Figure out who to call and see if the mother's contacts were in the box. Maybe I should've done a second random selection. Yet each case I'd looked at was one dead end after another. Remy claimed all of law enforcement was biased in some way. I'd assumed the same thing but hadn't learned its full scope until we worked the Fellows' serial murderer case. I just wondered how many brick walls I would run into before I either exhausted all avenues or found the piece of evidence that proved the other detectives' laziness.

2

DOC

COLD CASE
UNIT

W hen you're considered weird, you could get away with all kinds of behavior, but it was so much better being surrounded by other odd people because you could pretend you're normal. At least, that's what I'd always loved to tell myself. I sat on my friend Vega's back deck as we stared up at the sky. She was like me, gifted and unusual, but she played hers up as a positive. And me, well, I hid that I'd graduated medical school at nineteen and turned into a medical examiner instead of what my parents wanted me to be, a cardiologist or some well-respected specialist of some kind.

They were the top surgeons in their chosen fields. Dad was a plastic surgeon, and Mom a cardiologist. They traveled all over the world teaching in front of crowded classrooms between running their own lucrative practices. And there I was, lusting after a cuddly potential Daddy who had no interest in me. He was handsome with his honey-blond hair, lines beside his eyes, and the soft belly that rounded the front of his dress shirts. Stevenson always had mischief in his blue eyes, teasing and carefree. Which was odd for a man who worked Homicide for so long.

That afternoon when he'd shown up, I'd known who was there instantly. It was as if I had Stevenson radar. He'd stood there watching me for a few minutes, and I'd tried to sneak looks from under my lashes. I'd studied his expression, tried to determine if he had any interest in me at all, but his actions and expression all told me he saw me as an acquaintance, a friend at best. That was a well-placed kick in the balls.

"Talk to Mami. What's wrong, Doc?"

"As cute as you are, Mamis aren't my thing."

"Shut up. You know what I meant, brat."

"Stevenson came down to the morgue today."

"Ah, the hot, blond detective with unknown Daddy potential. Did you try to jump him?"

"Of course I didn't. I'm more than a decade older than him, and who wants an old Little?"

"You're not an old Little. Cash is older than me, and I'm her Dominant and Mami. It's all a state of mind, and you know that."

I sighed as I turned my head to find her watching me. "I know, Vega. But every birthday past forty, and you're farther out to pasture. Don't get me started on my diminutive size and weird personality."

"Your personality is adorable."

"Adorable…middle-aged men aren't supposed to be adorable." I pouted and threw a mini tantrum.

"Again, you're letting society's pressures on what and who we're supposed to be, mire you in some archaic system of propriety. Older Littles and Submissives and younger Daddies and Dominants are a thing. Gay culture has decided if you're above a certain age or Body Mass Index, then you're less than. It's bullshit, and you're smart enough to know it."

"Fuck, I know. But knowing and accepting are two different things, especially when it comes to the practice of said theory. Also, I involuntarily flirted, and he rolled his eyes at me." That was such a mood killer there.

"I don't even know why you set your sights on him in the first place. Davian would be a totally better bet."

"Davian is a complete bottom with no interest in me as anything other than a friend. It's just fun to flirt and have it returned, you know?"

"My sweet, sweet Doc, what am I going to do with you?"

"Drown me in pity?"

"No pity for you, little man. We need to get you back out there."

"Do you know how many men have run the other way when I say I'm a medical examiner? The ones who don't run want a true crime special during dinner. Victims need advocates, and in some cases, I'm the first one to care what happened to them. Civilians don't get it."

"We deal in death, Doc. And sometimes, that's gruesome, and people have a macabre fascination with their own mortality. That's why *true crime* shit is such a draw to them."

"I don't want to always talk about my work. Sometimes I just want someone to fuck me, but the ones I actually get back to my place or theirs...they don't give me what I need. Not everyone has Daddy Dom tattooed across their forehead."

I'd bore a lot of shame for my kinks through my twenties and thirties. I'd seen it as something wrong with me, and maybe in some ways, I was still embarrassed about my sexual needs. Three years had passed since I was in some man's bed I'd picked up at a club. One who hadn't looked at me with my silver hair and wrinkles as a deterrent. But as he'd fucked me, the word Daddy had slipped out, we'd finished, yet he'd asked me to leave as soon as he removed the condom. I'd given up after that. I left my releases to my own hand and a fortune spent in toys that, to be honest, I hadn't played with in a long time.

Getting off in the past few years hadn't seemed worth the hassle, and how pathetic was I that masturbation was too much effort?

"Why not go to Xanadu this weekend? Dress up all cute, bat those adorable silver lashes, and hump a Daddy."

I giggled at her baby talking to me and shook my head. That's why I've always liked Vega. She had a way of making everything right, and on occasion, she played Mami to me and Cash. It fed a bit of my Little and Submissive sides and took the edge off for a short time. I just hated that my head and heart were stuck on someone who I shouldn't even look at.

"Doc, think about it. Look at Remy and Robert. They're both men of a certain age. Robert loves his bratty boy, and being Daddy for Remy makes him happy. Why can't you have the same thing? As much as you know I hate the thought of fate and timing, maybe it's just not your time yet to find the Daddy of your dreams. Yet, I'm sure he's out there for you. The universe doesn't give us what we want when we want it. Sometimes it waits until we need it the most."

"Platitudes, my friend. Inspirational bollocks."

"You're not British. Bollocks doesn't sound right coming from that cultured southern deb voice of yours."

"Ouch, you're just mean tonight. Cash away on a gig, and you're just cranky."

"I hate when my girl goes away, all those groupies."

"She loves you and worships the ground you walk on, Vega. She texts you every hour. Calls for her goodnight story. You've been married a decade. It's weird marital bliss."

She wagged her finger at me as she glared. "Nothing wrong with marital bliss. Don't be a bitter brat. I told you what to do, but you're not going to."

"Clubs have run their course. The last time I went, it was too loud...too much chaos. I barely finished my drink before I wanted to go home. I'll be fine, I promise, Vega. I'm just...my birthday is coming up, and it's always a trigger that I'm another year single. I look at Remy with Robert, and I'm so damn envious of what they have. It's a romantic second chance with an adorable daughter. I never wanted kids of my own. With my work, it just doesn't seem fair, but if I'd had a partner, maybe it would've been different."

"Different isn't always best. Me and Cash are selfish in that we're enough, just us, but babysitting our honorary niece is fun. Just don't think about what you don't have. You have a great life. You do amazing things with your time...your volunteer work. You have awesome friends."

"I do, I have to admit that, but sometimes it just gets lonely."

"You're not your parents. They're so self-obsessed they have no idea how proud they should be. They're in their seventies and still image-obsessed and comparing their success with monetary gain. That's not you. You made a life for yourself outside that world. And no matter how hard it got, you did it. You know I'm more capable of knowing what you're dealing with than most. Being us is lonely. We're the weirdness in all those what-isn't-like-the-others scenarios. And there's nothing wrong with that."

"I try to remind myself of that, I really do, but I've always been the odd one out. I'd just like to belong."

"And you do. You belong with Cash and me, Robert and Remy, and their kids and grandkids, even with Stevenson and Graves, were the weird Cold Case Unit. It'll happen, little man. You just have to be patient and open-minded to what's to come."

I nodded, and she stretched her arm across the space between us, and I laced my fingers with hers as we once again drifted into silence. I was lost in my thoughts of all that I was missing, and her with whatever she used to get herself to the next call or text from her babygirl. I craved what Remy and Vega found with their people. But no matter how intelligent or gifted I seemed to be, I was clueless when it came to my love life. That wasn't due to change any time soon.

3

STEVENSON

"You're staring holes in that file." Remy plopped down on the edge of my desk and made me take my attention away from the file I'd read a dozen times.

"There were two interviews on this case. Father of the missing boy and the homeless man who found the body of Barnes. There isn't even a report to say the mother was visited in jail to be informed of her daughter's death or the disappearance of her son."

"Do we need another lecture in bias?"

Working the serial case, I'd thought I'd understood bias in law enforcement and the judicial system, but I had to face my own privilege when I learned just how little investigating actually goes into cases involving victims from marginalized communities. That was probably my biggest reason for the transfer. I'd lost my purpose a long time ago and wanted to find another one. Solving cases no one else cared about seemed to call to me.

"Please, I haven't had enough sleep or coffee for that. I went to see Doc yesterday, and he remembered the case."

As soon as I mentioned him, a memory of his playful flirting came back to me. That wasn't the first time since the previous day that it had popped into my head. He was smart, highly educated, and even in his fifties, strangely cute. We'd spent a lot of time together during the Fellows case. I guess I'd started to view him as a friend. But as soon as the case was over and we'd all gone back to our respective corners, I hadn't made an attempt to hang out unless Remy and Robert invited him, and we met up in a group.

"It's one of his many talents. Doc never forgets anything. What did he have to say?"

"Even after the victim was disemboweled, from the evidence, it looked like she fought until she lost too much blood and died at the scene. He also said that no one thought to get a DNA swab from the father."

Remy tsked and took the file I held in a death grip and started scanning the frustrating lack of information. It had taken a few minutes at most.

"Not surprised, if they determined his whereabouts at the time of the murder and possible abduction, then they wouldn't have gone much further than that without more proof. It looks like his new girlfriend and her minor children gave him an alibi, that he was home with them for dinner and a family movie night."

"If for some reason he's abusive, or she believes herself in love with a loving and caring man, she'll say whatever to cover his ass. Taking the DNA would've determined the identity of possible remains, and if he refused, it would've given some cause to request a search warrant or at the very least to take a closer look at his alibi."

"You said you didn't want the lecture."

"Fine." He placed the closed file back on my desk as I leaned back and laced my fingers at the back of my head. I tried to stretch the tension from my shoulders.

"Did you find any cases of unidentified remains in any of our unsolved cases down here?"

"No John Doe within the age range and height of our missing boy. It's like he disappeared off the face of the earth. I even did some searches within the state, and still no John Doe fitting Maxwell. But there are rural towns that are still in the damn dark ages. I have an entire list of towns to call and inquire."

"Call Doc about that. He doesn't mind helping out."

"I'd prefer to not do that."

"You have a problem with him?"

I grimaced at the sudden harshness in Remy's tone. The man rarely got pissed about anything. "No...I don't know."

"Come on, talk to Therapist Remy about all your problems."

"Fuck, I forget you're a psychologist."

"Yes, unlicensed but still capable of giving advice. You seemed to get along with Doc when we worked the Fellows' case."

"I did. I mean, I knew Doc. You don't work homicides and not become familiar with the medical examiners, but something about him just puts me on edge, and I have no idea what it is. It's driving me crazy." I'd tried to figure it out. I'd broken it down, and I'd even gone on runs to pick up dinner several times when we worked together. I'd spent time with him because I hated the not knowing. For me, not knowing the five W's was almost physically painful.

"I know what it is."

"Please, oh wise one, enlighten me."

"He's an enigma. Working closely with him...with us, you have an inability to function without knowing the details. Like the evening in Vega's pit of a command center. We all knew each other. You felt left out. Let me see, you were popular in high school, on a sports team, football, but not a quarterback, you're too bulky for it, and that popularity carried over into college. You were in the loop, the king of the crowd. Could do no wrong and then something happened, maybe your divorce."

"Well before the divorce, actually. I dropped out my first year of law school and joined the academy and completely shamed my parents who bragged about their son at Yale Law."

"Ouch, Ivy League. Doesn't fit you, really."

"The gay thing didn't go over well either but only second to dropping out with the highest grade-point average and on my way to the dean's list. I just didn't feel it, ya know?"

"Nothing wrong with not wanting to go into a career that you're not connected to. I mean, you've done well as a cop."

"I have no regrets. I was happy in my career. I had a boyfriend I lived with, and then we married, and it all went to shit." Joseph cared only about appearances, and it seemed like when the slumming fantasy wore off, he'd lost all interest in me. Since we'd spent so much time apart, I hadn't understood how far the distance between us had grown until he'd asked me to move out. I'd learned not long after I'd left that he'd moved someone in a lot more suitable for his position as a partner at his firm.

"Why?"

"He knew me before, at university. We hadn't dated but ran into each other a few years after I left. We didn't know each other was gay. I didn't come out until I became a cop. If I was going to live in shame, why not be a lowly gay police officer."

"You have such a low opinion of yourself."

"Some people would say I'm arrogant." I grinned at him, but his eye roll told me what he'd thought about my joke.

"Only people who don't know you. So what happened?"

"Shit, I don't know. We dated for a few years and moved in together. He was an attorney with a busy schedule, and I was working to make detective. We seemed suited."

"Suited is boring, I was suited with Harry, but that didn't mean it was right."

"I sucked as a detective. I should've noticed something."

"Did he cheat?"

I didn't know for sure, but I had a feeling he had. There was no proof except the quickness he'd moved on. "Maybe? He sure as hell wasn't getting it at home, but I guess, the last four years or so, he'd started to ask was I going to go back to school, wasn't it time to find a safer career, and so on and so forth."

"He thought being a cop was a phase."

"I don't know what he thought it was, but when we moved in together, I settled into his place. He stopped inviting me to work things. I'd started to see myself as his dirty secret."

"Your pride was hurt. You worked hard to get where you were. You thought you were equal partners, and he kept shit from you. Which made you need to know everything. Our Doc is exactly what you see. He's a sweet, adorable, way too smart for his own good brat. He's not like your ex. He's not keeping any secrets. He's pretty open."

"So you're associating me being betrayed by my ex-husband with my discomfort around Doc."

"Why not? You think he's adorable, and don't think I didn't notice you checked out his cute ass several times."

"I did not. If I looked at him, it had nothing to do with looking at his ass." Remy gave me a bratty smirk. "Don't even get that thought in your head. The man isn't my type. That Daddy stuff is all well and good for you and Robert. That's not my kink."

"Eww, vanilla. I had higher hopes for you." He eased off my desk and backed away.

"Smartass."

"What if Doc is just a happy, flirty little man who saw you as a new friend? Stevenson, we all need friends, and some friends flirt with each other. It's nothing more than that. Be a big boy and go make friends with a man that could help you out a lot with this case, and you might need Vega. If you're not nice to Doc, Vega will not help you at all."

"Those two scare me." I groaned at the thought of being trapped with Doc and Vega.

"They scare everyone. It's a lot of over-caffeinated energy right there. What they lack in height, they make up for in

19

mischief. They've been like that since they met. So make nice, or I'll tell Vega you don't like Doc, and you can fend for yourself."

"Dammit." I huffed and stood, jerking my jacket off the back of my chair. "I'll go make friends, but I have to call the victims' mother and see if she's willing to talk with me."

"If you need anything, let us know. We're working with Vega to get some testing pushed through on a few cases where it looks like they let the cases go cold with several suspects. We could close them."

"Doc said he was going to talk to Coleman for me. I need to see what he found out."

"To be friends with the ex-wives, he's a dangerous little man."

I left Remy chuckling behind me as I escaped, I needed decent coffee, and then I'd deal with Doc, Vega, and talking to the mother. I'd rather deal with Coleman than Vega or Doc, and that should tell me something was going on with me. I had to figure it out, or it was going to bother me into madness.

4

DOC

COLD CASE
UNIT

"Is there a reason you're just staring at me?" I asked Vega as I turned off the recording. I placed my hands on the edge of the table and rested my weight on them. Careful not to shift the step stool under my feet. I needed to replace the non-skid pads soon.

"You're distracted today. Why?"

"I'm not. I just didn't sleep well last night." It was a partial truth and close enough that my friend wouldn't call me on it, but my luck might not be the best.

"You need to get laid."

"Not everything is about my sex life or, in this case, lack thereof."

"That's an excuse the sexually frustrated give."

"Not all of us are meant to find their happily ever after like you and Remy. Some of us grow old, bitter, and stay single."

"Someone's cranky and in need of spankings."

I groaned because I missed spankings. I missed sex. I missed a Daddy's voice making everything okay. I was a Little without a Daddy. A Submissive without a Dominant. Yes, finding a temporary one would be easy enough, I had great friends, but I didn't want short-term. The thing was that if I couldn't have a committed Daddy Dom, I'd deal with being lonely.

The more I thought about it, the more I'd come to accept that a relationship of any kind wasn't in the cards for me. That broke my heart. Yet I needed to let the hurt and pain go. I was too needy and bratty, so my praise and Daddy kink was out of control. I needed to find better things to focus on. I had my volunteer work, Boss's Outreach Program, and my work there in the morgue. I was good, I was happy—I was a liar.

"What are we doing for your birthday? Strippers? Paddle? You think you can handle fifty-six spankings?"

"My birthday isn't for another month. Plenty of time to plan some extravagant party."

"Maybe a masquerade ball at the funeral home?"

I snorted. My family's funeral home had been deemed an historical landmark as it was one of the first buildings constructed in the area. It had been remodeled and expanded several times in the last two hundred years. But at its core, the house was still the same. A few years earlier, they'd placed in on a historical tour. It was filled with antiques and period pieces that had passed down through my family. The tours caused me to move out of the home to the groundskeeper's cottage about an acre away from the main house.

My uncle had been the funeral director, just like his father and grandfather before him. My dad hadn't cared about the tradition, and I'd spent a lot of time there growing up. My Uncle and his business partner spent their entire lives in the closet, but in the safety of their home, they considered each other husbands.

"Your Uncle would approve."

"Cyril definitely would. He did like a party, no matter what Leonard had to say about it."

"Leonard did whatever made your uncle happy."

Vega briefly met them before Cyril passed away. Leonard had taken an overdose a month later, unable to deal with losing his partner of sixty years. My dad had been a late-in-life baby, and my grandmother had thought she was going through menopause only to discover she was almost ready to give birth after visiting a doctor about abdominal swelling concerning her.

"They had the greatest love story."

"It was tragic. They lived in the closet for several decades."

"No, don't think about the end of it. Think about how much love they shared, through the stress and fear, they loved and were loved."

"Yeah." I went back to sewing up the Y-incision after making sure I had all the samples to finalize my finding of natural death. "Do you think it's weird that you sit on the table there while I sew up a cadaver while talking about love stories?"

"Honey, we work closely with death. We all have our coping mechanisms. We have nonsensical conversations or philosophical discourse to distract us that the world is shit, was shit, and forever shall be shit."

"God, that is so depressing." I covered the body, gathered my samples, and crossed the room to place them in the fridge until my assistant could take them to the pathology lab. Once they were stored, I removed my coat and cap and washed my hands as Vega came up behind me to hug my waist.

"We're taking you out this weekend. Cash has a local gig. You and me, we're going to go." She kissed my nape.

"Feminist Death Metal, I think I have too much testosterone for the lesbian bar."

"Aw, you know they love you. They did the last time."

"They treated me like an adorable gnome. Leather-clad, heavily tattooed lesbians pinching my cheeks for hours was not my idea of a good time."

"Not all were lesbian. There was that pansexual Dominatrix that wanted to take you home with her."

I sighed. "I was almost tempted."

Vega cackled behind me as she gave me a squeeze then released me. I turned to find her taking a seat at my desk.

"I love you."

"I love you, too, Doc. Always have and always will. But that's not going to get you out of a fun-filled night at the lesbian bar."

I snarled. "Fine, but if my cheeks are permanently bruised Sunday morning, it's all your fault."

"Depends on which cheeks." I snorted as she waggled her brows. "Okay, I'm out. It's Mami and Cash's special night. She's been excited all day about what she chose. I can't wait to see what it is." She jumped up and gave me a hug.

"Have fun," I yelled after her as she disappeared out the door, only to see Stevenson slip in before the automatic doors closed. "You're making a habit of visiting me, Detective."

"I brought you coffee."

"Bribe?"

"No, not a bribe. I stopped on the way over for coffee and picked you up one. Figured you'd still be here."

I took the to-go cup he handed me and smiled my thanks. "I should change this to my permanent address, but you almost missed me. I was on my way out in a few. What can I do for you?"

"Did you ever get in touch with Coleman?"

Of course it was about work. "Yes. He said he'd rush them after I mentioned wives number three and four invited me to brunch. I can't tell you what his idea of rush is, but I think you shouldn't have to wait too long. Have you talked to the mother yet?"

"I called her, but she wasn't too interested in speaking with me."

"Ex-con and her daughter's murder and son's possible kidnapping were barely a blip. She's a bit burned by anyone with a badge."

"You have any advice?" I could see the exhaustion in his eyes as if he weren't sleeping enough. To me, Daddies needed comfort too, and my compulsion to hug him came naturally to me. I needed to ignore it, though. In my gut, I knew he wouldn't appreciate my comfort.

"You work with Remy. You know the best way to approach. You're an amazing detective, Stevenson. You're compassionate. Just be honest when you talk to her. Don't make promises but let her know you're sincere about trying to find answers."

"Thanks. Not a lot of people say I'm a good cop and mean it."

"You're a special breed, Detective. It's a shit job, but it takes special ones to still have a heart after decades and not let bitterness take over." I smiled at his shock and held back my natural inclination to flirt with him. He wasn't interested, and we weren't besties, but we were friendly, and attraction or not, I liked him for the man he was.

"My ex-husband wanted me to find a better job, well, he said safer job. He was made partner at his firm, and a lowly cop wasn't fitting the image, I guess."

"That was his problem, not yours. You're well-respected, and you care about the cases that come across your desk. That means a lot, especially to the victims' families."

"You want me to walk you out?"

"You don't have to. I'll be fine."

"I stole the parking spot beside yours anyway. Not like it's out of my way."

"Doctor Montague would knife your tires if he was in the building. He has a bit of a temper. Rumor is his wife is screwing around with his twin sister. Apparently, they were seen in a very compromising position on a *lunch* date a few months ago."

"Is that all that goes around the lab, gossip?"

"We have to pass our time between tests and corpses somehow."

"Come on, get your stuff. I passed Vega. What trouble are you two up to?" he asked as I grabbed my jacket and called my assistant to put Mr. Flannery away for me.

"Cash is playing a local show Saturday, a night of Death Metal and feminism, and Vega insists I go. A pansexual Dominatrix tried to take me home the last show I went to."

He chuckled. "You, Vega, and Remy, and the rest of the crew of yours I've met lead very interesting lives."

"It's not so bad. It breaks up the monotony. That's what I get for having Vega as a bestie. We've been attached since we met. We're almost like twins, same IQ, graduated at the same age, both short in stature. Both extremely annoying to outsiders. What about you? Haven't seen you at many of the outings since y'all closed the serial case."

I turned off the lights and then walked through the door as they opened with him behind me.

"Usually, when I'm done with my day, I just want to go home, enjoy some quiet and decompress. I also don't drink, really. I'll order a beer and let it go hot or order a soda with a lime."

"Drinking is not required to hang out. Although, I will admit to being a complete lightweight when it comes to liquor because I don't drink often. The occasional glass of wine at home." We walked out of the ambulance bay and took the long way around to the parking lot. I inhaled the fresh night air and realized I didn't know how late it was.

"How did you and Vega meet?"

"That's an extremely long story that may require alcohol." I grinned as he chuckled. "Short version, she was hanging out on the strip with Remy, Davian, and Boss. I was running my weekly clinic down there. She ran inside to see what I was doing, saw we were almost eye-to-eye, said we're besties now, and proceeded to squeeze the life out of me."

"What is the painful version of that?"

"I screamed I was gay when she started kissing me all over my face."

"No experimenting in your formative years?"

"No, I was practically raised by my closeted gay uncle and his business partner slash husband. I wasn't out, but with my uncle and his husband, it was safe. They didn't grow up in a time when it was safe to even be thought of as gay. They were already in their sixties when I started spending the most time with them. My dad was a lot younger than Cyril. What about you, big production?"

"No, dropped out of Yale Law and then sweetened the blow by coming out as gay to my solidly working-class parents who used my Ivy League education as a bragging point."

"That was a knock-out if I ever heard one."

"It was, but I'm still summoned home once a month when my mother puts extra guilt into the invite." I turned as I reached my car and leaned against the driver's door, tilting my head back to look up at him.

"I'll repeat myself. You're a great cop."

"What about you?"

"My parents barely acknowledge my existence. They wanted a wealthy specialist, and I'm a medical examiner." I waved off whatever he was about to say. "It's fine. It's almost following in the family tradition that my father decided to ignore."

"And what's that?"

"Three generations of my family have run the first funeral home in this city, back when it was just a town."

"You didn't think about the funeral director route?"

"No, I wouldn't have turned it down, but Cyril and his husband, Leonard, it became too much for them as they aged, so they retired when my father absolutely refused to take over. I think most of my skills came from my uncles. They showed me how to treat a family and their deceased loved one with the utmost respect and compassion. You encounter someone on maybe the worst day of their life. Men usually think my choice of profession is weird."

"No, it's not, I don't think that, but I'm a cop that's dealt with the aftermath of violent deaths for twenty years. I've seen you on the scene. You care for the victim. Sometimes it's the first respect they've ever been shown."

"See, you're really good at your job, Detective." I lifted my hand and tugged on his tie. "You better get home. Thanks for walking me out."

"Thanks for talking to Coleman for me. It's gotta be a shit job to run go-between."

"It's not so bad. I would do it for any friend. Goodnight, Stevenson."

"Night, Doc. I'll wait until you get in and drive off, okay?"

"You're awfully sweet. Your husband was an idiot." I winked at him and hit the unlock button on my key fob, and opened the door. I slipped inside, and I barely looked away to back out of my spot and head home. Maybe Vega was right? Maybe I needed a night out to find someone to distract me from wanting a man who didn't want me back.

5

STEVENSON

COLD CASE
UNIT

I took the stairs in the five-story walk-up building and hoped Mrs. Maxwell would see me. She hadn't been receptive to my calls or messages. The Cold Case Unit didn't require suits and ties, so I was just dressed in jeans, t-shirt, and a leather jacket. My badge was on a chain around my neck.

Checking the address as I stepped off on the fifth floor, I strode to the end and knocked on apartment D. It was the middle of the afternoon, and except for a baby crying and children laughing from the floor below, there wasn't any other sounds.

I was about to take out my card and leave it tucked under the apartment letter, but the door slowly opened. A beautiful, full-figured Latina woman answered.

"Mrs. Maxwell, I'm Detective Carter Stevenson. I wanted to talk to you about your daughter and son."

"It's Ms. Barnes. I think I told you I didn't have anything to say to the cops."

"Ms. Barnes, I'm a detective with the Cold Case Unit. I found the case, and it was improperly investigated. And even though it was before my time, I apologize for how disrespectfully the case was handled. I just want to know more about Angela and Aiden."

I held my breath and exhaled audibly as she stepped back, pulling the door open to allow me inside.

"Thank you, Ms. Barnes."

"Call me Mary. I was just making tea. Would you like a cup?"

"That would be great."

"We can talk in the kitchen." I followed behind her, the place was neat, and there were pictures everywhere. A lot of Angela and Aiden. "You had beautiful children."

"I did. Do you have children, Detective?"

"Please, call me Carter, no, no children, but I do have an adorable honorary niece. Her parents call her Roo. Can I help with anything?"

"No, please sit." She turned away from me and started heating a kettle. "What do you think you'll get out of investigating a twenty-five-year-old murder?"

"Maybe nothing, maybe answers. A very wise man told me not to make promises, and I'm not going to. The investigation was shoddy, and I don't mind telling you so. Most of the forensics weren't run through the lab, and I'm unsure if any of what was stored is still viable. A friend of mine is making sure that happens no matter the result. What were they like?"

"Angela was a handful. It was just us for a long time. When her father died, I said I would mourn him forever. First loves are powerful things. She was independent, very much like her dad. Strong sense of self. At the time of her death, she was attending the local community college, hoping to transfer to a four year to get a business degree. She could've gotten a scholarship, but she stayed to take care of Aiden. I worked nights at the time."

"What about Aiden?" I thanked her as she handed me a mug and sat down in the chair across from me at the small two-person dinette table. She smoothed back a few strands that had escaped her bun.

"Amazing boy, nothing like his dad. He was bright and

compassionate. I was forever fussing at him for rescuing strays and sneaking them into the house. He was a good boy." Her laugh was sad and a bit brittle. "Maxwell was an immature man, but he was fun. And after struggling so long, I guess the fun was addictive. Carter, I made mistakes. I won't deny that I did things I shouldn't. But no one deserves to learn about their child's murder and the disappearance of the other on the news." She swiped away a tear, and I pretended I didn't see it fall.

"I'm truly sorry. The file didn't mention an interview with you. Did anyone come to the jail?"

"No. As soon as I got out, I went to the precinct demanding answers. They said the case went cold, and there were no new leads to follow. Every year I called Detective Sandowski for an update…tried to keep my children in his mind somehow until he retired. Every John Doe mentioned on the news I was at the ME's office, wanting to see if it was Aiden." She paused as she took a sip of her tea. "The doctor said his name was Morgan. He was very sweet…had a kind face. Even when he knew the person didn't fit my description, he'd let me view the body just to reassure me. After the first few times, he almost seemed to be waiting for me outside the elevator. Introduced me to a big tattooed detective. I think his name was Bosley. Heard his name around the neighborhood a bit but never knew if I could trust the rumors. Seemed a nice man, and if he came from here, then he understood."

"I work with Remy Bosley in the Cold Case Unit, and Morgan would be Doctor Warner. He's the friend helping me get the tests run."

"Do you know they sat with me, cried with me as I mourned? No one had ever done that for me before. Bosley wasn't in Homicide, though."

"He worked Sex Crimes and Special Victims. He moved to Homicide three years ago or so, his partner was hurt, and they went to Cold Case and decided to take over the unit when the old detectives wanted to retire."

"Why did you pick my children's case?"

"I randomly chose. There's a lot of unsolved cases. Doctor Warner, well, he remembered the post-mortem of Angela. Said she was a fighter until the end."

"That she was. I made sure she was prepared to protect herself. I guess I didn't stress that sometimes there would be someone stronger."

"It's not your fault. You could've been free when the attack happened, waiting at home for them to return. She could've still walked through that neighborhood at the same time. This was her area, a place she knew...that her and Aiden both knew. Did you do any asking around on your own?"

"You know I did, here..." She stood and disappeared and came back a few minutes later with a file box. "Every person to see or talk to them two days before and up until the night of the attack. Coltrane, he was the homeless guy, sweetheart, has a memory for shit, goes by Major, retired Marine, I think. The shop owners I knew gave me surveillance tapes that none of the cops asked for." She stroked the top of the box with thin, scarred hands.

"Hell, why didn't you become a cop?"

"Felons can't be cops. Something about us not being allowed weapons. Seems kinda hypocritical, you know? No offense to present company."

"Don't worry about it. My friends always mean offense. Cops with low expectations of their fellow law enforcement. Can I take this?" I pointed at the box, and she nodded, but I saw her reluctance to part with the last connection she probably had to Angela and Aiden.

"Sure, I haven't even looked at it in a few years. If it helps, but when you're done, I'd like it back if possible. I'm not holding out much hope, Detective, but if you can get me answers, maybe Aiden's body to bury next to his sister's, I'd appreciate it."

"No promises, Mary, but I'll do my best." I stood and reached for the box as she flattened her hand on the top again, giving me a sad smile with more tears threatening to fall.

"A lot more than what your colleagues did." I opened my mouth to apologize again. "It was before your time, and you're the first cop to actually come and talk to me. That means something. Do what you can. I've been living with the grief and the unknown for twenty-five years. If you don't get answers, nothing changes. If you do, at least I'll know what happened to my boy and why my daughter had to die. I hate to rush you, but I have to get to my factory job. I have a double tonight."

"Sorry if I woke you."

"It's fine. I don't sleep all that much anymore."

I thanked her again and carried the box to the door with her close on my heels. I turned the handle. "I promise to do what I can. I'll keep you informed as much as possible."

She nodded, and I stepped into the hall. I froze as I listened to the hinges creak and the locks click one by one. I held the box on one arm and dug my phone out, hitting the speed dial for Remy as I descended the stairs.

"Kauffman."

"Hey, Remy, do you know what Doc's address is?"

"He's on Statesville Road, the Warner Funeral Home. It's the massive monstrosity at the very end of the road. You can't miss it. Something wrong?"

"No. I need his and Vega's help, and I have to make nice with her precious Doc, or I don't get her help."

"You learn quick, Stevenson. If he doesn't answer the door, just call him. You have his number?"

"Yeah, thanks." I disconnected the call as I pushed through the front door and walked down the block to where I'd parked my truck.

After my conversation with Doc the other day when I walked him to his car, my curiosity about the man had reached obsessive levels. That irritation at the back of my brain kicked into anger-inducing levels. No one had affected me like he did in my life, and I had no idea why. But I was determined to figure out why the tiny man rubbed me the wrong way. First, I was going to find out why he didn't tell me that he knew Mary Barnes.

6

DOC

COLD CASE
UNIT

As soon as I'd pulled up to the house, all the lights in the funeral home were on, and I rolled my eyes. They'd told me they'd hired a new tour guide for the Friday tour. I used my key to unlock the door and found the alarm wasn't engaged. I'd call them the next day. At least it looked like they hadn't made a mess. I wasn't in the mood to clean. I just put my foot on the first step when a knock rattled the front door.

Turning, I crossed the foyer and saw a familiar shape through the sheer lace curtains and the etched glasses of the door. I grabbed the handle and turned it. "Hey, what are you doing out here?"

"Remy gave me your address. Are you busy? All the lights are on."

"No, come on in." I stepped back. "You can set the box right there."

"I'm not interrupting?"

"No, the historical society hired a new guide for Fridays. I was informed of it last week. I show up, and they left all the lights on and didn't turn on the alarm."

"Tours?"

"Yeah, it's on a tour of about ten properties that date back to the founding of the original town. All the tour guides dress up in period clothing and tell the history. You can follow me while I turn everything off, and I'll give you a free tour."

"I've heard about these but never saw a home on one of them."

"The house wasn't as grand at the beginning. It's been added on and expanded, but no remodeling was done after the early nineteen hundreds. The foundation and main structure are still in place. The embalming rooms and all are kept as they were. Casket display is through there, and we have two chapels where viewing and services would take place."

"You lived here?"

I laughed as he asked and followed me up the steps to the second floor. The third floor was off-limits as it was for storage and an office. "This was my room." I pushed open the door and stepped to the side to let him look. "I wasn't here full-time, so nothing was updated for me."

"Now, I get you a bit more."

I studied his tall frame, he wasn't overly tall, maybe an inch or two over six feet, but he was broad and burly. My mind instantly conjured the image of being cradled in those strong arms on his lap. His blond hair was getting longer than it was the year before. He looked more relaxed than he did when he worked Homicide.

"Is that good or bad?" I grinned as he glanced at me over his shoulder.

"Not bad, but you really didn't want to take over?"

"If I was asked, I would have, but I don't think in the end this would've made me happy."

He walked past me and out the door. I inhaled the scent of his cologne, it was faded, but it was warm and comforting. A lot of things I craved made me think of safety, and maybe that's what was so broken in me that I couldn't find it in a person—because safety didn't exist. Hadn't I learned that in my profession?

I turned off the light and closed the door behind me. "This

was Cyril and Leonard's bedroom, but if anyone asked, Leonard's was that one." I pointed over my shoulder as I turned the switch until it clicked and shut the heavy door.

"They were never out?"

I kept closing up the second floor with him beside me. "I think people assumed, but since they never made waves, it was just ignored. Two best friends spent sixty years living together with no wives, no kids? They did have a friend, a widowed lady. There was a story that they asked her to have a child for them. Leonard always chuckled when he told it because neither of them could do it. First Leonard went in and then Cyril, then they tried together. Nerves and maybe a little guilt...neither of them could get it up." I chuckled, remembering Cyril's face turned almost magenta with embarrassment. "If it worked, one of them was going to marry her."

"They had you, though."

"Yeah. They said I was the closest they were ever going to get. Cyril told me one night when Leonard went out to pick up a body of an elderly lady...he'd wanted a piece of Leonard to live on. Someone so good deserved to have a physical remembrance. They were sickeningly sweet."

He followed me downstairs, and the last room I needed to take care of was the parlor. The lights were low, and I froze in the doorway.

"You okay?"

"Yeah, yeah, they'd send me off to bed, but I'd hide in the shadows as they turned on an old radio. They used to dance right there, every night before they turned in. They had to spend most of their days pretending to be something they weren't, and when everything was quiet and everyone was gone, it was just them. Leonard would pull Cyril close, tuck his face right into his neck, and Leonard closed his eyes as if nothing else in the world existed besides them. Sappy, I know." I turned off the lights. "Come on, you can follow me home."

"You don't live here."

"No, I moved to the groundskeeper's cottage. It's not a long walk, just at the back of the property. Grab your box, and I'll set the alarm. I still own the funeral home and all the property. My parents didn't even come back for the funeral. Cyril passed away after a brief illness. Leonard took an overdose of sleeping pills a few months later. He couldn't imagine life without Cyril."

I descended the steps with Stevenson at my side. We walked around the side of the house along the pavers toward my cottage with the flowerbeds lined with solar lights.

"I'm sorry."

I waved it off. "It was a long time ago. Leonard made the choice that was right for him. Everyone has the right to die with dignity on their terms. If he would've asked, I'd have held his hand."

We made the rest of the walk in silence, and I unlocked the heavy, old-fashioned lock and entered my cluttered space. It was a single rustic room with a small basic bathroom. My books were piled everywhere. "Sorry, it's clean, I swear. My piles of books don't prove that, though." I rushed forward to throw the covers over my unmade bed and made sure no toys were embarrassingly left out. I didn't need to add that to the list of stupid things I've done around a man I like.

"Would you like some coffee or tea? I know I have some bottled water and maybe some sodas."

"Water would be great."

"So, what brings you out to my home?"

"Why didn't you tell me you knew Mary Barnes?"

I spun at the accusing tone of his voice and watched as he slowly lowered the file box to my small kitchen table.

"Who?"

"Mary Barnes, Angela and Aiden's mother. She used to come in checking every John Doe that was announced on the news.

Don't pretend you don't know her, Doc. You remember everything."

"She hasn't checked on a John Doe in fifteen years. We never talked about her case. I let her look at the bodies of young men who she'd hoped were her son. I implied that I knew her. I *did* mention that she called the old detective. Sandowski was and still is a bastard. Last I heard, he was drinking himself to death while chasing down cheating spouses. Is that her work?" I pointed at the box with one hand while I handed him the bottle of water with the other.

"She appears to have done a lot better job than seasoned detectives. She mentioned the homeless man, Coltrane."

"Not his real name. He got it because he plays the sax in the park for money. His name is Major Adam Grigori, retired Marine. Sweetheart of a guy but loses himself way too much."

"Do you know where to find him?"

"There's a few places, but you're not getting near any of them."

He sighed heavily and rubbed his hand over his face. "I'm going to need a chaperon?"

"I could go with you. I've treated Major a few times for infected wounds. He trusts me."

"Am I going to owe you another favor?"

"Tempting, Detective, very tempting." I forced a smirk as I let my gaze move over him from head to toe. I played a good game when I needed to.

"If that's what you want, you're not my type. I won't play Daddy for you. Look somewhere else. You can either help me or not, doesn't matter to me."

I barely suppressed a flinch. "I may be a pathetic, old man, Detective Stevenson, but I don't need to bribe anyone to be my Daddy. Get Remy to take you or ask Boss where to find Major. I think it's time for you to go." I turned away as my eyes started to burn and pretended like I was making myself coffee. I resisted the urge to wipe away the tear that slipped down my cheek. I wouldn't give the asshole the satisfaction of knowing he hurt me.

I counted his heavy steps on the wide, plank flooring and how the creaks were muffled beneath the area rugs. As the door slammed, I went to grab my phone from my back pocket to call Vega, but I stopped. It wasn't his fault I'd pushed when he didn't want me. Vega would try to protect me. I finished setting the timer to start the coffee when I awakened the next morning.

All I wanted was to shower and go to bed. I turned off the kitchen lights and stripped in the dark. By memory, I turned on the water in the small stall. I kicked the clothes aside, not caring where they ended up. I assumed he didn't like me or find me attractive, but to find out he thought I was desperate hurt. Words hurt, but I knew something that hurt a lot worse. I stroked the scars on my belly, tracing the ragged edges that I'd stitched myself. I'd learned what happened when you let the wrong man in. No one knew, not even Vega or Remy. I lived with my lessons. That was the bitch about remembering everything.

7

STEVENSON

COLD CASE
Unit

I walked into Cold Case with my backpack slung over my shoulder and froze as I found Remy seated on the corner of Robert's desk with his husband's arm rested across his thighs. Robert was rubbing soothing circles on Remy's hip.

"Bad news?"

"Shh, Doc is sleeping," Remy whispered, and I glanced to the couch tucked against the wall between two filing cabinets.

The thing was too short for anyone to sleep on, but it seemed the perfect size for Doc. He had a blanket wrapped tightly around him like I'd seen Remy and Robert do with Roo. He was naturally pale due to his line of work and mostly being on duty at night, but the dark half-circles under his eyes were stark against his porcelain skin. "What happened?"

"Seventeen car pile-up on the freeway. He was in the morgue until a few hours ago, taking dental x-rays to identify the deceased. He also had to take impressions of living victims at the hospital. A few were burned so badly they can't be recognized right now. The swelling of the tissue, well, he had a rough night. Vega called to inform us, and Robert went and got him to sleep here with us."

"Is he okay?" I eased the strap on my backpack off one shoulder and quietly set it down on my desk.

"He'll be fine. He just needed to be made to sleep. He was on forty-eight hours without. He attended a double murder scene two nights ago. Our poor Doc just needed some TLC. You should have some lab results in your email. Doc called in some favors for you."

The last time I'd seen him, we hadn't left on the best of terms, and I was shocked he'd kept his promise to help me. I still didn't understand why I lashed out at him. It wasn't in my nature to do that to someone. The flinch he'd tried to hide was as clear as if I smacked him. He hadn't done anything new. He'd flirted, and it had irritated me. I couldn't blame it on lack of sleep or bad news; he became my target, and I insulted him for no reason. For days I'd tried to decide how to apologize, but the few text messages I'd sent were ignored, or I just received an *it's fine*. It was anything but fine.

A pitiful little whimper came from the couch, and as I made a move to check on him, Robert was already up and knelt beside the couch. Robert stroked Doc's shoulder-length hair back from his face, and Doc grinned in his sleep.

"Hey, little man, you ready to wake up?"

I felt my brows draw together as I frowned. Robert only used that tone with Remy when his husband was stressed. Remy occasionally had panic attacks at work or nightmares, and Robert went into instant caregiver mode. His gruff voice naturally softened.

"No." Doc's voice broke, and I shoved my hands in my pockets.

"I know, you can sleep for longer if you want. I'll tell you another story."

"I need to shower. I'm so gross." Doc struggled to sit up until Robert helped him untangle from the blanket.

"Well, Mami Vega brought you fresh clothes, and you can shower in the locker room."

"I should go home."

Robert pinched Doc's chin and made him look at Robert. "Morgan, you will get up, shower here, and then I'll make sure you have a good breakfast. Do you understand me?"

"Yes, sir." I frowned at the almost sense of instant calm that came over Doc. There was no mania or brattiness, just an overwhelming sense of peace.

"Good boy, now, come on, I'll take you to our locker room. It's deserted except for us. I'll get you in the shower, and if you're a good boy, I'll even wash your hair. You liked it the last time."

I nearly stepped forward as Robert pressed his lips gently and playfully to Doc's several times until Doc giggled. I clenched my fists as Robert helped Doc to stand and took the pile of clothes Remy handed him. I jerked my gaze to Remy as soon as Robert and Doc disappeared.

"Problem, Stevenson?"

"How can you let Robert—" I motioned to the empty doorway.

"Doc needed a Daddy to center him. Robert asked if I would mind, and I said no. Vega normally takes the lead in these things, but she's trapped in a funding meeting and couldn't be here. It's not like my husband is going to get turned on. That isn't what our friend needed. If he had a Daddy of his own, then we would've called, but that's not the case."

"But doesn't it bother you?" If I had a man of my own, I don't think I could allow them to kiss another man or cuddle and bathe them. Although, I'd never seen myself as possessive. I hadn't been with my ex-husband. He'd come and gone as he wanted, and I did the same.

"No, there's something you don't get. You see, Doc is a Little and Submissive. Those things aren't always mutual. You can be a Little

43

and not Submissive. Doc's like me. He does so much for everyone else that he needs that calming presence a more dominant person can give him to make sure he takes care of his needs without thinking about everyone else. In this case, my husband. That need isn't always sexual, it's comfort and safety, and Doc trusts Robert to give him that. Did it bother you that my husband kissed Doc? Because it isn't the first time. He's bathed him. Cuddled him."

"No, I just wouldn't let my boyfriend or husband do that with someone else."

"I trust Robert. If he can be a nonsexual caregiver to one of my friends and we're okay with it, then why not? He's the most caring man I've ever been involved with. I don't mind sharing that with someone else who's in need. For someone who's been around me and Robert, Cash and Vega, you're not very knowledgeable, or does the whole Daddy and Little dynamic make you uncomfortable?"

"I have work to do." I sat heavily in my chair and logged into my computer to get to my email.

"Did something happen between you and Doc? Because he's telling me to give you messages and Doc was never shy with you."

"No, nothing happened."

"Keep your secrets, but I love Doc, and I won't have him treated with disrespect. So if you fucked up, apologize. He's very forgiving. I won't say the same for Vega or myself."

"He flirted, and I was irritated. I told him if he was looking for a Daddy, it wouldn't be me. I tried to apologize. He just keeps messaging me that it's fine."

"What's your issue with being someone's Daddy? It has to be more than just not being your kink. Which is understandable. Everyone has their thing. Robert wasn't that way before me. I was surprised. I just used it as a bratty endearment because it made him smile, and then after a while, he would drop his eyes to my lips every time I said it. So what's your aversion?"

I collapsed back in my chair as he seated himself on the edge of my desk and waited me out. "I have no aversion towards it. I never even thought about kink. You said it. I'm vanilla."

"And nothing wrong with that, but you can't lash out at someone. Explain it to him. You could've simply said you weren't interested."

He looked like he was going to say more, but giggles and deep laughter preceded Robert and Doc's return.

"Now, there's our adorable Doc." Remy slipped off my desk, and I watched him as he approached Doc, cupping his cheeks. "You okay now?"

"Yeah, I feel all better. Although, I'm gonna take the rest of the day off. The boss already told me to take it. Forty-eight hours was too long without sleep. Thanks for loaning me Robert."

"Little man, any time, you just have to call." Robert hugged Doc from behind and dropped a kiss on his damp hair. "Want me to drive you home?"

"I'll drive him home. I have someone I need to meet." I offered, and as Doc started to protest, I arched my brow, and he closed his mouth so quickly his teeth clicked. "Get your jacket and your things."

"Doc, are you okay with Stevenson driving you home?" I didn't miss the look Remy and Robert shared as Robert asked.

"Yes, Robert, I'm fine."

"Call us when you wake up, and we'll bring you dinner. Or you can come to the house and play dolls with Roo."

"I'll be by the play with Roo. I miss my niece, and she doesn't think it's weird I like playing dolls."

Doc kept his head down, and I watched him as he grabbed his stuff, put on his coat, and I clenched my jaw as Robert buttoned him up. He got that serene expression again, and all I saw when I looked at him was the way he flinched or refused to even look at me. I fucked up, I'd admit it, but I still didn't get why.

Once Robert had Doc ready, I motioned for Doc to go first,

and I followed him from the building and then led him to my truck. I opened the passenger door. "Do you need help?"

"No, I can climb in just fine."

I stepped back and observed as he struggled to get his short leg up enough to step on the sideboard. I rolled my lip between my teeth as he grunted and then threw a glare over his shoulder. "Are you done?"

"I can do it myself."

"I'd like to get home before it gets dark out."

"Fuck you, Stevenson." I widened my eyes as he mumbled a series of curses as he struggled.

"Stop, honey. I'll lift you." I grabbed his sides and lifted him into the seat, and then I got him settled. He sat there stiffly, still refusing to look at me. "Doc, I'm sorry about the other night, okay? I was frustrated, and I took it out on you. There is absolutely nothing wrong with you." I lifted my hand to pinch his chin and forced him to turn his eyes to mine. "Honey, you are not pathetic. Let's get you home so you can get some real sleep."

"I'm sorry I made you uncomfortable with my flirting. I won't do it anymore."

"Flirt all you want. It's kinda nice. No one's flirted with me in a long time. My ex-husband wasn't the type."

"Isn't the beginning of a relationship all about the flirting and the fun, finding out about the other person? Robert and Remy were adorable when they were first getting together. I'd never seen Remy like that with anyone. I was happy for him and jealous as hell."

I stroked my thumb across the curve of his lower lip as he smiled, but the smile fell before he turned away, jerking out of my hold. "Let's get you home."

I closed the door and walked around the front of my truck, paused to take a breath, then a second, before I got into the driver's seat to take Doc home.

"Doc, can I ask you something?"

"Sure."

"Does anyone ever call you Morgan?"

"No, hell, some days I forget that my name isn't Doc Warner. I don't think I even know yours. It's something with a C because you sign your reports C. Stevenson."

"Carter, but like you, I forget that my name isn't just Stevenson."

"Carter is a really nice name."

"You can use it if you want."

"Maybe."

"Fair enough. Did you want to stop and get something to eat?"

"No, I have stuff at home. I'm ready to get into comfortable clothes and curl up in bed, and then go play dolls with my favorite niece." He started to smile at me, and then it fell, and that was my fault.

All his shame and fear were my fault. I just didn't know what to do to fix what I'd done. "Would you help me find Major? Tomorrow night?"

"Um, I have a clinic from two to six, but I can help after that. I'll be on the strip between sixth and seventh. I can lock up the van after and take you to find Major. We can check the soup kitchen at Boss's Outreach first. From there, I know of about five places he usually beds down for the night."

"Thanks."

He went quiet, and I backed out of the spot, heading toward his place. I'd fix it tomorrow. I'd make up for being an asshole because I had some fences to mend. I just had to get it right, but past experience told me I wasn't exactly the best at making a man happy.

8

DOC

COLD CASE
UNIT

M y last patient for the day shifted on the exam table in the too-cramped van. I needed to upgrade, but I just didn't have the time, and while I kept my medical license up to date, my clinic wasn't exactly approved. I flushed the infected wound and grimaced behind my mask. "Phil, you have to change your socks more often. Your wound isn't healing. You're going to lose it. I know you don't want to, but you need to go to the VA for the wound care clinic."

"You know I've been waiting months for a damn appointment."

"I know, but I want you to wash and change your socks daily. Go see Boss to use the Outreach laundry room. I want to see you again next week." I cleaned up and dropped everything in the biohazard bin. "Here's a prescription for antibiotics. Take them. I already priced them." I handed over the script and a ten-dollar bill.

"Doc, it's too—"

"And I don't want to find you dead from sepsis. If you need me before the next clinic, get Boss to call me. Promise me, Phil."

"I promise."

I patted his knee as the van shifted, and I turned my head to find Stevenson watching us. "Hey, I'm almost done." I wrapped the wound in clean gauze and then set a paper bag with supplies beside his leg. "Here's a wound kit and some extra socks. If you need more, Boss is stocked. Use it." I carefully eased the clean sock over his bandages and put his walking boot back on. "Cree is across the street serving soup and sandwiches. Go get something to eat and then go fill your prescription. The corner pharmacy is open for another few hours."

"Thanks, Doc."

"No problem. I'll see you next week." I smiled at the man who was in bad need of a shower and new clothes. I straightened from the stool I was seated on and helped him down. Removing my gloves, I threw them in the trash and took off my mask. "Sorry, I'm running a bit behind. Line was longer than normal. This time of year, a lot of ear infections for the little ones. Just let me clean up, and we can walk to the Outreach building."

"Take your time. You do this every week?"

As I started sanitizing the space, I shrugged. "Every Saturday, same spot, and Cree sets up across the street to serve a hot meal while they wait or for afterward. Sometimes I get calls from Boss if someone shows up there. A lot of people can't afford to go to the ER or a regular doctor. Sadly, most of the people I see are Vets who are waiting for appointments and tests at the VA. All visits and care are free, and I pay for scripts when I can."

"That's a lot, Doc."

"I don't have many needs, Detective, a few hundred won't break me, but a generic script can mean the difference between losing a limb or their life. And trust is a big thing down here, and they trust me to make sure I try my best."

"I learned that from working closely with Remy. Did you want to grab something to eat before we start our search?"

"It's meatloaf night at the Outreach."

He opened his mouth to argue and then stopped himself. I

cleaned myself up and removed my white coat, and dragged my hoodie on.

"I'll just lock up. It's safe, I don't keep anything in the van other than over-the-counter meds, and everyone knows it. When I first started, it got broken into several times. Do-gooder, supposedly rich doctor and all that." He motioned me past him, and I turned sideways to avoid touching him. "We'll hit the Outreach first. Major sometimes shows up on Saturdays for his dinner, but like I said, there's about five or so places he beds down. Hide the badge." I pointed to the shield clipped to his waistband exposed by his unzipped leather jacket.

I glanced behind me as I descended the two steps to catch him zipping up, and I turned back forward, waving at Cree. She was a longtime volunteer with Boss. She'd been a sex worker back in the day before she met her girlfriend through a job fair.

"Did you catch up on your sleep?" he asked as he stepped up beside me as we started the short walk to the Outreach center that was housed in three remodeled warehouses.

"I slept until one...barely got here in time. Learn anything from the lab results?" I didn't want to admit that I hadn't slept until well after I got home from having dinner with Remy, Robert, and Roo. The sun had already started to rise by the time I'd stopped tossing and turning.

"Not a lot. There was no semen on the swabs you took in the rape kit. The other samples were degraded from poor storage."

"Sorry."

"I kinda expected it, ya know? I was told about twenty years ago there was a power failure, and the generators didn't kick on, so the evidence was compromised. And what they thought they saved was useless. Thanks for talking to Coleman, though."

"Threatened him more like it." I tilted my head back to grin up at him as he chuckled and shook his head.

"Whatever you did, I appreciate it. I've never been to Boss's

Outreach before. As many times as I've been to the strip, just never made it over here."

"He's worked miracles in the last thirty years. It's an entire compound. He does everything from job training to sliding scale childcare. He runs afterschool programs. The meals are prepared by low-income or homeless people from the neighborhood, and since he trains, they can use it as job experience. Pretty much any volunteer work can be used as work experience or training. The city council sees the Outreach as a revitalization of the area, and with private and government grants, Boss keeps making the safe haven a lot more beneficial to the neighborhood."

"And you volunteer?"

"I teach a sexual health class once a week, help organize the mobile testing clinics for the sex workers, and really teach overall health and nutrition programs."

"And the mobile clinic."

"That, too. But I keep my medical license up to date in order to be able to provide prescriptions and general practitioner medical care, but my clinic isn't exactly approved. The one run through the hospital won't write prescriptions. They do basic triage and referrals, which a lot of the people they see can't afford."

"Why not open a practice then you can do this full-time?"

"Wish it was that easy. The county and city want to keep their free health clinics under their control, which means independent mobile clinics beyond ones where medical students give less than basic care don't get the funding. Also, a lot of the patients I see have some form of mental health issue, especially PTSD, and the wait times for VA appointments are astounding. Again, they want to see someone they trust, and they always count on me to be here weekly and available for emergencies through Boss."

"That's a lot of time you volunteer."

"Fills my downtime."

"Honey, do you even have any downtime?"

I tried to ignore the way him using an endearment made me feel. "Not really, but it's fine."

"No wonder you crashed and burned yesterday." I flinched as he tucked my hair behind my ear, and I sped up my pace.

"It's not always like that. Did you see those people you mentioned yesterday?"

"Yeah, again, wasn't much help. I tried to track down Sandowski to question him and see if he had any notes not included, but no one's seen him around his office."

"Did you take a break at all since yesterday?"

"Mindless TV and a frozen dinner. Comes with being a divorced bachelor, I think. Kinda cliché, really. Did you have fun with Roo? She share her favorites? You always seem to get the best ones."

Was he making fun of me? I didn't want that. My eyes burned, but I bit back the tears. I breathed a sigh of relief when the Outreach entrance came into view. I made myself smile as Stevenson reached the door before me and opened it.

"Doc, rescue mission." Boss's deep baritone reached me, and I shook my head, rolling my eyes.

"Where?"

"The tunnel. We have a traffic jam."

"Wait here for a minute, okay?"

"Sure." His thick brows drew together in confusion, but I didn't stop to explain as I took off running for the daycare room.

I hoped he didn't follow because crawling around in plastic tunnels to rescue kids that got stuck and panicked wouldn't show him that I was capable of acting like an adult. Laughter sounded around me as I dove into a shallow ball pit that smelled of antiseptic and then crawled into the first tunnel. I heard kids trying to talk someone into moving. As I reached a turn in the tube, there was a little girl of about two, sitting there whimpering as three older kids tried to help.

"I got her. Go on. We'll be out in a minute." I shooed them

away as I smiled at her red, tear-stained face. "Hey, sweetie, did you get scared?"

With some smiles and a soothing tone, I got her moving at a snail's pace. We reached the first exit, which was a slide, and she went down, and I followed once one of the workers picked her up.

"Doc, you're the only one who'll go into the tunnels."

"I think y'all just like laughing at the grown, little man."

"That, too."

I stood up with a snort and headed for the door. I froze in place seeing Stevenson standing beside Boss. I shoved my hands in my hoodie pocket and closed the distance.

"Don't even make fun of me." I warned Stevenson and turned away to catch Boss's frown; that expression meant I'd be subjected to an interrogation at a later date.

"So, Doc, what do I owe for the visit? Other than it being meatloaf tonight."

"Major, you seen him around?"

"He was in last night, no show today, but it's a little early for him. He likes to sneak in for a to-go when it's quieter. Reason you're looking for him?"

"Witness to an old cold case. Stevenson asked for my help in tracking him down. You know he doesn't like strangers."

"He stopped his meds, so I don't know how much help he'll be. You know they stop when they *feel* better."

"I know. And it's a long shot, but what could it hurt to ask, right? He hasn't come by to get checked out in a while. I'd like to see how he's doing."

"Just be careful, Doc, you know how he gets. And you had a helluva shiner last time."

"He didn't mean it."

"If he's dangerous, we're not going, Doc." Stevenson's voice rumbled dangerously from behind me.

"I moved too quickly. He wasn't present, and you'll be there. It'll be fine."

"Go grab some food, grab a container for Major, too. Just in case he forgot."

"Will do, thanks, Boss."

"Anytime, sweetie. Go take care of what you need to do. I heard Vega was gonna hook you up with some Dominatrix tonight."

I giggled as Boss leaned down to kiss the top of my head and patted my backside to get me moving. I ignored Stevenson as I led him through the maze of hallways to the kitchen and cafeteria.

"Doc, here for your usual?"

"You know it, handsome." I winked at Bart. He'd been there almost as long as I had. He was easily three times my size but was as gentle as could be.

"You know I'm too old to keep up with you. Who's your friend?"

"Bart, meet Stevenson, Stevenson, meet Bart. He's the kitchen manager around here. Feed me, Bart."

The big man jumped to action filling two containers with that night's special.

"Could you do one up for Major, too? I'm going to check on him."

"Sure. I'll throw in some brownies for him. He seemed a little off last night. Don't expect him to show up tonight. Me and Boss tried to talk him into letting us get his meds refilled, but you know how it is."

"Thanks."

He placed one of the containers and a paper sleeve of brownies in a takeout bag and handed me the two other containers with two packs of plastic silverware. I jumped up and kissed his cheek, and then I went out the kitchen exit. I handed one of the to-go boxes to Stevenson.

"Thanks," he said as we walked and ate dinner while we made our way to Major's first hideout. "Is it like this every night?"

"Yeah. They provide breakfast for the kids before school, bagged lunches for those who need them, and full dinners seven nights a week. They have some of the students from the local culinary school work weekends for credit. People come in for a full menu, for lunch and dinner. People pay what they can, and if they can't, they get a free meal no judgment. Some of the local high school kids act as waitstaff and dishwashers for a little pocket money. They also let people buy meals and tack them up on a board in one of the offices so people can grab a ticket."

"Y'all do a ton around here. Still shocks me even after knowing everyone."

"We don't make a big production about it. There's no shame in needing extra help sometimes."

Praise for helping made me uncomfortable, and I was glad when he didn't make a big deal about what he saw. When I finished, he took my container and dropped it in the trash as we passed. Just because I didn't go without didn't make me any better than someone else.

As it turned later, I lost some hope that Major was around and was about to start asking at a few of the homeless camps. There was one more place to check, though. I reached down to grab the heavy, metal doors that led into the steam tunnels. The city had condemned them about forty years earlier, but one of the sections still housed a community. They were pretty tight.

"Watch your head. Keep your coat closed." I warned as I started down the metal stairs and felt the earth close around us. Stevenson stayed silent, but I felt his focus on me as I talked to a few people I knew, asked them did they need anything, and reminded them to come by the clinic.

I didn't miss the wary expressions of a few of the more antisocial residents. They had their own hierarchy down there, and even though they knew me, Stevenson was a stranger. Tents and sections were blocked off into territories, and smoke from burning barrels teased my nose as I went to the very end.

Success, Major was tucked into a corner, his duffel bag held to his chest.

"Hey, Major, how you doing?" I announced my presence, and he opened his eyes. I waited for recognition and smiled as a crooked grin tilted one corner of his thin lips. "Bart sent you something to eat. Is it okay if I come closer?"

He only nodded, and I tensed as I moved forward, and Stevenson fisted his hand in the back of my hoodie. Without thinking about it, I pulled away and grabbed a wooden crate. I moved it in front of Major and lowered onto it.

"Here, Bart threw him some of those brownies you like. You doing okay?" I handed over the bag.

"You know, same ol' same ol'."

"You feeling alright? Anything you need me to check?"

"Nah, that knife wound healed up right good."

"Good to know. This is my friend, Stevenson."

"Cop?"

"Yeah, but he's a friend of mine and Remy's. Can he talk to you about something?"

"I guess that a'ight."

"Why don't you eat while we talk?" I urged him to unpack everything, and I grinned as he called over a few kids, handing over the brownies and telling them to share with the others.

"Major, like Doc said, I'm Stevenson. I work the Cold Case Unit. There was a case where you were a witness. I know it was a long time ago, but maybe you remember. Angela Barnes and her brother, Aiden."

"That was too long ago." Major complained as he slowly shoveled food in between words.

"I know, but even a little something would help."

I relaxed and let them talk. Unless Major seemed to lose himself, I wouldn't interfere. The thing with Major was the meds kept him level, but they did shit for his memory. It was possible he'd remember something, maybe not fine details of what happened but maybe a little something he hadn't wanted to share with the investigating officers at the time.

"Angela was a sweet thang. Always had a smile for everyone and always had her brother in tow. Tough as fucking nails, too."

"That's what her mother told me too. Said she was a fighter." Stevenson smiled as he eased closer to Major.

"Didn't do her much good."

"No, no, it didn't. The cops did a shit job investigating."

"That's one way of putting it. I was an MP back in the day. They talked to me about two minutes...gave me a half pack of smokes. Didn't care what happened to that girl."

"Yeah, did you see what happened?"

"Nah, man, I just saw the trail of blood. Like two feet being dragged and then hit a dead end like someone got tossed in a truck or something. Folks talked about hearing screams. We ain't nosy down here. Best not to get involved. Saffy," Major yelled, and a young, pregnant girl scurried over. "Finish this. That baby needs it more than me." He handed over most of his dinner. "Can you check her out, Doc?"

"Sure, I'll leave you two to talk." I got up and went to talk to the girl. I kept one eye on Stevenson as I did what I could without my bag. By the time I examined Saffy and felt good movements from the baby, I got asked to check on a few more people.

"Doc, you ready?" I looked up to find Stevenson studying me like he'd never met me before. As if I were an experiment he couldn't figure out, and I was used to those looks.

"Yeah. Saffy, come by the mobile clinic. I'll borrow an ultrasound, and we'll get a better look next Saturday, okay?"

"Thanks, Doc."

"You're welcome, sweetie, but the baby has really good movement in there. I'll set you up with some prenatal vitamins, too. Just remember to stop in to see me and maybe go by the

Outreach for your meals. You're a little underweight but not bad from what I can see. Major been taking care of you?" She gave me a shy nod in answer.

I pushed up from my crouch and brushed off the seat of my jeans. We made our way through the dark, only lit by barrels and solar lanterns until we reached the exit.

"Did he have anything for you?"

"Not really. He was there after it was over. Nothing that wasn't in the limited report. He did say there was a series of attacks in the weeks leading up to the murder and kidnapping. Mostly young women with kids. I'll have to check the files to see if anything was reported, or they just didn't bother. Again, over two decades ago." He raked his fingers through his hair, and I saw the stress etched into his features. "Let's get you back. You got a date with a Dominatrix."

"Don't tease. I might call Vega and say I'm too wrung out to go to party tonight. Bars ran the course for men my age. Why don't you go ahead? I think I'm going to head back to the Outreach and see what everyone's up to, maybe help with dinner clean up. Boss will make sure I get back to my van."

"Doc, I don't—"

"It's fine, safe enough around here for me. Comes with being a familiar face. I'm sure you have better things to do than be my bodyguard. Goodnight, Detective." Before he could protest, I slipped into the crowd and disappeared. I glanced back to find him staring, but his bulk didn't let him follow.

I couldn't keep spending time with him. It was too hard and embarrassing to pine for a guy like him. I was too old to keep torturing myself. I forced a smile as a familiar body loomed over mine and tucked me under their arm as I headed back to the Outreach and the safety of friends who didn't think I was too much.

9

STEVENSON

COLD CASE
UNIT

I groaned as I fell back into my recliner with the contents of Ms. Barnes's investigation spread out over the coffee table and the pathetic case file from the official investigation. I combed my fingers through my damp hair and checked my phone for messages, but I didn't have any. Picking up my cup of coffee, I settled in to work on the case. Another exciting Saturday night in the life of Detective Carter Stevenson.

Part of me tried to ignore the fact that Doc ran from me earlier. I'd thought we'd started to get along. That he'd accepted my apology, but then he slipped into the crush of the crowd. He flinched again when I touched him. As if he expected me to hurt him, and of course, that was my fault. I'd shamed him, and I had to do more than use my words to make him understand I was truly sorry for what I'd done.

I shook my head as I tried to focus on the job. That was the only thing I could count on in my life. There would always be another case—another victim that needed my sole focus. I moved around papers and read account after account of Angela's whereabouts. I'd had all the surveillance tapes transferred to thumb drives, and I was still waiting on a few of the VHS cassettes to be moved to digital, but I watched what I had on my laptop as I tried to ignore the elephant in the room. All I had to do was tell him—explain—but self-preservation caused me to shut down.

I didn't want to admit to my hang-ups. In high school and college, I was so terrified someone would find out I was gay that I'd played up the hyper-heterosexual masculine athlete persona. It had never felt right. I'd betrayed a huge part of myself with my internalized homophobia, envious of the out gay men I knew on campus.

Fuck, how I'd wanted to be out, to be the man I secretly fantasized about being. When I'd dropped out of law school, I figured I couldn't fall any further from grace with my Catholic family, so why not come out. I did, and it still wasn't right. I'd hid it during my time at the academy and my first few years on the job. Meeting Joseph, I'd thought everything fell right into place.

In the beginning, I'd been super affectionate, but he'd hated it. I'd just determined that he wasn't one for the public displays of affection or anything spontaneous. That had been fine. I was okay with respecting his boundaries. Marriage had seemed the next step after you date and live with someone for years. I'd asked, he'd accepted, but even after the vows were made, it wasn't a fix. He became partner, and I'd wanted to make a whole production of it—special dinner to celebrate.

I'd sat there with food going cold until I realized he wasn't coming home. We became roommates. Yet a lot of cops and their spouses had to compromise to make things work. I used to love sex. But when your husband was your first—because before him, you were too scared of getting caught—you didn't have much time for experimentation. I did some of that after the divorce, though. Made up for lost time, but I was apparently happier as a monogamist. I got off, but the sex just wasn't great.

I'd spent the last few years flirting and pretending that I was a carefree bachelor. Hell, I'd flirted with Remy just because I'd known he was taken. It hadn't been hard to see he had a thing for Robert from the beginning. He was safe. I knew I hadn't had a chance of getting his attention other than friendly banter.

At my age, I was speeding toward middle age with my waistline expanding and still dreaming of shit I couldn't have. I'd put my needs on the back burner. Hell, I'd ignored them so long maybe they no longer existed. Doc fucked with my head and my status quo. He was so sweet and selfless he couldn't be fucking real, and I'd thought Remy went above and beyond when I'd finally learned about him outside the job.

Studying Doc that night, I'd noticed something I'd ignored before. He didn't see anything he did as a big deal. He didn't view himself as special. He sure as hell didn't expect me to respect him. Everyone he met got a smile. And he'd been so cute taking the slide from the play area in the Outreach daycare, and then he told me not to make fun of him. He could've gutted me with his sharpest scalpel and caused me less damage.

I'd discovered in that moment that I'd hurt him long before the night at his place. The difference in him was night and day. He didn't flirt or grin at me, batting his long, thick silver lashes at me. I'd never anticipated that I'd miss something that seemed natural for him.

The walls he'd built were no more apparent than when he stopped being the Doc I'd come to know while working so closely with him. I remembered the night of the tour of his family home, the wistful expression as he talked about his uncles. The way they'd danced together every night to simply connect. Yet I was clueless as to how to fix all the damage I'd inflicted as I unknowingly tried to protect myself from the pain and wanting and not have that desire returned.

How the hell did you break a two-decade cycle of being unwanted? I could solve cases with ease, but solving my own issues, well, I was clueless. I set aside my mug and picked up my phone. If I was going to fix what I'd broken, I needed to be man enough to ask for help.

I found Remy's contact and connected the call.

"Dammit, Stevenson, we're no longer in Homicide. Middle of the night calls are unnecessary."

"Let me have husband time." Robert's cranky voice yelled in the background.

"Tell me how to make Doc like me again."

"Oh, fuck, you're calling me at"—there was a slight pause—" one AM on a Saturday night to asked how to get your friend back? Don't you single gay men have better things to do?"

"Um, if you'd tell me how to get Doc to stop flinching when I touch him, it would help with that issue."

"Oh, shit, Mr. Vanilla wants to play Daddy."

"I didn't say that, and don't be an asshole." I heavily sighed as I relaxed back in my chair. "He won't even flirt with me anymore. I apologized. I was *nice*. I don't know what else to do besides grovel at his feet, and he needs to let me close for that."

"Doc doesn't need all that shit. You just made him self-conscious, but it's not all your fault either. When you get to a certain age and you have a particular set of kinks, one of them being praise, he's a bit burned by his inability to have the intimacy he craves. And it's not all about sex. That's what people get so wrong about relationships. Sex isn't everything. Now, don't get me wrong, sex is really, really, really good with the right partner, but our adorable Doc craves intimacy. You've seen it."

"The way Robert was with him? And the way Vega mommies him?"

"You see, anyone can have sex. You go out. You find a hookup. Have your minutes of fun or hours if you're extremely lucky, but when that moment is over, well, what's left? You might stay until morning, or you're gone by the time the sweat dries on your body. Why am I explaining to a grown-ass man about platonic, nonsexual intimacy?"

"Because I have no point of reference, okay? My husband wanted both of us to wear a condom because he didn't want to deal with the mess on his expensive sheets, and he'd still change the sheets afterward."

"Oh god, you've got to be joking?"

"Hell no. Would I willingly embarrass myself with this information, especially in your hands? He was my first because I was so scared of anyone thinking I was gay I became physically ill whenever I visited a gay club. My parents are Catholic."

"Eww, Catholic guilt. No wonder you're all fucked up."

"Thank you. I so enjoy these conversations of ours." Remy laughed at my thick sarcasm.

"Man, you're so bitchy right now."

"I didn't realize how much fun Doc was and how I enjoyed his craziness until it just stopped. I'm not saying that I want more than friends. Although, he is adorable and sexy when he bites at his bottom lip." I huffed as both Remy and Robert started laughing at me. "Great. Both of you now."

"We're sorry, we'll stop. So, you want your friend back?"

"Yes. We've always been friendly when we meet up at crime scenes or autopsies, but working with him closely made the job bearable even when it was shit. I went with him to the Outreach Center, and he helped this cute toddler out of the tunnels, and he told me not to make fun of him. He's stopped being himself around me. My stupid hang-ups over sex and intimacy shouldn't make him pretend that he doesn't like to play dolls with Roo or giggle when he's happy. I fucked that up, and you've known him forever, and you get the Little thing. I understand that it feeds a need, the way he was so serene when Robert woke him up the other morning. I have to make it better."

I was to the point I'd beg if I needed to, no matter how much it would kill my pride, but to make Doc be Doc again, I'd do about anything.

"Okay, you want to make it better, then tell him all that you told me. That the issues are with yourself and your past, and not with him as a person. Lay it all out for him. Be honest with him so that he can be authentic with you. Does that make sense?"

"Yeah."

"What brought on tonight's conversation?"

"His hair had fallen forward to hide his face, and I tucked it behind his ear. He flinched like I was going to hit him. No one should ever be that scared, and maybe that's not all about me. He could have shit he doesn't want to talk about, but he expected me to hurt him."

"Maybe he likes when you touch him too much?" Remy suggested.

"What?"

"Doc is very tactile. He likes to touch and be touched, intimacy, most of us crave it. I know I do, and I spent a lot of years denying it, putting distance between myself and anyone who might touch me. Doc has never been one for casual sex. It's not his thing. But the cuddles he gets and the touches, having the care of another human wanting to connect on a platonic level. It's being cared about beyond what someone assumes you can do for them. Doc does so much for others and the Outreach, and he never asks for anything in return. But he also needs guidance, someone to make it okay to be selfish. And it hasn't escaped anybody's attention except yours that Doc kinda has a crush."

"On me?"

"What's so shocking about that?"

"I'm a middle-aged, overweight man with intimacy issues."

"Worse things. And maybe our Doc thinks you're cuddly, his own personal teddy bear."

I groaned. "I really don't like you right now."

"And I really don't give a damn. You called me at one AM for advice. You don't like it, call Vega next time."

"No, she'd destroy me. Probably post our conversation all

over the internet, especially if she thinks I was mean to Doc. I'm surprised I'm not a target already."

"He wouldn't snitch you out just because you don't like him or find him attractive. He expects it. I have it on good authority that he's off tomorrow, no clinics, no volunteering. You know where he lives, go make up with your adorable, little man, and if there's dirty, sweaty details, I require a very expensive thank you."

"How are we friends?"

"I didn't give you a choice. Goodnight, Stevenson. You got this."

He didn't wait for me to say bye before he disconnected the call, and I tossed my phone on the table. Could I tell Doc everything? Would he think I'm an idiot for thinking he cared? Whatever the outcome, I had to make him know that he was perfect no matter how much of an idiot I was.

DOC

COLD CASE
UNIT

I stoked the fire as I reminded myself that I needed to get someone out to reseal the windows. The old stone and plank cottage was as old as the main house, but I loved it. I sipped my coffee as I started to work on some semblance of order with my books. I'd already put a third of them on the shelves I'd installed a year ago. It was odd to have downtime with no volunteering, and I wasn't on call. Boss was told to call me in case of emergencies, but he rarely did unless he had to.

I'd already changed my sheets and done a few loads of laundry. My plan for later was to watch a movie or two. First, though, I wanted to get some organizing done. It was all a means to distract myself, but to be honest, all I'd thought about since I'd gotten home late the night before was the stroke of Stevenson's fingertips as he'd pushed my hair back.

Having the ability to remember almost everything was a curse sometimes, especially when that curse came with anxiety that made you play out every mistake you made in perfect detail. I missed the interaction with Stevenson I'd had, the way he'd laugh when I flirted with him. There was no way it would've gone anywhere, but I'd felt safe to do so until I'd pushed him too far.

I jumped at the knock at my door, and I set my oversized mug aside, pulling my long sweater tighter around me as I peeked out the window. Stevenson stood on my stoop, and I frowned. I opened the heavy metal slide lock that I used while I was home alone and pulled the door open.

"Hey." His smile was unsure as he looked down at me, a takeout bag held in his hand.

"Hi, did I miss a call?"

"No, no, I just wanted to stop by."

"Okay, come in. It's getting chilly. I think they mentioned snow on the news this morning." Great, talk about the weather, I rolled my eyes as he stepped past me, and I closed the door, lifting it a bit to get it to seal. Another thing I needed to have fixed.

"I'm not interrupting, am I?"

"No. Rare day off. I was just cleaning up. Finally getting around to putting my books on the shelves. Only a year late."

"You have a great place. Mine's a shit hole. Very bachelor chic."

I laughed as he pivoted on his toes to smile at me. "Mine's just absentminded professor. This place is as old as the original funeral home. The assistants used to live here. It was part of their employment package. I just made a pot of coffee. Would you like some?"

"That would be great."

I nodded as I crossed the room to the kitchen and tried not to remember this was almost exactly like the night I fucked up. "You can take your jacket off and put it anywhere you find a spot." I motioned over my shoulder. I glanced behind me when I heard him step away, and he draped his jacket over the back of the overstuffed couch in front of the fireplace with a battered wood coffee table I'd cleared of books earlier.

His bulky upper body was highlighted by a navy cable knit sweater with two buttons at the collar exposing a t-shirt beneath.

The jeans he wore strained against thick thighs, and I jerked my gaze away before he caught me looking.

"Black, right?"

"Yeah, thanks."

I turned around and held out the mug, and I jerked away before his fingers could touch mine.

"I bought an early lunch."

"That was nice. I hadn't even thought about food yet. A man who can't forget who forgets to eat."

"Doc, um, I wanted to, I guess, I don't think I made it clear how sorry I was I hurt your feelings. I'd never make fun of you like you thought I would yesterday."

"It's fine, really. You didn't have to go to the trouble."

"Morgan." I jerked my gaze to his as he used my name for the first time. "I don't think apologizing for being an ass is trouble. Me blowing up at you had nothing to do with you."

"It's okay. I'm just too much, I annoy people."

"Dammit, honey, you don't annoy me."

I flinched, and he cursed. I wrung my hands together as he set his mug down on the kitchen table too hard.

"Would you please stop doing that? I made you think I'm an asshole, but I'd never hit you."

My hands shook as I shoved my hair behind my ears and lowered my gaze to the floor.

"I'm good at pretending. I do all the right things to make people believe that I'm just this flirtatious goof, but I'm not. I was in the closet until my mid to late twenties. My ex-husband, Joseph, I don't think I told you his name. He was my first relationship, sexual experience. I was so excited about being out and having a boyfriend. I wanted to be affectionate and do all those things gay teen and college me couldn't."

"It's normal for a person who comes out of the closet to have a sort of puberty, a discovery period. It's completely natural."

"I know that, but being inexperienced, well, I guess I thought I was too much because he didn't like it. So as much as I flirt and put on the act of the out and proud gay man, another out and proud gay man made me ashamed. He didn't like when I touched him. Didn't want public displays of affection. So I respected his boundaries and ignored my wants and needs. God, I had so much fun with you, you were so open and happy, and I ruined that." I opened my mouth to protest, and he shook his head. "Let me finish. There is nothing wrong with crawling through a ball pit or a tunnel to go on a rescue mission. You were so cute in your victory slide. I just want you to know that I never looked down on you for playing dolls or cuddling on anybody's lap that would let you. I miss the friends I thought we'd become before I got frustrated with my own hang-ups and took that out on you. Morgan, you did nothing wrong, and I want the old Doc back. The one who flirted and batted his lashes at lightspeed to the point I wonder how you didn't get dizzy."

My lips twitched at his description, but I wouldn't look above the center of his chest, which was right in my eye line. "It's a talent, takes decades of practice."

"Well, you're exceptionally good at it. Please look at me." I flinched as he placed his fingertips under my chin and urged me to look up. "I made up for some of that inexperience after the divorce, but it never felt right, so I just quit. I'm a very sad and middle-aged, monogamist."

"Worse things to be. Sleeping around isn't all it's cracked up to be. Sex is okay, but I like the other stuff more. Remy says it's about finding your right person. It would feel better. Vega says it just takes practice."

"I can see her saying that. Can I say, I like you with the longer hair."

"Midlife crisis thing." I laced my fingers to avoid reaching for him. And I refused to lean into his touch when he tucked my hair back where it tended to escape. I let out the breath I realized I'd held as he dropped his arm to his side.

"Worse things to do. My dad bought a motorcycle and wrecked it the first ride, broke his leg in three places."

"At his age, that was probably a long recovery."

"It was, and he bitched the entire time. Are we okay?"

"Yeah, with people who've known me forever, and, you know other Littles and their caregivers, other kink practitioners, it wasn't a big deal. A man my age shouldn't want to play with dolls. Or cuddle on someone's lap. Or giggle like a teenager."

"Hey, if Remy taught me anything, it's that the need you have has nothing to do with age. I think he said it was a state of mind."

"Still, it doesn't get easier when you're older and still single. And you find a really nice guy, and then it goes bad." I refused to touch the scars through my sweater and t-shirt. "I went to a club, it was nice, and I met a guy. We hooked up because I was lonely, and it had been a long time. I said the word, ya know, and he got rough to finishing getting off and then kicked me out. Since then, I've been kinda sensitive. So it wasn't all you."

"He was wrong."

"He was, but he wasn't the only one. I'm going to be fifty-six in two and half weeks. Maybe it's time to grow up."

"Don't do that. I like you as is, and your friends love you. You think Robert would've taken care of you like that if he didn't want to?"

"No, but they're my friends."

"Don't change, and don't let me being an ass ruin the fun you had. I used to watch you and Roo play. You were really cute."

"You don't have to say that."

"I don't, but I want you to understand that my issues aren't your problem, they're mine to fix, and I will. Just be patient with me while I figure it out. So, what do you say about us having lunch? I'll help you organize all your books, genius, and we see if I can make up for being a major dick?"

"That would be nice. I planned to catch up on movies which I'm probably also a year or more late watching."

"You and me both. I'm home so little I don't even bother with a TV."

"Your coffee is probably cold. I'll get you—" As I went to grab the mug, a calloused hand slipped under my hair and curved around the back of my neck. I tensed as he pulled me close, and I inhaled the scent of man and cologne, and my eyes slammed closed as his lips brushed the top of my head.

"I'll make it up to you, I promise."

I nodded because my throat closed up, and I fisted my hands in the sides of his sweater. This could be the best thing that ever happened to me or the start of the worst mistake of my life.

STEVENSON

COLD CASE
UNIT

It was barely five AM, and I was standing beside Doc's bed, fully clothed and ready to leave to get back to my place to change for work. Weeks of stress had me passing out on his couch in the middle of our second movie. He'd made dinner, and it was the first time in years I'd spent most of a day and all night with a man just talking, joking, and having fun.

He was curled up in the middle of the bed, his sheet, comforter, and quilt tucked up tight under his pointed chin. He didn't even have any stubble on his face. He was so beautiful, and I knew he wasn't for me, but I couldn't get the feel of him cuddling to my chest after I'd apologized out of my head. His hair had smelled like lemon shampoo and woodsmoke, and the few times I'd smoothed it back behind his ear, I was shocked at how soft the silver strands were.

The delicate man needed something I wasn't sure I could give, but I still wanted his friendship. The freedom his flirting gave me. When the house had warmed up the previous night, he stripped off the long, baggy sweater, and his t-shirt and thin pajama bottoms had shown off a trim body that his usually ill-fitting clothes or lab coats hid. I wasn't ashamed to admit to myself that I had a brief moment where I wondered what his much smaller frame would feel like under mine, and my body had reacted. I couldn't remember the last time that had happened.

He shivered, and I worried the cold would wake him up so I backed away from the bed, and I went to add more wood to the fire. His home was beyond rustic, but I liked it. It was a home with all its piles of books and odd items he'd collected over the years. He'd proudly shown off pictures of his uncles.

Cyril had looked very much like Doc, short and slender, while Leonard had been a big, brute of a man. Heavy through his waist, and he'd said Cyril had spent a lot of time cuddled up to that bulk. His uncle had said Leonard had made him feel safe and loved. And once more, Doc had sounded so envious of that love. I wondered if he'd ever felt anything as close to that as Cyril had been lucky enough to find.

Even in the closet, they'd lived a lifetime together, and I was jealous of the stories. I picked up my jacket and headed for the door. I grimaced at the loud creak of the hinges and turned the lock, before I eased it closed. Yet not before I took one more long look at Doc, he moaned in his sleep and turned over.

I forced myself to leave and walk the distance to the main house where I'd parked my truck beside Doc's car. What I wouldn't give to be a different man? One that could give him everything he needed, but I had too many insecurities. Like I'd told him. I hid them well, and I'd figured out why he put me on edge. The alone time we'd spent together, I wanted him. Every adorable inch and quirk of him. Although, I knew he required a side of me I didn't possess.

Hearing about the man who hurt him and kicked him out, I knew I'd never physically hurt him, but I could emotionally damage him when he couldn't be the person he was. I'd rather be friends than be the man who broke another piece of him.

I hopped up in my truck and backed out. It was too early for me, but I still had to get home, shower, and gather up all the case files to take back to the office. The streets were deserted except for early morning deliveries and first shift people hitting the freeway. I propped my elbow on my door and rested my chin in my hand.

I'd taken Remy's advice, I'd done what he said, and I was confident I'd mended some of the damage I'd caused. Yet, in doing so, I'd created a larger problem, but that was my issue to deal with, not Doc's. He hadn't done anything wrong. I turned off into the parking lot of the unit of studio apartments.

As quickly as my tired body would go, I made it up to mine, unlocked the door, and stepped inside the barren space. I tried not to compare it to the warm, homey feel of Doc's, but he had decades of history there, and I arrived with the bare minimum. First, I boxed up the papers and my laptop and set them next to the door, and then grabbed what I needed from my single tote of clothes to get ready for work.

I turned on the water as I waited for it to heat as the pipes screamed. I studied my reflection and decided against shaving. I brushed my teeth and stripped. I grabbed a threadbare towel and again tried not to think about how shabby everything I owned was. It was as if my shit belongings, or lack of, were a depressing metaphor for what was my life.

I stepped under the water and hissed as I leaned my back against the cold plastic lining of the shower and let the water beat down on my hairy chest. My eyes drifted closed as I cupped my sac with my left hand and gently squeezed before dragging my palm up my thickening length. I moaned as I fisted my half-hard cock and gave it a few slow tugs as I curled my toes.

My brain brought up an image of Doc. I bet he was smooth all over. I'd already heard the teasing about the size of his dick for being so short. Just knowing him, he'd be a greedy bottom. My thighs tingled, and goosebumps covered my skin as my mind let me have him. Pushed to the shower wall, I bet he was tight as fuck, and I squeezed my cock, imagining the feel of him. The way he'd stretch around me as I loved on him slow and deep—because I knew that's what he needed—what I wanted to give him.

There was one barrier. I couldn't imagine kissing him. He had lush lips, and if I pictured it, I'd never be able to look at his mouth. I stroked faster as I brought up the memory of him pressed to my chest, the warmth and slight weight of him. I swore I could smell him, feel his small body clinging to mine as he begged me to make him come. I forced myself closer to the edge, fighting the need to linger and savor my first orgasm in I didn't know how long, but I wanted it too much.

My right arm shot out to brace myself as I jacked off as my chest heaved, and I groaned as I shot onto the shower wall. My thighs shook as I milked every second of pleasure as I fought the overwhelming need for the connection to be real.

"Fuck," I groaned out as I tipped my head back, letting the water sting my cheeks. I cleaned up, got ready for work, and tried to forget. A fantasy never hurt anyone. No one had to know but me. It could be my little secret; my bit of selfishness.

After my mental pep talk and the ride to the precinct, I was seated at my desk as Remy and Robert stumbled in.

"What the hell are you doing here so early?" Remy stared at me suspiciously.

"Wanted to get a start on pulling some old files, and I still have to track down Sandowski. I don't hold out much hope he has anything in his personal notes, but I don't have much else to go on."

"Did you talk to Doc?"

"Yeah, yeah, we worked everything out. Friends again."

"Good. He'll be back to his flirty self in no time."

I was dreading and looking forward to it. Maybe he'd let me hold him again, curl up on my lap so I'd know exactly what he felt like. I clenched my fists as I brought my attention back to my notes and decided where to start looking at unsolved attacks.

That's if anyone even filed reports or just took notes and let it go as some random thing. It was best to work the case and forget everything else, at least until I could be alone and allow myself the one pleasure I could.

I got up and grabbed the inventory board, flipped the pages back to almost the beginning of the files, and worked my way forward. Jotting down case numbers as Graves dragged his ass in, looking like he'd tied one on, which was weird for him. He sat across from me, and Remy and Robert started making calls to check on the forensics they and Vega ordered.

Work as usual. I could deal with work.

1 2

DOC

COLD CASE
UNIT

"Look at the walking dead." Remy's amused voice made me glare at him from over my mask as I put my newest case in the drawer and flipped him off as I closed the door.

"If you're here without coffee, you can turn around and leave."

"Someone's cranky, plentiful sex would cure that."

I flipped him off on my way to my desk where he was currently perching his oversized ass.

"Sex isn't a cure-all."

"You're just not having the right kind."

"Any kind would be good right about now." If I thought I was sexually frustrated before, after having Stevenson in my home had made it worse. When he'd fallen asleep on my couch, I'd turned the movie on mute and turned to watch him. He'd seemed so relaxed, like he'd been before our disagreement. I'd liked him in my house, in my space as he'd helped me make dinner. We'd worked to put all my books away, and he'd randomly picked one up and asked me what it was about. I gave him a play-by-play of each one.

He'd smiled at me and not like he was making fun because I'd

81

read and remembered thousands of books in my fifty-plus years. He'd seemed impressed, and I loved that I made him feel like that.

"Well, your favorite Detective is on his way with coffee. He said he was picking one up for you when he stopped for himself."

I looked down at my desk to avoid eye contact with my friend because he'd see shit I didn't want him to. I'd never been great at hiding my emotions. Although, I was great at masking them with sarcasm and flirting.

"What brings you to my lair?"

"Haven't seen you in a few days, which is odd."

"Been a busy few days, first snowfall and people lose their minds and can't drive for shit. Homicide is having a slow week."

"That is a rarity."

"Doc, my adorable ghoul. Your coffee. Remy was slacking." A smiling Stevenson breezed through the automatic doors with a large to-go cup in hand.

"You trying to seduce me, Detective?" I nibbled at my bottom lip as I took the cup.

"Am I not trying hard enough?" I batted my lashes, and Stevenson groaned. "Cute, Doc, but that's nothing unusual."

"What are you up to? I know this adorable ass is irresistible, but you're laying it on thick."

"Hmmm, that depends on how thick you like it. I may not measure up."

I dropped my eyes down his body. "I'm sure you measure up just fine."

"Okay, I'm hosing you two down." Remy pushed an arm between us and then turned to me and mouthed *really*, and I rolled my lips between my teeth that in no way hid my bratty grin.

Stevenson slipped around us and took a seat in my chair.

"So, since I'm not getting left alone to be seduced by the sexy detective, why am I special today?"

"You're special every day," Remy said as he gave me a

charming smile.

"Uh-huh."

"Graves got his ass chewed out by Robert yesterday, and the tension is ridiculous," Remy said.

I frowned. Graves was a bit of an asshole, but he was extremely by the book. So the fact Robert had to say something to him surprised me. "What did Graves do?" I turned to follow Remy with my gaze as he went back to sitting on my desk. Automatically I lowered to sit, and instead of ass meeting chair, ass met some seriously thick, strong thighs. I tried to jump up, but Stevenson fisted his hand in the back of my lab coat and tugged until I rested against his chest. The man was just being cruel, but I wasn't moving.

"He had a bit of a run-in with a new homicide detective that took over one of the four empty spots in the unit."

"And that's an issue, why? Cold Case Unit is kinda the black sheep of the department. It's the rainbow brigade down there, but I'm still unsure if Graves is bi or gay."

"The captain called demanding a reprimand. Robert said he'd take care of it. He wasn't going to give Graves shit, but as soon as he started to talk to Graves, our normally staid and straight-arrow unit-mate went off on Robert."

"About what? I need the gossip." I whined as Stevenson chuckled and rested his chin on my shoulder.

"I think he's as bad as I am." His scruff teased the side of my neck as he spoke.

"Well, Graves left an open case that he'd worked his ass off on, had it ready to go to the DA's to see about issuing warrants."

"And?"

"The guy kicked it down to Cold Case and said the investigative work was shoddy and hoped the detective was no longer working for the department."

"Ouch, them's fighting words." I sipped at my coffee as I swung my feet and stared at Remy.

"Very much so. So, when the case was on Graves's desk Sunday when he came in to pick up something he'd left over the weekend, he went straight up to Homicide. Apparently, they almost came to blows."

"My money would've been on Graves."

"See, my little man agrees with me. That's what I told Remy, too."

The automatic doors opened, and all three us panned behind us to see a big, dark-skinned man in an expensive suit walk through the doors.

"Am I in the right place? I'm looking for Doctor Warner."

"That would be me. What can I do for you?"

"I'm Detective Marcel Douglas. I'm a new detective in Homicide. I was told you did the post-mortem on one of my cases."

"Name?" Stevenson turned the chair to face the grim-faced detective.

"Gerald Perkins."

"Forty-six-year-old, African-American male, six-foot, one-hundred eighty pounds. Found deceased in his home from severe burns and smoke inhalation from a ceiling collapse. No underlying disease or injury. Happily married with one child. I ruled the death undetermined until further information could be presented by the arson investigators. They determined faulty wiring that Mr. Perkins and his wife had complained about on several occasions. Without the safety issues of the dwelling, our victim would've, with reasonable certainty, been able to flee the home."

"Don't you need to check your notes, Doctor?"

"No, Detective, I do not."

"Be polite, little man." Stevenson warned.

"Do I have to?" I pouted.

"For now," Stevenson whispered in my ear, and I slipped off his lap from where I was very comfortable.

"Due to water damage to structural beams and a short in the wiring, the ceiling collapsed not long after the short caused a fire in the insulation, which was a result of the fire retardant being essentially washed from the fiber. He was a perfectly healthy adult male before the house came down on him."

"So medically, if he was able to escape from the house, he would've lived."

"Yes, at the very least, the landlord is guilty of criminal negligence."

"And is that your professional opinion, Doctor?"

"Oh, you might want to put a leash on Little Man." I heard Remy say behind me.

"No, I think he's got it." I grinned at the confidence in Stevenson's voice on my behalf.

"I've been a medical examiner for thirty-six years. I was doing this job before you were out of diapers. So yes, that is my professional opinion that Reginald Trass is a slumlord whose properties are so in disrepair he should've been tried twenty years ago. Because he keeps getting off every time someone makes a complaint because his tenants can't afford to move, and they recant their statements. Witness tampering and intimidation, Detective."

"God, has he always been that sexy?" Stevenson stage whispered.

"Hush, you're ruining the effect your boy's going for."

"He's not ruining any effect on me." Remy's snort was loud at Stevenson's statement.

"So, as you can see, I'm well versed in the case you want to throw out because it wouldn't be high-profile enough, just like the three ego-maniacal detectives before you who have come down here to get me to change my opinion. If that's all, I was very comfortable on that sexy detective's lap, enjoying my coffee. Are we done here?"

"Shouldn't you show some more professionalism, Doctor?

Spend time with your boyfriend on your personal time."

"Oh shit," Remy and Stevenson both whispered.

"Honey, this is as professional as you're going to get. I can point you in the direction of my direct supervisor if you'd like to lodge a complaint, but I assure you it'll be a nice addition to the other hundred or so complaints from detectives and commanders that I've received since taking this job. I'm a killer on the stand. The conviction rate with my testimony is almost hundred percent." I smiled sweetly at Douglas and returned to my perch on Stevenson's lap. "I can call my supervisor to come here if you want?" I lifted the receiver of the phone on my desk.

"I think I can find his office myself. Good day, Doctor."

He pivoted on his toes and left, and I rolled my eyes.

"You going to get in trouble?" Stevenson asked as he looped his arm around me and handed me my coffee.

"Remy?"

"Forman worships the ground Doc's tiny shoes walk on. Prosecution gives the Doc whatever he wants, whenever he wants it. It's not news that Homicide is filled with over-inflated egos. Do you know how much schmoozing went on to get someone with Doc's education and qualifications? I swear they would've promised first-born to get him to take the job. A medical examiner with almost perfect recall and can't be tripped up with trick questions on the stand? Doc is golden no matter what. And I can see why Graves went the hell off, though."

"Shit, I'm gonna have to work with him on a regular basis."

"If you're a good boy, I'll give you all the rewards you want?"

"Will you two stop? I swear, hosing you both down. Come on, Stevenson, I'm not leaving you two alone."

I giggled as Remy pulled me off Stevenson's lap, and I got hugs before they both left me to my work. All the detectives had learned that they couldn't bully me, and Douglas wouldn't be any different. He'd learn as soon as he tried to complain to my boss or his captain.

13

STEVENSON

COLD CASE
UNIT

Fuck, I cursed to myself as I entered the office to find Douglas seated at my desk looking as put together as if he'd stepped off a damn runway. What did I do to deserve this early morning visit?

"Detective Douglas, what brings you to the dungeon?"

"I was looking for Graves."

"He's in court today. And if you're looking for the Detectives Kauffman, they don't come in until they drop their daughter off at the babysitter after breakfast." I removed my jacket and hung it on the coat stand behind the door, and then I went to start a pot of coffee. The first one in made caffeine for the others, or there was hell to pay.

"Ah, so, this is where four of the so-called best homicide detectives came to hide."

As I rolled my eyes, I didn't bother turning around to give him my attention. "We see it as giving voices to those who no one else cared about. Still smarting after Doc handed you your ass?" I smirked over my shoulder.

"Your boyfriend could learn some decorum."

I didn't bother to correct him. It wasn't any of his business that Doc and I were just friends, no matter how much I'd recently started to wish we had more. "Would ruin his adorable personality." Seeing my adorable little man go toe-to-toe with a man almost three times his size was sexy as fuck. From Douglas's temperament, I was sure I'd see them go at each other a lot more in the future. "If you're homophobic, you're in the wrong unit. I'm sure you don't need directions back upstairs."

"I kinda wanted a look at the unit that took down a serial killer no one even thought existed."

His tone implied we were beneath him for whatever reasons that played out in his head, but it wasn't the first time and wouldn't be the last we were ostracized for something that wasn't in our control. Being gay or different in any way wasn't always acceptable in the boys' club that was law enforcement.

"That's because he went after homeless kids and sex workers. No one cared because it wasn't one of their kids. So, we've established you're an asshole, and you look down on us. Was that all?"

"Fuck, I should've called first." I grinned as I turned to find Doc standing in the doorway.

"Hey, honey, what brings you here?" I asked as I put myself behind him and Douglas. He was wearing a baggy winter coat, a slouchy rainbow beanie, and his cheeks were pink from the cold. As had become my habit, my gaze dropped to his full lips, and I wanted to know what they felt like under mine.

"I got you Sandowski." He tilted his head to the side as one of the waves of his silver hair touched his cheek.

"I'll reward you with whatever...I don't care how expensive. Where?" I closed the distance between us. I'd practically staked out the bastard's office and asked around, but no one knew shit about where he was. It would figure my little brat would find him for me.

"Tempting, very tempting. Here." He handed me a piece of paper. "It's his favorite bar, office away from office. You can find him in a back booth after eight. Bouncer is gonna lock the back door to bar his escape. Sandowski is hiding out, he owes a bookie his soul right about now, and there's also an ex-wife trying to get him served for about a century in back alimony. Skull owed me one and said he'd keep him there for you."

"And why would a bouncer named Skull owe you one?" I didn't like the bratty grin that curved his lips at my question or the way he leaned slightly out of my personal space.

"Wouldn't you like to know, Detective? You're not the only one who finds my ass adorable." He stared up at me through the heavy fringe of his lashes.

"I see spankings in your future."

"That's just an incentive." He tried to back away, and I snagged his jacket and tugged him close. His pupils expanded, and he held his breath. His small hands settled over my love handles.

"You're so asking for it, little man." My cock ached but thankfully decided to behave. If we hadn't had an audience, I didn't think I would've resisted pushing him a bit.

"Maybe, bring me coffee, normal time. I have a double homicide waiting for my undivided attention."

I leaned down and kissed the top of his head. "I'll see you in a few hours, and thanks."

"Anytime, have to keep my gorgeous detective happy." He rubbed my chest and lower over my belly, stopping just before he reached my buckle.

I growled, and he let out one of his cute giggles at my expense. "Get going, you're too distracting, and I do have to work."

"Stevenson?" The flirty tone had disappeared from his voice, and I held his jacket a little tighter.

"Yeah."

"Wear your vest. Sandowski has a quick trigger finger. Please."

"Of course."

"Thanks."

He didn't bother saying anything to Douglas before he was

backing away with a bratty wink. I turned back to find Douglas's nose snarled. "You're still here."

"He can't be as good as everyone claims." He was staring past me to the empty doorway Doc had disappeared through.

"He remembers cases from thirty years ago as well as he remembers one from yesterday with nothing more than a name and date. You can't trip my man up, and if you're gunning for him, you won't have to worry about getting settled into Homicide." He opened his mouth. "Listen, I've been a cop for twenty years, most of those in Homicide. I know we all want to make a name for ourselves and move up the ranks. But if you fuck over your support people, you won't get cooperation. And this isn't a threat. If you don't make nice with Doc or Remy, these streets are not going to be kind to you. Most of them won't talk to you without Remy or Doc's word that you're trustworthy."

"They run these streets, huh?"

"You could say that. They've been around here for over thirty years. They've earned the trust of all the people you're going to want to interview at some point." He started to open his mouth probably to argue more, but we heard footsteps coming down the hallways.

"Uncle Stevenson." I spun at hearing Roo's voice, and she darted into the room. Some of her enthusiasm disappeared when she caught sight of a stranger.

"Hey, Roo, can I get a hug?" She nodded, and I picked her up. "You just missed Uncle Doc."

"Aw, but I can't go to his work." She pouted.

"I know, sweetie. But his office isn't appropriate for little girls." She still didn't understand why she could visit our office and Vega's but never Doc's. "So, why do I get to see your beautiful face today?" At the flattery, her lashes went into hyperdrive. Remy and Doc had to have taught her the power of the fluttering lashes. Both of them used it to their advantage any chance they got.

"Doctor appointment, therapy," she said in a whine.

"But isn't today art therapy day?"

"Yes, I'll draw you and Uncle Doc a picture."

"He'll love that. Remy, why the early appointment?" I asked with a little concern because shouldn't her appointments be lessening than increasing in frequency. Doc had said Roo was having a hard time with the thought of school coming up next fall. She was working with tutors and online classes to try to get her up to speed on what she'd missed out on during her recovery.

"With school coming up, she's having some issues with the change, so we're doing three days instead of two for a while. And we had to shift some of her appointments with the new schedule. Detective Douglas, this is not a pleasure."

"Baby." Robert's Daddy voice was clear.

"Sorry. Also, Vega's on her way." Remy sent me a pointed look, and I narrowed my eyes as he grinned like a damn fool.

"Yay, Auntie Vega! Is Auntie Cash coming with her?" Roo practically twisted all the way around in my arms.

"Shit, I'm out. Love you, Roo." I kissed her soft curls.

Remy couldn't laugh louder if he tried, and I wasn't happy with his amusement. "How are you still scared of the five-foot-nothing computer geek?"

I shifted Roo to my hip as I pouted at my friend. "Remy, she holds my fate in the palm of her sadistic hand. If she doesn't like me, I'm back to square one with Doc. Those two are besties. She holds all the diabolical power."

"If you make sure Doc is a very happy little man, she'll worship you."

"Man, that evil grin of yours doesn't elicit comfort. Roo, yours and Doc's coloring books are in my bottom drawer." I set her on her feet, and she muscled her way into my chair, making Douglas jump. He watched her like she was a pigtail-wearing perp ready to pull a weapon at any moment from her tiny pink, sparkly backpack.

"Detective Douglas, I haven't heard very many flattering things about you," Robert said with the professional smile he'd perfected over the years of covering Remy's ass.

"I assure you, it's mutual. I was coming to see Graves, but it appears he isn't here. That one had some verbal foreplay with Doctor Warner before that menace left."

What was his deal with not liking any of us? He'd barely been in the department long enough to have that much disdain for us. We'd burned some bridges when we blatantly threw decades of bias in our fellow officers and detectives' faces, but damn.

"Again, why do I keep missing this new development?" Robert smirked. "I was given some very interesting intel of yesterday in the morgue. I have it on good authority that my husband wanted to hose you two down."

"If he'd only left us alone." I smirked as Douglas cleared his throat. The man wasn't going to survive if he had to work with us very long, especially if he didn't loosen up some.

"Well, well, well, if it isn't Doc's overnight visitor."

"Shit." I hissed at Vega's voice and refused to turn around. I was sure I'd read somewhere not to make eye contact with a dangerous predator. Even if that wasn't true, I wasn't taking any chances.

"Overnight? What overnight? I heard nothing about overnight." Remy's focus on me became almost uncomfortable.

"His truck was outside Doc's place. I was stopping by to drop something off the other morning after an all-nighter at the office." The tiny woman walked around with a dangerous, maniacal glee in her eyes as she stared at me.

"So, maybe it's too late to hose you two down." Remy leaned into Robert's side and crossed his arms.

"We had lunch, dinner, and I helped him with a few projects. I fell asleep, and I spent the night on the couch. Innocent, he was very much alone and comfortable in his bed when I left. Don't embarrass him." I wouldn't let them make Doc uncomfortable. I knew how they were when the teasing started, and while I imagined crawling into bed with him, our day together was innocent and about us becoming friends again.

"Why would I embarrass my Doc? Even though he kept this from me, expect a visit from Cash." She warned

"Remember assaulting a police officer."

"Aw, my babygirl will be so amused by your fear of a pat-down."

"That wasn't a pat-down. She was so thorough she could probably tell how many inches I'm packing." I accused as she giggled.

"I know, she told Doc."

"I hate you. You know that, right?"

"You better love me because I hold your fate in the palm of my hand." She held out said hand flat and then fisted it like she was picturing squeezing my nuts until they burst. I wouldn't put it past her either.

"See, Remy, I told you. Now, it's blackmail."

"Don't you people need to pass psych evals to do this damn job?" Douglas growled out, and when we turned to him, we saw him take a seat on the corner of my desk. At an annoyed throat clearing from our Roo, he jumped up and backed away from her. She wasn't shy about demanding her boundaries and personal space to be respected.

"Who's the stiff?" Vega approached him and circled the man as she checked him out.

I was glad her focus was no longer on me, but I knew that wouldn't last long. Like Doc, she never forgot anything.

"Please tell me Mr. Rules and Regs isn't joining us."

"Detective Douglas, meet our forensic genealogist, and Doc's best friend, Vega Carlyle. Detective Douglas is one of the new homicide detectives they hired to fill one of our spots." I introduced them.

"What did he do to Doc?"

"I'll leave you to fend for yourself, Detective. My little man is expecting his coffee. Roo, me and Doc are looking forward to our picture."

"Stevenson, I'm not done with you." I grabbed my jacket and made a run for it with Vega yelling behind me.

I should've come in my regular time, but then I would've missed Doc or left him alone with Douglas. I'd admit to a new sense of protectiveness, maybe possessiveness. I'd never felt that for a man before. Not even in the early days of my relationship with Joseph. I'd discovered there was a side of me I'd never experienced before. As if I was learning about a new man, but even with the oddness, I still wasn't confident I could give Doc what he needed no matter how much I'd started wanting to try.

14

DOC

COLD CASE
UNIT

"We have to stop meeting like this, Douglas." I greeted the detective but didn't look up from the reports I was finishing. The day had dragged on after seeing Stevenson at the Cold Case Unit and then when he'd brought me coffee. My cheek was still sore from me biting it to rein in everything that wanted to slip out.

Flirting was all well and good, but I couldn't let it go too far. I couldn't let him see. When he'd grabbed me that morning, my submissive side instantly wanted to curl up at his feet. That warned me I'd have to try for a bit more distance for a while.

"I wanted to apologize."

I spun in my chair. "Did that hurt?"

"I reluctantly moved here three months ago from Chicago. I wasn't completely up to speed on the case. After a little detective work, because that is my job, I saw what you meant about Trass."

"He owns several buildings on the strip along with about a dozen or so homes in some of the lower-income neighborhoods. His tenants can't afford to move to better neighborhoods, and he makes sure they know it."

"I was told I was supposed to make friends with you and

Remy if I wanted cooperation. I've learned some very interesting things about you and Detective Remy Kauffman."

"Rumors travel fast, but all are well-known and no longer leverage."

"You're extremely suspicious, Doctor."

"Please forgive me. Continue."

"Listen, I'm an asshole, always have been and probably always will be. And just for your information, I was well out of diapers before you started this job."

I grinned at him, and he shook his head.

"I was on my way to my Sergeants badge before this move derailed that. So yeah, I'm more of an asshole than normal, but I read the Fellows' case files, the investigation was top-notch. For an odd bunch, you know your jobs."

"Flattery usually happens before someone asks me for something, and sorry, Detective, you're not my type."

"I'm not that into brats anyway, so I think my heart will survive. I need intel."

"Sorry, try someone else."

"Listen, I knocked that case down to the Cold Case Unit, but I sure as hell didn't think Graves would take it as a personal insult. There's another case, officer involved. I don't know the players, and strangely enough, the odd crew is my most unbiased information train."

"Graves is an excellent detective. His father is the District Attorney, and his mother is State's Attorney. Anything less than perfection isn't in Graves's makeup. He worked his ass off to get the evidence for that case. You saying it was shoddy police work make him look bad, and that isn't the way to make friends."

"You and the Cold Case Unit have your own method. Whatever madness it is, it works, but I need to know how he came to his conclusions."

"And you're getting frozen out. Interesting."

"Come on, tell me about the case."

"Fallon Comstock, forty-three-year-old single mother of six. Worked two jobs. No criminal history. Not even a parking ticket. All witnesses said that since she turned up dead, her abusive ex-husband did it. His only alibis were his drinking buddies and fellow officers."

"What were your findings?"

"She had several decades' worth of old badly healed breaks. Crush injuries to the right hand and fingers. There was a hairline fracture at the front of her skull that was two weeks old at most. There was still blood pooled between the brain and cranium. She would've suffered some effects from a severe concussion. There was a call-out to the Comstock home for a domestic disturbance. The Brotherhood of Blue barely took a report. No medical attention was noted, or photos of injuries were taken. When she found her way to my table, her ribs and sternum were shattered due to blunt force trauma. I determined they were possibly made with an expanding baton. The pattern of injuries matched. She had numerous lacerations to the face, fractures to the orbital bone, cheekbone to the right side, which would make my findings that she was attacked by a left-handed assailant. When I performed the internal exam and checked her stomach contents, I found four teeth."

"And your opinion?"

"Graves showed me his report and asked what I thought. I agreed with his conclusion that she was beaten to death by her husband, Officer Comstock. Due to the frequency of nine-one-one logs that proved there were no less than twenty instances where she called for help, help that didn't come."

He was about to open his mouth when the door opened behind him, and I jumped up as I saw Major carrying Saffy, who was pale and her face was bruised.

"What the hell happened?"

"She went into labor on our way to the hospital, Doc. It's too early, and we were already here. The hospital was another mile."

"Okay, okay, this is not the place, but put her on the table there. Detective, grab some gloves." I rushed to the table, grabbing a sheet to lay it out so she wouldn't be on the cold table. "Saffy, where are the pains, sweetie?"

"All over." Her voice broke, and she looked so young.

"Okay, you have to be calm and breathe for me. I'm going to tell you everything step-by-step. Major, help me get her pants off."

"It's okay, baby, it's going to be just fine," he whispered to her as he did what I asked, but I saw him slipping.

I grabbed his face and made him look at me. "Major Grigori, you're a Marine, you're going to hold your shit together, and we're going to get through this. You have a baby to welcome, right?"

"She's too young…I shouldn't have but…"

"Hey, the deed has been done. Now we just have to make sure you two have a beautiful baby to hold, okay?"

"EMTs are on their way. Do you have any idea what you're doing?"

"Won't be the first baby I've delivered, Detective. First in my morgue, but we work with what we have." I moved to the foot of the table. "Saffy, I need you to scoot down to the edge of the table, okay? Remember, I'm really short." I pushed up her dirty shirt and saw more bruises forming on her stomach. "Detective, get through to the Cold Case Unit and get Remy and Stevenson here now."

I took deep breaths and tried to keep myself from freaking out. "Saffy, remember you've been coming to me. We did the ultrasounds. You're farther along than we thought. The baby was healthy, and she's a little early but still good. Major took such good care of you. Okay, I'm going to touch you. I need to check dilation. I won't touch you in any way not medically necessary."

Her sweaty hair stuck to her face as each breath puffed out

her cheeks. She was at thirty-four weeks at the time of the last ultrasound—I kept repeating the stats.

"Sweetie, she's so ready to make you two happy. You better start thinking about names."

I barely registered other bodies entering the morgue, Stevenson's voice calling my name between Saffy's screams and Major's whispers that his woman was so brave. The paramedics handed me clamps and scissors as the tiny form finally slipped free.

Panic hit me as I heard no cries, saw no movement. I grabbed her and moved to the next table.

"Okay, sweetie, don't do this to Uncle Doc." I start compressions, roughly rubbing her thin chest. A paramedic attempted oxygen as I tried to ignore Major's curses and Saffy begging me, and Remy doing his best to calm the situation.

I held my breath as a single gasp barely moved her chest.

"Come on. Your parents really want to say hi to you." It seemed like hours passed as I watched her gasp until a weak cry echoed in the space. "That's right. The world needs another survivor."

"Doc, we're going to transport everyone. She's looking good. See her color. Listen to that cry. She's going to be keeping her parents awake for the next eighteen years with that much fury."

I barely saw him through tears as the paramedic tried to take over. I straightened and noticed the shaking.

"Hey, honey, just lean on me. You're fine. You did so good." Strong arms came around me, and warm breath teased the top of my hair.

"Remy," I yelled.

"Already called Boss, they have housing waiting and all the baby stuff they need. Just relax and let Stevenson take care of you."

I was scooped into Stevenson's arms, and the next thing I knew, I was seated on his lap in my chair.

"Could you get us some water and rags to clean him up, please?" Stevenson's voice was soft and soothing as he wrapped his arm around me, my chin tucked into the bend of his elbow as he stroked my hair. "Once I get you cleaned up and nice and calm, we'll go to the hospital, okay? We have to meet the newest member of our family properly."

"Doc, give me your hands." Douglas's voice was strangely sweet as I offered my hands. "A little too much excitement for me. I knew you'd be a menace."

I let out a broken laugh. The adrenaline fled with the intensity of being hit by a train going off the rails, and I shook. "I'm…I'm sorry."

"Baby, you have nothing to be sorry for. We'll get you some caffeine and something to eat, and you'll be as good as new."

I shivered as if I were freezing to death. "I…I have to clean up."

"Your assistant is here, and he's doing it. You don't have to worry about anything but letting me hold you." Stevenson kissed my temple between each word as Douglas finished cleaning my hands. "I'm so proud of you, Morgan." I slammed my eyes closed as Stevenson's lips moved lower to my cheek. I savored it, the caring and the praise, but it was all too much.

15

STEVENSON

COLD CASE
Unit

S affy had hemorrhaged on the way to the hospital. They'd immediately taken her to the operating room for emergency surgery. All the doctors said if they hadn't have gotten to Doc when they did, she and the baby may not have survived. My man wouldn't have been able to handle that. Boss was currently attempting to keep Major calm, which wasn't an easy feat.

I looked into the nursery at Doc gently tracing tiny features of the still-unnamed baby in the incubator.

"You think he's okay?" Douglas asked beside me.

I'd been surprised when he followed us all to the hospital, but no more surprised when I saw him helping take care of Doc. I hadn't been able to let my little man go to tend to him other than to keep him from breaking apart.

"He'll be fine as soon as Saffy's out of surgery."

"That Boss guy is making a lot of arrangements, and there's a lady named Grier from social services here. Is that gonna be trouble?" I glanced at him to find him staring through the glass as well.

"Fran, she's just arranging for some assistance. She was Roo's social worker. Boss owns an apartment building where he keeps several units free, Saffy can stay, but Major will have to stick with his meds as a condition to live there until they get on their feet with jobs and all."

"He was amazing. He didn't even hesitate. Anyone else would've looked at them and…"

"That's not Doc. He does a mobile clinic every Saturday. Saffy's been coming in for a few weeks for exams. He's always been too good to be true. I just didn't realize how much until we worked the Fellows' case so closely together."

"So, you two a couple?"

"No, friends, one of my best ones, we're…" I paused. "He needs something I can't give him."

"I think you gave him what he needed just fine." He turned to lean his shoulders back against the glass.

I ignored his comment. "Thanks for helping out. Damn, look at him." I smiled sadly as Doc practically beamed when the baby was placed in his arms. "He wouldn't have been the same if he lost them. I saw it breaking him the longer she wouldn't breathe."

"Stevenson, one of the nurses I know is going to let me get Major showered, and Robert brought him some clean clothes so he can hold his daughter. She'll be ready for visitors soon. Doc got special treatment because Major wanted someone in there with her." I quickly glanced over my shoulder to see Remy taking in the same sight as us.

"Okay, I'll stay here. If something comes up, I'll have them page you."

"Saffy's doctor should be out soon to give us an update. Intel said they were about ready to close her up. They were able to fix everything without the partial hysterectomy, but you didn't hear that from me."

"Shit, does anyone have clothes and stuff for Saffy and the baby? I can run out and do some shopping. I'll probably suck at it."

"We got that covered. I called Gladys and Carol. They're going to bring some clothes, and Carol still has our granddaughter's clothes bagged up, so we'll have some stuff for our newest baby soon."

"Is Major alright?" I glanced at the man talking with Boss.

"I think he's feeling guilty. He left her alone to go see about playing in the park for some money. She was craving ice cream. Came back to her beat all to hell. Doesn't help he's feeling a little ashamed of knocking up a girl half his age, but he did his best to take care of her. Sometimes love makes us do strange things. I think he really does love her and wants the best, so we're going to work on getting him back to his life. He wants to make his girls proud."

"He should be entitled to benefits."

"He is. Boss is going to contact the VA and see about getting everything set up. Major has an address to get his mail and set up a bank account now. It's not an instant fix, but we'll do what we can. Until then, we have the Outreach programs, and Fran is working on things from her side. Graves got Boss's keys and went to get the apartment cleaned up. Some of the volunteers are going to stock the kitchen and gather some clothes to last for a few weeks. Bart is making some meals they can just heat and eat. We have a crib and changing table arriving. We rallied the community almost as soon as our little girl took her first breath. Let me get the proud new daddy. He wants to look good when his girls see him."

"Tell him congratulations. As soon as Doc is ready, I'm gonna take him home. He has the clinic tomorrow, and you know he's not going to miss that." Remy patted my shoulder and called Major. The man followed, looking like he needed about a week's worth of sleep.

"So some of the rumors weren't exaggerations."

"What?" I asked Douglas.

"All of you ready to drop anything at a moment's notice to rally the troops. I was thinking it was all legend and bullshit."

"I thought so at first, too. I didn't understand how people could be so selfless. After everything Remy went through, what they've all seen, they still see so much good in people the rest of society gave up on. I didn't believe until I was immersed in it during the Fellows' case. The people on the strip have so little and still so willing to give. We're not a bad community to be a part of, even if most of the department looks down on us for our sexualities or the way we work against the system from the inside."

"I'm starting to see that. I better get home. My daughter is blowing up my phone."

"How old?"

"Thirteen. I swear I wasn't prepared to deal with her hormones. I was raised by a single dad and only had brothers. I was not ready for estrogen. Me and her mom tried to make it work, but our careers took us to opposite ends of the world, literally. Her mom is in the military. That's where we met. We were both stationed in California and Savannah. Well, she didn't want to move again and leave her friends. So, what's a good dad to do? I packed up and transferred here."

"It's a good city, well, parts of it are. Once Doc's done cuddling his new favorite little girl, I'm getting him home. Thanks for the help and coming to hang out. I bet we're a bit weird to you."

"Weird ain't a bad thing, Stevenson. Weird is sometimes the best in the world. Tell Doc I'll be by to see him soon to finish our talk. I was consulting with him on a case when the big event happened."

"I'll let him know."

As I was left alone, I brought my full focus back to Doc as he carefully placed the baby back in the incubator, and I tracked his movements until he appeared, removing the paper gown.

"How's she doing?" I opened my arms, and he instantly walked into them.

"Definitely a fighter. Where did everyone go?"

"Remy took Major for a shower and a change of clothes in one of the locker rooms. Boss and Fran were doing their thing. Graves's getting the apartment ready. Robert went home to Roo. Douglas had to get home but said he'd come by to see you soon to finish your talk. A nurse told Remy that they were finishing up with Saffy. I figured after you knew she was okay, I'd take you home to sleep."

"I really need it."

"Yeah, you got some good-sized bags going on here, honey." I stroked my thumbs across the dark circles.

"You're not supposed to insult the traumatized doctor."

"Traumatized, as if you'd lose your cool."

"God, I so did, Carter. All I can think about is how close I came to losing her."

"But you didn't. She's going to live a very long life. And can you imagine the stories she's going to hear from her parents about how and where she was born?"

"Yeah, I'm sure the little girl wants to know she was birthed on an autopsy table."

I felt better when he laughed and tipped his head back to look up at me. "I'm so proud of you, Morgan. You did an incredible thing. You saved two lives, maybe three because I don't know if Major would've survived without them. Did you know the baby was his?"

"I assumed with how he interacted, and he did come to her appointment for that first ultrasound. You should've seen his face when he saw the screen. It was love at first sight."

"Who's here for Saffron Weatherby?"

"We are," I announced and laced my fingers with Doc's as we met the doctor halfway.

"She's going to be fine. We were able to repair the rupture.

She's going to be in recovery for a few hours or so and then moved to a room. Is her husband here?"

"He's getting cleaned up, he wanted to see his daughter, and he can't wait to see Saffy," Doc answered.

"She's in terrible shape. The beating she sustained—"

"I'm Detective Carter Stevenson. She was attacked, and we've already taken the reports. She's safe with us...her family."

"Okay, with her beating, I wanted to make sure it wasn't a case of spousal abuse."

"Not at all. Major Grigori can't wait to see his wife and daughter." I assured him.

"Who delivered the baby?"

"I did, Doctor Morgan Warner."

"Aren't you the senior medical examiner?"

"I am. I know Adam and Saffy. They were closer to me than the hospital when she went into labor. I'm a licensed general practitioner on top of a well-respected medical examiner."

"Well, her husband did the right thing. A delay of even a few minutes, she might not have made it, her or the baby. Congratulations, Doctor."

"Thanks for that and taking care of Saffy. I know how excited she was for her daughter's arrival."

The doctor nodded, and I threw my arm over Doc's shoulders, "Let's text Remy, and then we'll go home. You need a bed. I'll make you something to eat while you shower."

"That sounds great." He leaned into my side, and we briefly stopped to get one last look at the baby, and then I led him from the hospital and to my truck. He didn't protest when I picked him up to settle him on the seat. It was lightly snowing as I drove carefully through the city to the turn-off to reach the funeral home. He pointed to a narrow gravel drive and said I could park at the cottage.

He was barely awake by the time I parked, and I almost had to carry him inside. The fire was completely out.

"Get you some warm clothes. I'll get the fire restarted and then make you something. You have any soup?"

"Yeah, there's some cans in the cabinet, but you don't have to go to the trouble."

"No, trouble. I know how you like to forget to eat."

He started to turn, and I grabbed his arm. "What?" he asked.

"Nothing, if you need me, yell, okay?"

"For the most part, I'm a big boy."

"That's not what I asked."

"Yes…sir." He dropped his gaze, and I let him go. He needed to get clean and relax, and I had to take care of him.

I heard the shower turn on as I removed the ashes to a bucket on the hearth. I was a city kid, but I wouldn't embarrass myself by letting a damn fire beat me. The night I was here, I'd watched him tend it, so after a few false starts, I got it going and straightened to heat up some soup. My cooking skills were rusty but heating up soup shouldn't be too hard, and I found some tea.

Just as I finished setting the table, he appeared in a pair of sweats, t-shirt, and that long, heavy button-up sweater he'd worn the other night. He was finger combing his damp hair, and the strands were darker, almost dark gray, but I knew they'd dry to an almost impossible silver. I'd only seen the color when people went and had it professionally done.

"Just in time, sit down." I pulled out a chair for him, and he blushed a pretty pink. "Can I ask you an odd question?"

"I don't think there's much that would be considered odd in our friend group?"

"As long as I've known you, your hair has been that pretty shade of silver. What was it before?"

"I was this color since I was twenty-eight. Before that, it was black. Here." He reached to a box of albums, and he flipped through the pages before handing it to me and settling in to eat.

I stared at the picture. It was a group one, and I recognized a much younger and painfully thin version of Remy, Boss, and several of the other people I'd been introduced to in their lives. Doc's hair was professional-short, but he wore tight-fitting jeans and a black band t-shirt. Except for the lines at the corner of his eyes, he looked almost the same. The same bratty grin and tilt to his head. "Damn, you haven't changed. Although, I think you've gotten cuter as you aged."

"Flattery gets you everywhere, Detective. I was twenty-six. God that was a long time ago, almost thirty years. Remy was sixteen in that picture. I'd met him a year earlier when he was brought to me to stitch up his back the first time."

"It shocks me how far you, Remy, and Boss go back." I set the album aside as I ate, but I made sure that he was eating enough.

"I was nineteen and doing my final residency in the ER when I met Boss. It was a lifetime ago, but also, like time hasn't passed at all. When I met Boss, it was like this connection clicked into place. He'd brought in his boyfriend at the time, who was a sex worker. Got worked over pretty badly by a client. He was shocked I'd treat him and his partner with respect. Even in the nineties, it wasn't safe to be out. The community was still reeling from the AIDS epidemic that no one wanted to see as a human issue and not just a gay one. We must have seemed pretty out there to you when you stumbled into our craziness."

"No, it was actually freeing. My parents were and are strict Catholics. I was going to graduate from Yale Law, pass the Bar, and marry a good Catholic girl, have babies. I just smiled and agreed because no one in our neighborhood was like *that*, and I was so scared for so long. And then I accepted who I was and came out. I thought it would fix everything. It didn't, and then I met you and Remy, and then everyone else, and I did that whole contrast and compare."

"Not everything works out on the timetable we want it to. I'm almost fifty-six. I thought I'd have a husband and Daddy...a Dominant, by now. I never thought about having kids, my career and all is way too demanding, but I'm a great uncle." He smiled so sweetly. "Roo, and Becca, and Sammie and Teddy, Remy and Robert gave me nieces and nephews. My life is good, though. I'm doing what I want. Couldn't ask for better or crazier friends… family. You're only forty-three, you have plenty of time to find your happily ever after, and, Carter, you really deserve one."

"You think?"

"Yeah, I really do." He wouldn't look at me when he said it and seemed determined to stare a hole in the bottom of his bowl. His hair fell forward, and I reached out as had become my habit and tucked it behind the perfect shell of his ear.

"I've wanted a man just mine for so long. He'd be beautiful." I stroked my fingers down his cheek. "He wouldn't think my affection and love were too much. He'd be so sweet…I'd have to remind myself he was real." I traced the delicate line of his jaw.

"I'm so tired," he whispered as he closed his eyes and I pulled away.

"Finish a little more of your soup, and I'll turn down your bed." I pushed up from the table and hated when he didn't look at me again. I rubbed the center of my chest and forced myself to swallow around the lump in my throat. By the time I got his covers turned down and the bed ready, I felt him behind me. I straightened. "I'll bunk down on the couch again, just in case you need me, and I'll take you to get your car."

He stepped in close, his forehead came to rest on my chest, and he wrapped his arms around my waist. I hugged him with my right arm, and my left sunk into his soft, thick hair.

"Thanks for tonight. You've gone above and beyond the friend code." He turned his head to lay his ear right over my heart, just like Roo did when she wanted comfort from one of her favorite humans.

"Morgan."

"Goodnight, Stevenson." His goodnight and withdraw were abrupt, and then he crawled into bed with his back to me.

"Night, Doc, I'll clean up and turn off the lights." I stepped away from the bed with my heart breaking worse than when Joseph told me he didn't love or find me attractive anymore. Why couldn't I remember my promise to be his friend? To do what was best for him? Fuck, why did it hurt so much to do the right thing?

16

DOC

COLD CASE
UNIT

I sat on the hearth with a throw blanket wrapped around me as I watched Stevenson sleep. I'd run out of tears two hours ago, but I couldn't make myself even take a nap. My fingers kept stroking the exact spots he had. My brain conjured the exact feel of his callouses, the warmth of his touch. I'd imagined he'd called me beautiful and perfect, but I knew I was neither of those things.

I'd pressed my ear to his chest so I could take in the rhythmic beat of his heart. He deserved so much, but I'd sell my soul for him to be mine. Daddy had nearly slipped past my lips, and I'd barely suppressed it in time to replace it with sir. I hadn't wanted to make him mad and have him leave me. I was a pathetic old man, just like I'd known. I closed my eyes and leaned my head back against the fire-warmed stone.

"Baby, why aren't you in bed?"

My eyes shot open to find him watching me with heavy-lidded eyes. "I couldn't sleep."

"Come here." He lifted the blanket, and helplessly, I got to my feet.

I held my blanket tightly as he grabbed my hand and pulled

me down until I rested on top of him. He tucked his blanket back around us. I'd dreamed of being held by him. Feeling his warmth and burly frame, the cushion of his belly. I closed my eyes inhaled the scent of him, me, and my home combined.

"You have to sleep. You had a lot of stress last night. And we don't want you cranky. You're only supposed to be a bratty boy, baby."

I couldn't hold back a sob as his lips brushed my forehead, just the barest of a caress.

"Hey, what's wrong?" he whispered softly in the dim light from the fire.

"I'm just stressed. I'm fine, really. I should go back to bed."

"No, stay right here. I think you need a cuddle, and since Remy or Vega or Robert aren't here, I guess you'll have to suffer through my half-assed attempt." His arms circled me, and he laced his fingers at the small of my back.

"You're not doing too badly. You're perfectly built to give the best cuddles."

"Am I?"

"Uh-huh. I'm a genius. I've done the calculations."

"I was wondering, your birthday is soon. What do you have planned?"

"Vega said paddling was definitely in, but wondered if I could handle fifty-six of them."

He chuckled, and it vibrated his chest beneath me. "You've talked about spankings a time or two."

"Brats like spankings. It's an incentive for my bratty behavior." I bit the inside of my cheek as his fingertips stroked up and down the indent of my spine, and the only thing keeping my body from reacting was the fear that he'd stop. "We don't have to talk about this."

"Morgan, don't hide with me. I've known more about Remy and Robert than I ever want to, but that doesn't mean I don't like knowing my friends are happy. What's one thing you've always wanted?"

"Mmm, loaded question there, Detective."

"I'll take my chances." His husky voice seemed more appealing in the hushed intimacy of my fire-lit home.

"I've wanted to be made love to."

"Explain."

"I'm needy. I loved being fucked, taken, made to submit. Being desired is the best feeling in the world. To have a man so overcome that he forces you to edge until you leave marks down his back, over his ass, I've done that plenty in my life and well before I should have let someone inside my body. But I've never had someone want to cherish me, savor it, make it last because he can't imagine being anywhere but between my thighs...inside me. We can crave what we already know, but there's a desperation for that unknown variable...that experience that you've only played out in your fantasies and dreamed of. That moment when he's so deep, and you know, can see it in his eyes, the strain in his features that you're the most amazing and safest place he's ever been."

"And..." He cleared his throat, and I grimaced, thinking I'd gone too far. "That's what you want?"

"More than anything. What about you? If you could have anything in the world, what would it be?" I asked as I completely relaxed and took advantage, drawing patterns on his chest, feeling the cushion of hair under his t-shirt.

"This, right here. A man letting me hold him without timing it. Without mentally planning his next day or what opening or closing argument he'll make in court, just waiting for me to get off so he can go clean up and go to sleep. His back to me, a barrier between us more tangible than if he'd gotten up and went to sleep in the guest room." He slipped his big hand under my hair and massaged the back of my neck. "Which he did. He hated the feel of me, the roughness of my hands…the excessive body hair. I was made to feel privileged that he let a brute like me on top of him. We all want things we never had or maybe never will. But, baby, a lot of us are too scared to allow it to happen because what if that perfection doesn't live up to the dream of it? What if we ruin that experience for the other person by not being enough?"

"You'll find that one special person who's everything you've always wanted. You're too exceptional to not be treasured." I let out a soft sigh as he combed his fingers through my hair to curve around the back of my head. He lifted to bury his face in my hair, and his chest expanded as if he was taking me in, committing my scent to memory exactly how I'd done with him.

All of that was nothing more than wishful thinking. The want of the unattainable. He didn't want to be my Daddy or my Dom. He simply didn't want to be mine. And I understood. It was like an old uncomfortable blanket, but it was a familiar, safe in its sensory memory; it was a thing you could always count on. Oh, how I wanted to be that person to let him be him—to keep him. The person who always made him feel wanted and not like a burden or a chore. Because I knew exactly what that felt like, and it never failed to kill a small piece of your soul.

To me, as I laid there, savoring that soft cushion of hair, it was real, and the way my flat, yet soft belly conformed to the curve of his. It was as if two pieces were finding the exact place they belonged, but in the end, fate was a cruel mistress, sadistic in how she presented you with all you dreamed of wrapped up in a perfect sparkling package that was so sweet and good; yet she always held it just out of reach.

"Go to sleep, baby. I know you're exhausted…we both are. You have important work to do and so many people counting on you."

I nodded as I tried to take a breath without it breaking. There would be no sleep for me, but as the minutes turned to an hour, I listened to the way his heart beat that steady, strong pace, and his breathing became deep and even. I synced my own to his, tipping my head back to watch his face in sleep. The heavy stubble that had turned to a dark blond beard over the last several months, the shadow of his lashes, and I painted them to my memory. He had so many years left to find happiness, but all I had was years of loneliness.

One day he'd come in with my coffee, a smile on his face that lit up his blue eyes, and tell me about the amazing man he'd met. And I'd congratulated him because I would be happy for him. I'd tell him how I couldn't wait to meet this man lucky enough to call him theirs. And I'd mean it because he deserved it all, but first, I held my breath as I eased up his chest until I could reach his full lips.

A tear slipped free as they gave under mine, and I felt the involuntary reflex of him kissing me back. I whispered in my head how much I loved him and then tucked my face against his neck. Lost myself in his scent until the sun began to rise, and I forced myself to ease out of his arms and went to get ready for my day.

17

STEVENSON

COLD CASE
UNIT

"Is there a reason you're hiding in my office?" Vega asked as I sat on the floor of her dark office and tried to get my thoughts together.

"Trying to think." I leaned my head back and looked up at the ceiling, drew my legs up to rest my forearms on my knees. The more I investigated the Barnes-Maxwell case, the less I knew and the more questions I had without any answers. I'd read and gone over everything in the official case file and the one Mary put together so much I'd practically memorized everything.

"Can't do it somewhere else?"

"An innocent young woman is just walking down the street with her little brother, and next thing anyone knows, she's dead. No one even started looking into it enough until they realized her brother was with her. By the time they put out an amber alert, it was already too late. The original detective, Sandowski, when I tracked him down said he didn't know shit." I pushed a heavy breath through my teeth as I flexed my hands.

"Listen to me…" She spun her chair. "You're talking about the strip. A young woman that isn't white disappears, then she must have been fucking around."

"I know. I've worked with Remy long enough to get the bias lectures. I went into this case thinking it would be a case of a parent kidnapping their kid, and shit went wrong. I didn't promise to solve it, but..." I muttered curses under my breath. "I want to solve it."

"Closure rates of cold cases are low, like fucking embarrassingly low, and we got a backlog of them. Forensics are missing. Some evidence is so degraded that it can't be processed. Witnesses are dead, missing, or simply unwilling. Like I tell Remy, you can't solve them all. Sometimes they just have to go back on the shelf. Are you doing this because you believe you can solve it or your ego is too big to give up?"

I thought over her question. I'd admit to anyone that I was stubborn and egotistical when it came to my job, but working the Cold Case Unit had brought me down several pegs. I just needed one new piece of evidence, someone to remember something, no matter how small. A knock sounded, and I turned as the door opened, and Graves slipped inside.

"Am I just getting all the visitors today? Why am I so lucky?"

"Homicide Detective Douglas, I want to strangle him. Could I get away with it?" Graves fell into a chair.

"You worked Homicide, forensically aware, if anyone can get away with it. But why don't you just get over the sexual tension and finally admit you're ready to ride that man into a mattress?"

I snorted as Graves flipped her off, and he grabbed her bag of chips. Lots of things changed in a year. Health nut Graves was all over the junk food and out of his suits. It was weird seeing a relaxed Graves. His once buzzed head was covered in thick waves of dark hair, and his face was covered with stubble.

"So, what's this meeting about?" he asked.

"My case."

"The murder-kidnapping?"

"Yeah, there's practically nothing in the official file, the victims' mother did a better job, but I've tried to track down some of the people she spoke with. Their memories are hazy, or I can't find them at all."

"Have you tried talking to Boss? A lot of people are off the grid, but he does have people who still check-in." Graves spoke between each chip.

"The pretty boy isn't wrong. Boss is a helluva source when needed. He does take safety into account, so some people go underground for a reason."

"I'm not pretty. If I thought I could get away with it and not have to deal with Cash, I'd make you disappear."

"As long as my babygirl frightens you, I'm safe. Fuck with me, though, I'll steal your phone and sext your big detective."

"You're obsessed with my sex life. And quit being mean. I thought we were friends."

"No, I'm not, I just think you're wound too tight, and we're only friends with you because you can't make any others." She made a grab for the chip bag.

"I'm eating all your chips now." He pushed off and slid across the office away from her.

"I need new friends and co-workers." I got off the floor and straightened. They boo'ed me, and I rolled my eyes.

"You know what to do, Stevenson. You're an excellent detective, and if you tell anyone I said that, I'll make sure you never get your hands on my Doc."

"Doc and I are friends."

"Yeah, keep thinking that. Now, could I have my office back?"

"I'm headed to talk to Boss. I have no control over Graves."

"I'm leaving, but I'm taking the chips." He jumped up and made a run for the door. She yelled his name as he slipped through.

"Do I need to buy you more?" I watched a grin widen her lips as she reached under her desk and pulled out an entire bag. "I can see you're covered."

"I live here, man. Sometimes I forget what my house looks like."

"If I could get a fresh DNA sample, do you think you could do your magic?"

"Get it for me, and I'll do everything within my power. What's on your mind?"

"I know bodies disappear, some victims just disappear off the face of the earth, but if they just wanted to snatch the kid..." I took a deep breath and then exhaled. "My gut says this was done by more than one person. Angela was a fighter. She was going to do some damage. They went to so much trouble to grab Aiden. If they went through all that trouble, there has to be a reason."

"You're hoping his DNA gets a hit."

"Hoping."

"Get me a sample of the mother's DNA and the fathers. If, and I mean if, the boy is still alive, I can possibly get a familial hit and work my way from there. Unless he's completely off the grid."

"I'll call in Mary. I'm sure she'll be willing. But I have to track down Aiden's dad. He left the city and no forwarding information with the original investigators."

"Like I said, get me what you can. Should I search for John Doe murder cases with DNA on file?"

I nodded. "Thanks, Vega."

"Not a problem. Normally I can let shit go. People get murdered...some just disappear without a trace. But kids? They didn't do shit, and if I can actually help bring one home... highlight of my fucking job."

I thanked her again and left her office, which was almost as pit-like as her basement office at her place. I squinted my eyes at the bright hallway lights and strode through the empty hallways until I reached the exit of her building. Visiting Boss was a good idea. But I also knew that if it endangered anyone, he wouldn't tell me anything. The Outreach he ran occasionally helped abuse victims disappear and start all new lives. I respected him and the

Outreach's mission, but I needed this case solved. Even if that meant telling Mary her son was dead, at least give her closure and maybe bones or ashes to bury.

I climbed into the driver's seat of my truck and turned the key, backed out of the spot, and drove across the city to the Outreach. All crime at its base was senseless. No matter the circumstances, no one deserves to die as violently as Angela did and not receive justice. I needed that, and even if eventually I had to put the case back on the shelf, I'd still think about it, always looking for answers.

I smiled as I pulled into the parking lot and watched the little kids playing on the equipment right in front of the basketball courts. I parked, and after grabbing my case notes, I jumped out of the truck, slamming the door. I said hi to several people I knew.

"Hey, Lorna." I headed for the reception desk. "Is Boss around?"

"Hey, Stevenson. Um, I think he's in his office, but if he's not there, he might be in the pantry. Bart's going to be late today."

"Thanks." I walked toward the maze of hallways, checked his office first, and of course, he wasn't there. I went hunting him down in the pantry, the door was open and his back was to me. The short, powerfully built man wasn't someone I wanted to take on, so I knocked on the metal doorframe. "Hey, Boss."

He glanced at me over his shoulder and then went back to work. "Stevenson, Doc isn't here."

I rolled my eyes. Everyone seemed to think Doc and I were always supposed to be together or looking for each other. I would admit that since I slept with him in my arms, my need for him had grown. Focusing on the case had put some distance between us, but he was such a big part of my everyday life at work and personal. "I know, he's working with a federal prosecutor today, some appeals thing. They needed an independent opinion."

"Then what has you looking troubled?"

"Angela Barnes and Aiden Maxwell."

"That's ancient history."

"Yeah, but what's your opinion?"

"Mary is a bulldog. She knocked on more doors than the cops."

"I know, she gave me her case file, and I was amazed at the work she'd done. Some of the surveillance videos are at the lab getting cleaned up for me. What was your opinion on the victims?"

"Angie wasn't someone people fucked with, especially men." He paused as if thinking. "She had a girlfriend."

"I didn't know that," I said as I watched him continue to unpack and organize the pantry items.

"No one knew. Angela hadn't come out to Mary. She used to come to our group for queer teens. She was scared they wouldn't let her raise her brother if they knew she was gay. I do know that the girlfriend wasn't exactly happy about being kept a secret, but she loved Angie, and figured once Mary got out, Angie would tell her mother the truth."

"Do you think it could've been a lover's dispute that went wrong?"

"No. Angie and Di were very much in love. They treated Aiden like he was theirs. Di came to our group for people who lost a loved one for a long time after the murder. I don't think she ever got over it. If I remember right, they were about to get a bigger apartment in a nicer building...a better school for Aiden. Angie was thinking of asking for full custody of Aiden, but she didn't think his dad would sign the papers giving up his rights."

"What did you know about Maxwell?"

"Outside world, respectable businessman, kid from the streets that made good."

"To everyone else?"

"Couldn't get the powder up his nose fast enough. Everyone

warned Mary to stay away from him, but she was struggling so much after her first husband died. And like with a lot of people, their grief…their loneliness makes them search for relief from the pain."

"Mary used?" I already knew that since she'd gone down on drug and distribution charges.

"No more than a lot of people. Would it have been more socially acceptable for her to use alcohol as a band-aid?"

"I'm not judging, Boss. She already admitted she did things she regretted, but could the killing and disappearance be a form of retaliation?"

"She dealt to pay for her habit, but as the saying goes, don't get high on your own supply. Easiest way to fuck-up. I always felt Maxwell got her hooked and then used her to keep them supplied. A scapegoat. She had Angie and Aiden. There's no way she would've been carrying that weight on her when she sold to the undercover if she wasn't pushed to do it. She went down, and Maxwell looked squeaky clean and went on with his life as if nothing happened."

"Why wasn't Aiden put in his care?"

"The woman he was seeing at the time, as high-maintenance as they came, she didn't want to share, not even with a kid. So he didn't fight when Angie was made guardian of Aiden. At least that's what Di told me. Anything new on this case that has you looking into it?"

"I just picked at random, and I read the shitty official file. Most of the evidence wasn't even tested, and what was stored was degraded. Mary didn't even get to go to Angie's funeral. She had to learn about her daughter's death and son's disappearance on the fucking news. The work on this case was shoddy."

"Most crimes committed in the vicinity of the strip usually are. There was even some pushing from the cops to say she was an addict…sex worker. Others wanted to say she traded Aiden for drugs. It was bullshit, and no one believed it, but she was brown and poor. She was an amazing young woman. She was on her way to doing great things when she was murdered."

"Any other rumors on the streets?"

"Just stupid urban legends, trying to say it was another Jack the Ripper since she was practically cut in half. Then you had the human trafficking angle. They tried to grab her, and since she fought, they killed her and took Aiden. You know the usual shit. If we have anything down here, it's an active grapevine. What did Doc say about the case?"

"He could practically recite the damn report. That man is too smart."

"He is."

I went through a list of questions, writing down his answers, but while there were a few new things to check out, most of the information I already had. I put away my notebook and pen into the inside pocket of my leather jacket.

"Thanks for answering my questions."

"You're welcome. You got something else on your mind?"

"What should I get Morgan for his birthday?" I knew it was coming up, but I kept looking, and I just couldn't find anything. I knew Vega was planning a big party. I'd thought about taking him to dinner, like a date, but kept telling myself no.

"He's happy with anything. He likes antiques, odds and ends, just random old stuff. But if you want to make his Little happy, he likes soft things."

"Would giving him a Little present be weird?"

"No. He's been ignoring that part of himself for a long time. He needs to be reminded occasionally that there's nothing wrong with being in your fifties and being a Little."

I thought about it and remembered all the antiques littered around on his shelves. Old cameras, medical instruments, and dolls. Maybe I'd hit a few stores over the weekend, and it would come to me. I knew he liked his cuddles and the way he smiled when I brought him coffee and treats. It always seemed so easy to please him. "Why is he self-conscious about being a Little?"

"He had a few bad experiences, and it made him insecure. I heard you two had words."

"It wasn't words. I was having a bad day, and I was idiotic and took it out on him. We made up."

"He told me that, too. There isn't much that happens with my people that I don't know about."

"I may have heard that a time or two. Graves is the one that told me to come talk to you."

"Graves has been a bit of a surprise. I didn't think he'd survive with all of you, especially Vega."

"He *has* changed a lot the last year. It's kinda weird."

"He's fine. He needed to relax some."

"That's an understatement. Okay, I'm headed back to the department."

"Don't hesitate to call me if you need info, but there are some things I won't talk about."

"I understand. Groups are private."

"The only reason I talked to you about Angie is because I want to help. Mary has been lost without her kids, and not knowing where Aiden is tortures her every day."

"When I've spoken with her, I can tell. The uncertainty. I want to give her answers, but I'm terrified I won't be able to."

"You're caring about what happened to her son and daughter... that's more than she got from the cops before you. I went to visit her."

"You did?"

"Yeah, she called me after she saw the news. She begged me to tell her it wasn't true, and I went to visit her a few weeks afterward. She nearly gave up. There wasn't a reason to make it out of prison anymore. Her investigation gave her purpose, but she worked it as far as she could."

"I told her she should've been a cop."

Boss laughed. "I told her that once, too, and she said something about being a felon."

"She told me the same thing. Thanks again, Boss. If you think of anything, call me, okay?"

"You'll be the first one."

I took the same path back to the front exit and thought about calling Doc to see how his day had been. I knew the prosecutor and agent that contacted him stressed him out. I'd text him when I got home for the day. Mostly I wanted to go to the coroner's office and check on him. I wasn't feeling friend-like toward him, but I still didn't think I could give the beautiful man what he needed. I couldn't endanger our friendship and make him miserable in the end. No matter how much I wanted him, I wouldn't hurt him.

I pushed it all aside and focused on what I needed to, and not my little ghoul and his adorable giggles.

18

DOC

I hated consults. I loved my job even though the hours sucked, sometimes it was beyond disgusting, but I didn't know anything else. What I hated about my job was having to look over someone else's work and see how they fucked up the case. There were five death row appeals, and the autopsies were all done by the same coroner.

His reports were filled with supposition from personal beliefs and not facts proved by the evidence. How did the prosecution let him on the stand or defense not file motions to remove the coroner? I scanned the trial transcripts, and the defense attorneys barely objected. Which meant that I had five cases to redo. I'd packed up the files for the oldest case into my vehicle to take home.

I opened another energy drink and settled in, there was way too much information to go through, and I'd told them I couldn't guarantee I would agree with the original medical examiner's opinion. They were worried about every case the doctor was on would come under scrutiny, and in a forty-year career, that was a lot of cases.

Connecting my phone to my Bluetooth speakers, I turned on

my music and settled into work. I hesitated as I reached for the top on the first file box and dropped my hands to the cushion on either side of my thighs. My birthday was only days away, and I always looked forward to the party. One night of letting everything go, work and stress, just spending time with my best friends. Yet there was something about that birthday I wasn't ready for.

I didn't know why fifty-six turned into a contemplative milestone, but it had. All the dreams a teenaged me had. A life like my Uncle Cyril, but out and proud, married maybe—and it had almost happened in my twenties. No one ever knew. It wasn't even something I'd shared with Vega. Leif had been a decade older than me. It was those impossible meet-cutes you read in all those romance novels. He worked in research for a pharmaceutical company, had nothing to do with law enforcement or death, he was rich and worldly, and it was nice... he was nice. We'd talked on the phone and had a few coffee dates before going on the big first date.

He'd been a beautiful man, so different from my friends and found family that I'd kept it to myself. At first, he hadn't minded my crazy hours or the emergency calls that would have me leaving in the middle of the night. He'd given me all the romance, and he'd introduced me to his friends and colleagues. He hadn't treated me like a dirty secret.

One night after dinner, we'd cuddled on the couch, and he'd asked me to move in. For the first time in my life, I'd been in love, and I hadn't hesitated to say yes. The moment I'd moved in, it was all I'd dreamed. He brought me flowers, took me on dates, and remembered all the milestone anniversaries. He spoiled me.

The night he proposed, it wasn't legal, but he said he wanted the ceremony and to have his ring on my finger. I hadn't realized how everything would change. He'd became cold and demanding, my need for affection exhausting. The accusations about me cheating due to all the nights I was out, the calls from

Remy and Boss. Dr. Jekyll and Mr. Hyde had had nothing on Leif.

I'd tried to conform and make him happy. Shame had kept me quiet after the first hit. I always counseled people to leave because mistreatment always escalated. Yet I'd stayed through it all until the night he tried to kill me. I could still feel the first slash of the knife, the sting as the skin split. The rage in his eyes so different from the adoration of only a year earlier. I'd wasted three years living a double life, kept my friends and family in the dark, and all I had left were the insecurities and scars to show for what I thought would be my happily ever after.

I'd gone to work, stitched myself up, and tried to pretend everything was okay. I hadn't lived there at the time, and he hadn't met anyone, so I'd run home to my groundskeeper cottage and hid there. I'd ignored the calls. The apologies were empty promises that it would never happen again.

Eventually, he'd lost interest, but I'd looked over my shoulder for years afterward. It was years before I'd let another man into my life, some had given me what I'd needed, and others shamed me just like Leif had. One-night stands filled my need for physical affection but nothing beyond that.

I was damaged goods. The one I'd wanted for years saw me as only a friend, but he was giving me the affection I needed. I just wished it went past platonic. I dropped my head back and nearly jumped out of my skin when the shrill ring of my phone played over my speakers. I leaned forward, disconnected the Bluetooth, and answered the call.

"Warner."

"Hey, baby."

All the heaviness of my thoughts disappeared at the warm, rough timbre of Stevenson's voice. "Hey, what are you doing?"

"Just got home and thought I'd check on my little man. You working?"

"Yes, but I'm at home."

"What did the Feds want?"

"Death penalty appeals."

He groaned. "On what grounds?"

"Incompetence, so far it's five cases."

"But if you find out he fucked up…" From his sudden silence, I knew what had popped into his head. The last time I consulted with the Feds, I'd spent most of two years reexamining one case after another when a case of corruption had put all the cases of a coroner and detective under scrutiny.

"Then we're about to have an epidemic of appeals. Any progress on your case?"

"They told me they'd transferred the rest of the tapes to digital and would have them to me tomorrow. Hopefully, I can see something strange on the videos in the vicinity of Angela's murder. I might have to borrow Vega's set-up to watch all of it. Wanna do me a favor?"

"I see what this call was about. Sweet talk me into talking to my best friend for you so you can play with her toys. My feelings are hurt." His deep warning rumble teased me.

"Don't be like that, baby. I missed having coffee with you this morning."

I pressed my cool hands to my suddenly hot cheek. "I did, too. Will I see you in the morning?"

"You will, nine AM like normal, and I'll bring you your snacks."

I knew he'd never be my Daddy, but, fuck, he had so much potential. "You take such good care of me."

"I do what I can. You excited about your birthday party?"

"That depends, Detective. Are you going to be there?" I nibbled at my lower lip as he gruffly chuckled.

"Would I miss it?"

"I hope not. Want to come over?" My eyes widened as the question slipped out in an almost needy whisper, and I froze.

We'd been getting along, and I didn't want to go back to the distance after our last disagreement.

"I wish I could, I love your place, and your couch is way more comfortable than my futon."

"I bet my bed would be even more comfortable."

"I'm sure it would be, little man."

I loved how his voice dipped lower, and I could picture that wicked smile he sometimes gave me when he playfully flirted with me.

"Morgan."

"Yeah?"

"You got quiet on me. Are you sleepy?"

"I'm always sleepy. I need a vacation."

"Where would you go?"

"Mountains. Nice quiet cabin. No cell reception."

"No white sandy beaches? No umbrella drinks? Hot men barely dressed?"

"Okay, you may have sold me on a tropical vacation, but I'd look like a lobster, so not sexy."

"That's why you take someone with you, an excuse not to leave your room."

"I can see what vacations with you would be like."

"I admit to nothing, baby. Okay, I'm going to bed, don't stay up all night…you need your rest, too."

"That I won't deny. I have an early autopsy scheduled. Goodnight, Carter."

"Goodnight, baby, and I'll see you in the morning. If you want anything special, text me, and I'll pick it up."

"Thanks, you don't have to, but I appreciate all the coffee and snacks."

"Gotta keep you fed and healthy and make sure you sleep. Don't open that file."

I rolled my eyes. "I promise." He whispered goodbye, and I reluctantly disconnected the call.

My sanctuary seemed colder and lonelier than normal without his soothing voice in my ear. A person shouldn't be your comfort item. Yet my brain and body calmed so much when in his presence. He made everything so right, and my past experiences urged me not to trust myself. My track record with men, especially ones I wanted for my Daddy Dominant, were bleak. Learning from my mistakes didn't seem to be my strong suit.

I leaned forward to grab the top of the box and froze with my arm suspended in the air as I remembered promising him that I'd go to bed. The next day would be soon enough to drive myself crazy going through the reports. From a quick scan of the contents of a few folders, I'd already braced myself for missing or incomplete data. I picked up my coffee energy drink and pushed up from the couch to stick it back in the fridge to chug when I woke up.

He wasn't wrong. I needed more sleep, but when I dreamed, he was there, and that made me want him even more.

19

STEVENSON

Masquerade Ball in a two-hundred-year-old funeral home, of course, that would be Vega's idea of the perfect birthday party for Doc. I'd already spotted Carol, Robert's oldest daughter, and Gladys, his ex-wife, who was wearing an obscene dress and having a drink with Shine, an old friend of Remy's. Those two had been attached at the hip for a year.

I hadn't run into Remy or Robert yet, but I knew they'd wanted to wait until they'd put Roo to bed. She wouldn't go to sleep unless her Papa read her no less than five books.

"Do I need to pat you down, Detective?" I spun as Cash whispered in my ear. "So jumpy."

She was dressed in a latex dress that hugged every one of her supermodel curves and had a latex mask with *Vega's Babygirl* embroidered above the right eye.

"No, I'm not on duty. I'm not carrying tonight."

"You do have a concealed weapon, though."

"For a lesbian, you're obsessed with my dick."

"I just like giving y'all shit." She let out a husky laugh as she turned to stand shoulder to shoulder with me. "Have you seen Little man yet?"

"No, I just got here. I was kinda floating around. I'm not much for parties. I don't drink."

"Plenty of sodas and bottled water. Doc made sure we had a lot of non-alcoholic choices. If you want to have a cover, there's non-alcoholic beers, too. Cover the label with your hand, and they'll never know."

"You're being nice. What gives?"

"I'm not much for parties either. I do so many bar gigs...I just prefer the quiet and shit, ya know? Just at home with my Mami cuddled on her lap. Heaven. But I have to admit the suit she's wearing and the crop she's carrying is really giving me ideas."

"How does that work?"

"You've been around us long enough you should know how it works."

"How does one realize they're a Caregiver-Dominant or Little-Sub?"

She hooked her arm in mine and led me away from the crowd and into the casket display room. Electric candles lit the room, giving it a creepy air. I kind of liked the aesthetic, it was very much Doc, and I'm sure it reminded him fondly of his uncles.

"So, how does someone know? It's different for everyone. God, when I met Vega, I was so touch-me-not *butch* it wasn't even funny. I thought I was a complete Top because, growing up, I learned to fight. I was too tall. Too Masc. Too everything, really. The first time"—she sighed heavily as she spun on the toes of her boots to face me—"Vega stroked my cheek and said, *tell Mami all about it*, I swear it's like all the walls I'd built around myself disappeared. Don't get me wrong. I fought it. I mean, Vega is a genius, like seriously smart, and I barely graduated high school. I sing and play bass in a band. I was living in a two-bedroom apartment with seven other people eating ramen noodles three meals a day. And here is this younger, scarily intelligent, successful woman who has her shit together. She came to every gig, walked away when I said no, but she always came back until one night I said yes."

"Was it easy?" I saw the serene look on her face as she talked about Vega's care. It was similar to Doc's when Robert cared for him.

"She took me back to her big house, led me upstairs, and stripped me down, gave me my first bath, and held me. No pushing for sex. She didn't even touch me in a sexual way. It was so fucking weird, but, man, it felt so right. Everyone has their thing. Some don't do kink. Some live the lifestyle twenty-four-seven, and for others, it's a little thing to spice up the bedroom. You have total Daddy potential."

I stared at her, studying her to see if she was making a joke. "I don't know about that."

"You do. You have an inherent need to care for your person. You're affectionate. You're playful, but you're stern, too. I've seen you with Doc and the way he talks about you. It's a title, yeah, but it's more than that. It's the actions of a Daddy. Someone to guide and make you focus. Make you stop when you're pushing yourself too much. It's knowing when to cuddle and when to correct. Praising and rewarding your Little for following rules. You've seen how people care for Doc."

"He gets so…peaceful. *Focused.* He loves playing with dolls. Coloring. He loves touches and kisses. He loves when I tuck his hair behind his ear. When I kiss the top of his head. He loves when I tease him and let him flirt. I love how selfless he is, but I hate that he doesn't take a moment to breathe for himself."

"Why are you so scared of letting Doc in?"

"My ex-husband." I'd spent more time talking about my ex-husband in the last few months than I had in the years since the divorce. Most of the time, I tried not to think about him at all except on the odd occasion we ran into each other at the courthouse or when he was arriving at the precinct to meet a client. Seeing him, I wondered about whatever had attracted me to him. As much emotion that was in his polite greetings, I may as well have been a stranger.

"There's always a reason they're an ex."

"He made me ashamed of my need to take care of him. You know, just little things, like on my dinner break, I'd come home to make a meal so he wouldn't have to. Especially if I knew he was in the middle of a rough case. The food wasn't fancy enough, or he had a business dinner. I wanted to hold him outside either of our need to get off. I'm scared I'm too much."

"Stevenson, that's where you have to change your thinking. He made you feel like it was too much to be taken care of, to be loved and cherished. The right one will think it's just enough. Not everyone is the same. If something ever happened between me and Vega, I don't think I could have that level of trust for another person. She spent nearly a year waiting me out. You want to be too much, and well, our Doc is a very needy boy."

"What if I can't be what he wants and I disappoint him?"

Cash shook her head and smiled at me. "Having a dynamic of Dominant and Submissive, or Daddy-Mommy and Little is all about communication, expectations, and rules, all written down, laid out, and agreed to. Everyone's different, and safe words are required and used at any time, not just during sex. People don't understand that a lot more goes into being a part of the kink community than leather, whips, chains, and scenes. It's about building trust and open, honest communication. Just ask your baby want he wants and see if it meshes. There's also a thing known as compromise."

"Do you know where he is?"

"With Vega. They have matching costumes and riding crops. Two short people with top hats and dressage outfits. They're like weird little twins."

"Why are they so close?"

"Like gets like. Twenty years apart, but their lives mirrored. They both graduated at nineteen, they both entered a field of forensics at twenty. It's like the universe created mirrored twins. Vega's Dominant to Doc's Submissive. Come on. We'll find your baby so you feel better."

Once again, she looped her arm through mine. Several times, she stopped to introduce me to people or just say hi to the ones I already knew. Even as I did that, I was still looking for Doc. He was short enough to get lost in a crowd. When we didn't find them on the first floor, she led me down a steep staircase, and I froze.

Doc and Vega were on embalming tables giggling. The room looked like something from a Victorian horror movie. I was still amazed how they'd recreated the original time. I caught Cash bringing her hand up and placing a finger against her lips as she leaned in the darkened doorway. The electric lanterns just illuminated the tables.

"So, what do you want for your birthday? Spankings?"

"That's a given. Big, rough masculine hands, but they gotta have callouses." He moaned. "I wouldn't be able to sit tomorrow." His top hat was rested on his belly, and he hugged it, tapping on it. I could only see a bit of his small smile. The perfect tilt to lush lips I was dying to taste.

"You like those spankings way too much. That's why corner time is your punishment."

"I hate corner time."

I smiled at the pout in his voice and the way he kicked his legs, the heels of his boots ringing off the table.

"I know. That's why I started it. You being still is torture for you."

"Vega?" I stiffened at the happiness disappearing from his voice.

"Yeah, Doc?"

"Do you think I'm too much? That I need too much? Like I just annoy men so much that"—he sighed—"that maybe I shouldn't color or play with my dolls or want cuddles all the time. Maybe I shouldn't be Little anymore?"

"Doc, Cash loves playing with her blocks. Fingerpainting on the walls of her playroom. She runs around in circles at bedtime because she doesn't want to sleep. My babygirl is never too much. Because when she acts like that, she trusts me. She feels safe to be silly and laugh. She can leave the outside world and that persona behind. I absolutely love to make my wife happy in every way. Because that's what a good wife, Mami, and Dominant does. They earn their person's trust and love. Doc, the right one will love all your quirks. Hell, I love all your quirks. The way you giggle when the tip of your nose is kissed. That bratty batting of your lashes and your outrageous flirting. Never apologize for who you are. Don't ever let anyone take away the joy you have in being Little, in being submissive. Those are your places of peace. The way you leave that cold morgue behind. The way you escape the death that constantly surrounds you."

"But, Vega, I'm fifty-six, and I want a Daddy so damn much. I want a lap to cuddle on. I want to be able to tuck my face into his neck and be safe. It's like it's too late. Like I missed my moment. Or that he saw me...saw me the way I am, and he didn't like it. I'm not handsome or fit. I'm adorable and tiny."

"Except for one part of you."

He giggled. "I can't help that my height was made up with dick size. Maybe it just looks big because I'm so short."

"I've bathed you. I know what I'm talking about."

"I love you, Vega."

"I love you, too, Morgan. You've been my best friend forever."

Cash stepped back to the steps and let her heels click loudly. "Mami."

Vega was instantly sitting up and searching for her wife. "Aw, did my baby miss, Mami? Come here." She spun on the table to let her legs dangle, and Cash slipped between them.

I walked into the room. "Happy Birthday, Doc." I crossed the room to the table and spread my hands on the steel on either side of his head.

"Stevenson, you came."

"Of course I did. Would I miss my favorite little man's birthday?" I let my gaze slowly move over him, taking in the forming fitting coat over a white dress shirt and caveat. Then down to pants that hugged every trim line of his leg. I nearly groaned at the sight of a long, thick cock shown off clearly. Even soft, that was a length that begged to be sucked. "And, baby, those pants are just inviting everyone to look."

"Gotta get my cheap thrills where I can, Detective."

I lowered to rest my weight on my forearms and brushed my lips to his forehead. I kept them there as I breathed him in. The scent that was all him. When I'd awakened the other morning, his presence was gone, but his body wash lingered in my clothes. I moved to his nose, kissing the tip as he wrinkled it as my beard teased him.

"I got you presents, but I left them in the truck for later."

"What did you get me?"

"You'll have to wait and be patient. Can you do that for me, baby?" I pulled away enough to see his expression change, the lines of worry between his perfectly arched brows eased, and the corner of his lips lifted into the smallest movement.

"Yes...sir." He nibbled at his lower lip and tried to look away from me. The insecurity and stiffness were back, and I hated I made him react that way.

"Did you get your spankings?"

"No." He pouted. "Unfortunately, no appropriate candidates."

"Shame, I know you were looking forward to that tradition. Maybe it'll still happen. The night is young."

"I really was looking forward to someone bending me over before this night was done, Detective. Maybe I'll wish for it when I blow out my candles, and a big burly man will make it come true."

"Is that right?"

"That's what wishes are for, right? To get something we really want?" I didn't miss the way his gaze moved to my mouth, and I wanted to kiss him, but without an audience. "Maybe you'd like to volunteer? Those hands of yours are just the perfect size."

"Jesus, no wonder Remy wanted to douse you two in ice water. The verbal foreplay is fucking fantastic, and him eye-fucking your dick was just obscene. Come on, babygirl, let's leave these two alone."

We were both watching them as Vega jumped down and grabbed Cash's hand as Cash put Vega's top hat back on, and they disappeared. Cash giggling all the way up the steps.

"You have weird friends." I grinned as I turned my head to look at him again. I cupped his jaw and stroked his cheeks. His skin was soft with a fine dusting of blond fuzz.

"*We* have weird friends. You look handsome, very phantom of the creepy opera massacre." He tugged at the white mask with blood splatter on it. "Never been to one of these before. Figured this might be appropriate for a party in a funeral home."

"Morgan?"

"Yeah, Carter."

"You look beautiful." He blushed and tried to look away, but I held his chin to he couldn't. "But you're always beautiful."

"You don't have to say that."

"No, I don't, but you are. So smart. Compassionate. Selfless. You deserve every wish to come true. You deserve it."

"You're so sweet, Detective, and sexy, it hurts to look at you."

My heartbeat increased in pace with need at the desire in his tone. "Can I come home with you tonight, baby?"

He just nodded, but I could feel the quickening of his breaths against my mouth. I groaned as I kissed one corner and then the other. His arms came up, and his slender fingers tangled in my hair.

"Let's go celebrate your birthday and then we can go home, and I can give you all your presents. Is that agreeable?"

"Yes...sir."

Before the night was over, my baby was going to call me what he really wanted.

20

DOC

COLD CASE
UNIT

I stumbled into my cottage giggling after we'd left the mess of the funeral home behind. Vega had arranged for a cleaning service the next day, but I had bigger issues than whether my home would be ready for tours Monday or not. The heavy slide of the bolt lock made me turn. Stevenson had two bags clutched in his left hand. He'd removed his mask on our walk across the snowy yard.

He looked so good in his tux, all big and handsome. He didn't even have to try to be sexy. And I felt so small and plain beside him.

"Do you want your presents?"

I nodded. I'd been thinking about what he got me all night. Patience wasn't one of my finer qualities when my Little was triggered, and he'd very much had a Daddy voice that night. It was also in the way he'd touched me, the press of his lips to my forehead, nose, and the corners of my mouth but never a full kiss. I wanted that kiss so much, one that I hadn't sneaked while he was asleep.

"Sit on the couch."

I skipped to the couch with him chuckling and listened to the creak of the wooden floors under his shiny shoes. I dropped onto the couch and locked my gaze on the two gift bags. He lowered, and he gave me a smile so indulgent I almost sighed in bliss.

"First, you'll open this one." He handed me the first one. It was an extra-large plain brown craft paper bag with twine handles.

I reached inside and felt the thick handles. I curled my fingers around them and pulled out the antique doctor's bag. Not one that you'd buy to look old, but an actual one. It was almost exactly like the one my Uncle Cyril carried. I opened it to find it fully stocked with turn-of-the-nineteenth-century implements. Everything a doctor would need at that time.

"Carter, this is too much. It must have—"

"It's your birthday, and I thought it would be something that would look good mixed in with your books and other odds and ends. Do you like it?"

"It's perfect. Thank you so much." I surged forward and brushed my lips to his cheek. "It's...it's amazing, really."

"Now, something for the baby." He handed me a bright bag with balloons and confetti printed on it.

I looked at him confused as I took it and set the doctor's bag aside. I held my breath as I opened it, and every muscle froze in my body. I couldn't breathe as I held the most beautiful doll. Dressed in scrubs with a tiny stethoscope. And I hugged her to my chest. "Carter."

"There's more." I pulled out a dozen outfits and a brush for her hair, along with tiny shoes. There was a pink cloth bag with my name on it. "One gift for Doc and one for your Little. I know how much you...did I do okay, baby?"

I bit the inside of my cheek as I hugged my doll tighter and tried to get words past the tightening of my throat. "She's...she's beautiful."

"I got the bag so when you go play dolls with Roo, you can take her with you. I looked at teddy bears so you could have something to sleep with, but I saw her, and she had your name all over her. Morgan." He whispered my name seconds before his fingertips tucked my hair behind my ear.

I was too helpless to deny myself as I turned my head and leaned my cheek into his palm. I held the doll closer as I whimpered when he brushed his thumb along my lower lip.

"I shouldn't touch you, but it's all I've thought about for months." He scooted across the cushions and lifted my legs over his thigh. "I've imagined kissing you. Loving on you so good you can't think about anyone else." He stroked his hand across my cheek to the back of my neck, he pulled me closer, his lips so close our breaths mingled. Both frozen as if we were both terrified the other would deny us. "I want to be everything you need, but I'm so scared I can't."

"I've wanted you for years. The first time I saw you, you were wearing a cheap gray suit, with a blue tie. There was a brown burn from an iron peeking out from the left lapel. I looked at you and couldn't speak...you were so handsome. You had a ring on." I moved our mouths closer, retreating right before contact. He tugged the doll from my arms and gently set her aside on the coffee table. I gasped as I was lifted to straddle his thick thighs, the seam of my riding pants pulled at the stretch of my short legs.

"Then, my beautiful baby, why don't you unwrap your third present?"

"Now, Detective, you did save the best for last." I licked my lips as I spread my hands over his broad chest and smoothed my hands over the fine linen and beneath the fabric of his jacket. As I studied his expression, and I was awed by the need in his eyes for me as I pushed the fabric off his shoulders.

He leaned forward until his cheek brushed mine, and he removed the tux jacket. "You going to let me kiss you, baby?" he whispered in my ear, and I nodded, nervous and turned on. "Thank you, but I think you may be wearing too many clothes." I smiled shyly as he leaned back enough to rake his gaze over me.

I couldn't look away, not when he pulled at the caveat, or

when he worked the buttons on my coat and shirt free. He stripped me until my upper body was bare, exposed for him. He dropped his gaze, and I tensed as he traced the scars across my belly. "Those aren't so beautiful, are they?"

"You're still gorgeous."

"I'll tell you the story but not tonight. I just want us. Please."

"It'll always be just us." He cupped my face in his hands as he closed the distance between our lips.

I whimpered at the first contact, the softness of his lips and the coarseness of his mustache and beard. He kept pressing our mouths together, each one longer than the one before, as I curled my fingers around the backs of his big biceps. When he opened, I did, too, the tips of our tongues teasing. A gasp slipped free as his rough fingertips teased my nipples.

"May I carry you to bed?"

All I could do was nod.

"No, baby, I want to hear it. I want to hear you say yes, I can carry you."

I arched painfully as he palmed my ass cheeks, and they fit perfectly in his hands. Being petite had never been as much of a turn-on as it was at that moment.

"Please, carry me to bed." I squeaked as he easily surged to his feet with me cradled against him. He never stopped kissing me as if it were his new favorite thing, and I didn't want it to end. I didn't know what would happen in the light of day; I didn't know if I only had that one night, but I hoped it was enough.

He tenderly laid me down on my unmade bed with my legs dangled over the edge. He straightened to loom over me, and he roughly pulled the tails of his shirt from his pants. I inhaled deeply and held it as he slipped the buttons free, and every inch of hair-roughened skin he exposed made my cock thicken painfully behind the zipper of my riding pants.

I whined as he unveiled the sexiest, soft belly I'd ever seen.

"You enjoying the show?" He smirked as he shrugged the item off and then went to unbuckle his belt.

"I have never seen anything sexier in my life, Detective."

"I'm not so sure about that, but my view right now is incredible."

And I could see the truth in his gaze, and when the rasp of his zipper filled the room, I drew my attention south, and I rolled my hips as several inches of big dick appeared, uncut, and I wanted to suck him. Before I could beg for it, he leaned over, and I gripped the sheets beside my hips as he suckled my cock through the stretchy fabric of my pants. I stared at the rustic beam ceiling as he popped the button, and he caught the zipper between his teeth.

I dropped my eyes to the top of his head as I watched him pull and slowly, carefully opened my pants. I grabbed his hair in my right hand as he licked my sac and up my length, hot and wet. "My baby *is* a big boy, isn't he?"

"Carter." I screamed his name as he sucked me to the back of his throat. He circled my wrists and pinned them to my sides as he bobbed quickly, pushing me toward the edge of all control, and I whined as he slowed, edging me. He abruptly stopped and then licked up my belly, traced the edges of my scars with the tip of his tongue.

"My baby doesn't come until I'm between your thighs, do you understand, baby?"

"Yes...sir." Even in my lust-addled brain, self-preservation held that word in check. In my head, I called him Daddy. He'd given me a pretty doll, and he called me his baby. God, how I wanted to be his baby in every way. Pre-cum pooled on my lower belly.

"I love how soft and smooth you are..." He lightly bit at my nipples. "How responsive." He straightened again and hooked his hand under my knee, lifting my leg in order to unzip my boot. And just as slowly as he'd removed my jacket and shirt, he stripped me until I was naked on the bed. He turned to the side and slipped his arms under my shoulders and knees, lifted me to settle me in the middle of the bed, my head on my pillows. "Baby, open wide for me." He pushed his fingers between my thighs and urged me to spread them. I nearly came as he pushed between my cheeks and teased my long-ignored hole. "That is all tight and small. You think I'll fit right there?" He circled it, increasing the pressure with every caress. "Was my baby made for me?"

I couldn't answer as he crawled onto the bed and lowered his weight on top of me, the hair on his legs teasing my smoother ones. His cock aligned with mine. My hands hovered over his shoulders. My submissive side deferred to my dominant man, unconsciously submitting to his control.

"Are you waiting for permission?"

"Yes…yes…sir."

"With me, baby, you never have to ask. I want those hands everywhere." He dropped small kisses over my face, forehead, eyes, nose, and lips.

I settled my hands on his shoulders, felt the impossibly soft hairs that dusted them, and lower over his back. A sigh parted my lips at the freedom to touch him; learn the textures of hair and skin. His weight was everything I'd known it would be. I tipped my head back as he arched his hips back and then forward, rutting our lengths together in a slow, easy rhythm.

"Hope you have today off because we're just getting started."

I parted my thighs to the point of discomfort and lifted them higher to squeeze his sides.

"You like your big man all hairy and heavy on top of you?" I moaned as he caught my wrists in one hand and pinned them above my head. "Holding you down, I can do whatever I want with your delicate body. Take it however I want. Isn't that right, baby?"

"Yes. S'good. I'd fantasized…" I stopped myself.

"No, be a good boy, and tell me what you pictured. Were we just like this?"

"Yes…sir. So big and heavy, I fingered my ass as I pictured you buried so deep." As I told him my fantasy, he rode my tiny body. I smelled his cologne and sweat that eased the slide of our bodies together. "So hairy." I lifted my head to nuzzle his chin with my nose and nudged his head up until he arched so I could rub my cheeks against the mat of hair on his big chest. I panicked as he rolled off me. "No, I'll be good, I promise."

He hummed as he kissed me, soothing me out of my anxiety. "Where's your lube?"

I didn't hesitate to answer. "In the drawer in the stand behind you." Fingers or cock, I didn't care which—I just wanted him inside me. He petted my hair as he laid on his back and rummaged around the drawer until he found my slick.

"I'm just gonna use my fingers, okay? I'm gonna suck that thick, pretty dick as I finger fuck you until you shoot down my throat, is that okay?"

"Yes, please."

He knelt between my thighs as I heard the snick of the cap. I observed his every movement, from slicking his fingers to him slipping his forearm under my knees. He pushed my legs back to my chest.

"I'm gonna be so good to you, baby. Just relax and let me in."

He spread the warmed lube around my waxed hole, and he got it nice and wet before I felt the pressure of a large, blunt finger easing inside. He groaned as his middle finger pushed all the way in. The stretch and burn were what I assumed heaven would feel like. I stared at him as he tapped my prostate, and I tried to roll my hips to get him deeper. The brace of his forearm restricted my movements.

"Damn, baby, you're such an obedient boy." His voice was barely above a rumble as he thrust in and out. I clenched around the digit every time he withdrew. "Now, you're gonna take a second one just as easy."

"God…sir, more." He pulled out enough to slip his ring finger in beside the middle one. That torturous slow thrust and withdraw kept the same pace, teasing but never giving me enough to get off. The pressure and pleasure increased as I rolled my head on the pillow. Submitted as his boy…his sub, as he controlled, praised, and loved me.

Sweat beaded on my skin—my skin—my body so sensitive I could feel the tickle of them caressing across my skin to fall to the sheet below me.

"Now, I'm going to release your legs, but you're gonna keep them open. My baby doesn't hide from me."

I obeyed as I lay splayed open, exposed for him the way he needed me to be. I was the only one to give him this, the one allowing him dominion over me.

"Baby, you look…god, the heat, the way that pretty little hole is already so stretched around my fingers. I could just watch and feel you clench around my fingers all night, but my baby deserves a reward for being so good for me." As he lowered, he leaned forward until his hot breath teased the underside of my cock.

I ached so badly it hurt, and I could get off just from his fingers fucking into me, hearing him praise me. And as I parted my dry lips to tell him, he once again swallowed the end of my dick, and then sucked until my toes curled into the mattress. He hummed and growled, bobbed as he fucked me. I screamed as a third, and then a fourth one, slowly pushed inside, slick drizzled down my taint as he forced me to take his thick, broad fingers. Stretched me open wide as I fisted my hands in his hair, and I jerked as he tapped my gland in an increasing rhythm as I grunted, and his right hand stroked up my belly, over my chest, and he gripped my throat.

I hissed as he gave it the slightest squeeze before he moved higher, his fingertips tracing the seam of my lips. I opened and sucked two. He reached the back of my tongue, pushing down until I gagged. As I did, my cock pulsed in his talented mouth. I lost all sense as I rutted against his face, made him swallow around the broad head of my dick. His hand slapped against me as he brutally took my ass.

My heels dug into his shoulder blades, and my thighs squeezed his head as the pressure increased. My release was coming, and I couldn't stop it. My sac drew up as I hooked my ankles while I sucked hard at his fingers, my body arched off the bed, then I shot down his throat, whined and whimpered as I felt each movement of his throat as he swallowed.

A silent scream locked in my throat as my breath stilled in my chest as I suffered through the most pleasure I'd ever felt as he sucked me off until my cock softened on his tongue. He surged up my body, my thighs cradling him as he slammed his mouth down on mine, and I tasted myself on his tongue. His right hand fisted painfully in my hair on the top of my head as he reached between us to grab his cock.

"I'm gonna mark that hole as mine." He growled as he pushed up onto his knees. "No one else, baby, no one's, do you understand?" he demanded.

"Yes...sir." I hugged his head as he kept kissing me, his breathing a harsh inhale and exhale through his nose.

"God, baby, say it. I want to hear it as I cum all over your ass. Say it!" His words were demanding and rough.

"Carter, I—"

His pace sped up. The power of his strokes rocked us along with the bed. "Call me what you want. You're safe with me." He grunted. "My baby." He kept pressing his lips to mine, suckling at the upper and lower curves. "Please, baby, trust me. Tell me what you want."

"Come on me..." Fear locked my throat, but I pushed it out. "Daddy, give it to me." I twisted my fingers in his hair. "I've been a good boy. I need it."

"Again."

"Daddy, please." I whimpered as pre-cum trickled down my taint where his cock head was pressed under my sac.

"Fucking again. Just like you did, all soft and sweet. Tell me who you are."

"Daddy's baby."

His forehead pressed to mine, and his eyes squeezed tight as his hips thrust forward, and his release covered my cock and balls, my slick, well-stretched hole, and my brain snapped into absolute peace. I never wanted to be anyone but Daddy Carter's baby.

STEVENSON

COLD CASE
UNIT

I groaned as I cuddled the warm, trim body to mine and nuzzled the side of his neck as I forced my eyes open. I glanced over my shoulder to find the sun blazing through the windows and then to see the fire had died down. The air of the cabin was cold on my face, but my boy was nice and warm.

My lips curved into a smile as he hugged my left arm tighter to his chest. His rounded bottom was cradled by my hips and thighs, my cock notched between his lush cheeks. That night played out in my head. I'd never felt so needed in my life. After I'd cleaned us up with a warm rag, he instantly cuddled back to me, not wanting to be separated.

Besides the sex, the highlight of the night was the way he reacted to his doll. He'd lit up and smiled so big that you'd have thought I'd given him the moon and stars. I curled my right hand over his thigh, stroking up to his hip, to the dip of his waist, and along his ribs. He was so trim and flawless. Yet he'd craved me, what I did to him.

The way I'd taken control had caused his pale skin to flush with arousal. I'd seen the physical change in him as I commanded him; it was a serenity I'd seen on Remy's face when Robert whispered in his ear. The way Remy's husband soothed his anxiety. I'd done that for my baby. I sighed as *my baby* played over and over in my head. I'd never seen myself as a Dominant or a Daddy.

I didn't think it would be something I needed until he fought himself not to say it; not voice his wants and needs. I'd seen his fear and wanted to soothe it, to make him trust me. I smoothed my hand around to his soft, flat belly. We were so physically different, but I hadn't missed the way he took in every inch of me as I'd stripped for him, and he'd wanted more. Stroking my hand lower, I palmed his heavy, fat cock. Sucking him off could become my favorite thing. I petted his smooth waxed groin.

"Mmm, Daddy." He whimpered in his sleep, and I circled the base of his dick and stroked him until his semi-erect length hardened fully and pulsed against my palm. He rutted his soft, bubble butt against my hard cock. I'd come all over that smooth tight hole.

I'd waited for the emotional hit as he complained about the mess that my sweat and scent were on his body. I'd anticipated a repeat of the past, of the few men before him that had found my bigger, softer, and hairier body unpleasant. That hadn't happened. I'd laid there with his legs open wide as I'd gently tended to him. Tenderly moved the rag over his swollen, tiny hole.

He'd never lost that peaceful expression as he'd shyly peeked at me under his pretty lashes. Yet I still wondered if that night, maybe once I left and the afterglow faded, we'd only have the one time. I wanted to keep him. Make him mine for however long he'd allow. Sex to me meant something; it was a commitment.

"So warm."

I chuckled as Doc turned over and burrowed under the covers, rubbing one cheek and then the other over my chest like he had the night before.

"What time is it?"

"I have no idea. I don't even know where my phone is." I lifted the covers enough to lower my head to brush my lips to his tangled hair. "And someone doesn't have clocks in his home."

"That's what we have phones for." His bratty whine made me hug him tighter. "Also, I didn't have it last night. There was nowhere in those pants for my phone."

"I will say, I did love those pants, loved them better when I was taking them off you." I pulled the covers over our heads as I scooted down. I pinched the adorable point of his chin and tilted his head back until I could bring our mouths together. "You okay, baby? I wasn't too rough?" As I asked, I slowly pushed my fingers between his ass cheeks and stroked over him.

"You were perfect. It's almost cruel how hot you are." He pushed against my chest, and I rolled to my back. He got to his knees and threw his slender leg over me to straddle my hips. He moaned as he sat his bare ass right on my cock. "I love how my knees don't touch the bed." His long dick rested on the curve of my belly.

I grasped his thighs and stroked his smooth skin with my thumbs. "Do you wax everywhere?"

"Self-care is important. Do you think it's sexy?"

"Yes, yes, it is."

"Daddy?"

"Yes, baby."

He nibbled at his lower lip. "I just wanted to say it."

I stretched out my arm and curled my hand around the back of his neck, his shoulder-length hair tickling the back of my hand and fingers. I slowly drew him down to me until our mouth almost touched. "Does saying it make you happy, my baby?"

"Uh-huh."

"I always want you happy."

"And, Daddy, do you know what would make your baby really happy?"

"What's that?"

"If my Daddy would let me suck him off. May I, Daddy?"

"It's all yours, baby." As his lips touched mine, I fought the urge to close my eyes because I didn't want to miss a moment. I kept my left hand tangled in his hair as he kissed and licked over my chest, my belly, and I smirked as he loved on the curve of it for a long time. His pink tongue peeking from between his plump lips.

"You were built for your baby to cuddle, Daddy."

Fuck, how I loved the sound of his voice all soft, sweet, and wickedly innocent. I could imagine a lifetime of waking up just like that but reined in my premature thoughts. I was still unsure what it all meant. Was I his exclusive Daddy, lover? Was I his boyfriend? My heart wanted everything.

"Shit, baby." I snarled and hissed through my clenched teeth as he tongued my loose foreskin and then sucked it over the sensitive head. "You love playing with Daddy's uncut dick, don't you?" There was a harshness to my tone I'd never heard before, and his shiver told me he loved it.

"I love playing with anything of my big, handsome Daddy's." His touch was feather-light as he circled the base and lifted my length. He opened wide, and I clenched my fist as he suckled the head. The shadow of his lashes dark on his cheeks as he worked inch after inch into his beautiful mouth. Stretching wide and the bliss on his face nearly became my undoing. He didn't stop until he buried his nose in my thick bush, his hands found mine, his fingers laced in my right, and his other curled over the fisted hand in his silky hair.

I held him to me as I ground his face into my groin, making him grunt and gag, his mouth opened, and spit running down my length. He rutted his cock where my calves met, and I used him. I forced him up and down my dick. And he submitted, trusted me to keep him safe. If that weekend was all I'd get, I'd be selfish. Take pleasure in being his Daddy—his Dominant.

"Next time, baby, you're gonna be stuffed with that fat dick you're slobbering all over."

As he sucked my cock, I controlled the pace, slow and fast. Taught my baby just how Daddy liked it, but at the same time, I was learning what I loved myself. I was spread out naked, in full daylight, and I was conscious of the jiggle of my belly with my quickened breathing and movements, the sweat that misted my skin, that made my hair stick to my face. It was freedom. It was all my fantasies rolled into one adorable, short package.

"Baby," I groaned out. "Baby, if you want to pull off this would…" I warned him as I felt the end coming. The jerking of my cock, the painful ache for release in my balls, and he just sucked harder as I tried to retreat. "You better swallow every fucking drop." I ordered him as I slammed his face against me and arched as I came hard down his constricting throat. At the corner of my mind, I felt the weight of him become heavier on my legs as he humped and rolled his hips until wetness spread over my hairy calves, and he whimpered as he gently suckled my cock.

I released him as I tried to catch my breath, but he didn't pull away. He lay there, letting go of all but a few inches of my cock. His head came to rest on my hip as he gently almost nursed my dick. I spread my hand over the side of his face, and he sighed through his nose as he hugged my legs. Then the pressure eased, and his lips fell lax. He snuffled in his sleep with the head of my soft cock still pillowed on his tongue.

My thumb rubbed a drop of cum into the corner of his mouth, and as much as I needed to get up, to get us both clean and comfortable, I couldn't move him. He slept so sweetly there with his knees bent and his little ass in the air. How the hell did I live without him for so long? How would I continue if this was just a moment for both of us?

DOC

I held my tablet as I swung my legs back and forth and enjoyed a slow morning in the morgue. Okay, it was a little grisly to be bored without bodies to examine, but with my brain, it was best to be busy. I should be going through the cases the Feds kept delivering. Then again, I should just move to the small town and set up shop in his office to get rid of the middleman.

"So, did you ride the sexy detective or not?" Vega whined where she was seated on the metal table across from my own perch.

As I'd gotten into my car that morning, Vega had pulled up behind me and then followed me to work. She'd started a huge side project that was keeping her up at night, and then the daytime hours were for the cases she did for law enforcement. Cash was in the middle of a studio project. She played bass for recording sessions as a fill-in. The band all had day jobs, and nights were the best time for all of them to work.

"He left this morning to go home for work clothes." I dropped my chin to my chest to hide my silly grin. He'd kissed me several times in the doorway, almost as if he didn't want to leave. I'd almost grabbed the front of his wrinkled dress shirt to drag him back inside, yet I refrained so I wouldn't overwhelm him.

"An entire weekend? How are you still walking?"

My face heated, and with my pale skin, I was sure I was bright red. "We didn't do that. We spent all Sunday curled up on my couch under a quilt, making out and napping. Then last night, he held me while we slept. But I will never look at his mouth the same way again."

"Look at you, you're all giddy, but there's something you're not telling me."

I knew she'd pick up on it. She'd known me long enough to pick out my tells. "What if it was just a weekend? You know one of those things. We're both single and…"

"Stop, you're analyzing without knowing all the facts, and you need to take a breath. Did you ask him if the weekend was all you'd have?"

"No, but that was probably because I was too scared to ask."

"Ask him." She checked her watch. "It's almost time for coffee."

I'd been there since six because I couldn't go back to bed after he left. Vega decided to keep me company until Cash texted her that she was on her way home. That moment I dreaded was coming up. I'd mentally calculated the time and wondered if he'd stick with our usual mid-morning coffee break.

I'd never liked the unknown, but I had a terror of my fears coming true. That we'd be back to our usual selves, friendly and flirty in front of everyone. Our new dynamic a secret. As if us talking about him summoned the man in question, the doors opened, and he came in with two coffees and a plastic bag hung from his forearm.

"I drove by and saw the crazy one was here." He announced as he entered. "Hey, baby. I brought you caffeine and snacks." He stepped up in front of me. As he leaned in, I offered him my cheek, and I nibbled at my lower lip as he handed me the coffees with a frown. He dug into the bag and turned to Vega. "Get lost.

Me and my baby need to talk. Go." He shoved an energy drink at her.

"What if I don't want to?"

"I'm three times your size. I'll carry you out of here and lock the door."

I snorted as Vega jumped from the table. "I could weigh you down in the harbor, and no one would ever find you." She hissed through her clenched teeth as the two of them mirrored each other until she was backed all the way to the door.

"She's a delight in the morning," he said as he finally turned back to me. "Now, that's not the face of an adorable man extremely happy to see me." He spread his hands on either side of my hips and lowered his head enough to meet my gaze. "Talk to me. What's wrong?"

"I didn't want to...well, I didn't know what the weekend meant," I whispered as I set the to-go cups aside and tugged at the front of his sweater. "I didn't want to assume."

"What it meant was, I don't have sex with people I don't have feelings for, and it meant something. Is that okay with you?"

I nodded, and he gave me his lopsided grin. "I didn't want you to leave this morning," I whispered my confession.

"I didn't want to go. Next time I'll bring clothes. That tux wasn't exactly Cold Case appropriate. We're working this backwards, baby. How about an actual date? I pick you up. Dinner and all the first date-appropriate things. Friday because I know Saturdays aren't the best after the clinic. You're tired."

"As long as people can stop murdering or dying suspiciously for one night, Friday night, I'm yours. I have to stop being the most popular ghoul."

"Not possible, and just so you know, you're mine every night." A groan rumbled in his chest as he softly pushed his lips to mine, easy and gentle. I slipped my arms over his shoulders. "Is that going to be an issue?"

"No, I'm a very needy and greedy boy."

"Yes, you are." He smiled against my lips, and I kissed that perfect tilt.

"Dr. Warner." Douglas's voice broke us apart.

"Can we ignore him?" I asked.

"Probably best to get it over with." He gripped my waist and lifted me from the table. He picked up our coffees and followed me to my desk.

"What do I owe for the pleasure today, Detective?"

"Here." He handed me a stack of files. "It's for both of you. I got nosy and checked out the cold case Stevenson was working. There was a series of disappearances twenty-five years ago, three women convicted of murdering their children and claiming it was a snatch and grab. No bodies were ever found, but scenes were discovered, forensics and blood evidence tied the DNA to the missing children. They assumed they were murdered at these other locations and the bodies disposed of in some way. The images didn't show nearly enough blood to prove homicide."

Stevenson and I both flipped through the case files. "All we're between eight and ten, different races and ethnicities, and all socioeconomic backgrounds. What ties them?" I asked.

"The mothers were knocked down. They were mostly carrying younger children and unable to fight off the kidnappers. Angela Barnes was a fighter. Literally, she went to a gym several times a week. She was the only one to be attacked without other younger children present. Since there were no actual bodies to examine, it didn't make it to your office."

"What made them think it was murder?"

"All were single mothers, recently divorced with absent fathers or widowed, all younger children in the home. They were all investigated by different detectives, and each one came to the same conclusion after speaking to witnesses and neighbors. The mothers were overwhelmed. All of them took an Alford Plea. I don't even know how they convinced the mothers to take it."

"So, these could be connected, the method is similar, they

were spread out over"—Stevenson took the files to get a closer look—"three precincts. Back then, they wouldn't have connected them because of the area. Angela was found on the strip. The others were all over the city...two were near upscale or middle-class neighborhoods."

"Who did the forensics on this, or do I even have to ask?"

"You don't, your favorite lab director," Douglas said with a shake of his head.

"That misogynistic bastard."

"Where are they all doing their time?" Stevenson asked.

"State, about an hour away. Mrs. Farrier just got denied parole because she didn't show remorse for a crime that she swears she didn't commit."

"I'll call and set up a visit with them to see how well their stories mesh before I get them in the same room. I've been looking at cold cases for weeks and found no similar one. Now, I know why. They were all convictions. Thanks, Douglas."

"No thanks needed. I owed him one." He pointed at me.

"What did I do?"

"You didn't let me railroad you into taking my side."

"You're delusional if you'd think I'd take your side over Graves. I worked on that case with him, and once again, my logic is flawless."

"Keep thinking that, brat, I got a suspect sweating in interrogation for me. Let me know how the info works out for you." He nodded and left, the door swooshing closed behind him.

"What do you think?" I lifted onto my desk, and Stevenson took my chair and rested his arm across my thighs.

"It could be all coincidence, but the time frame, the stories...I have to give the lead a go. Would you check over the forensics for me? See how the hell they even got this to court."

"You got it. Anything for my favorite detective. You know this is going to fuck up so many lives."

"It already did. If they didn't do it, at least three women were convicted of murder and spent over twenty years in jail for it. Why would someone snatch children of that age? It's usually babies."

"Could be a pedophile ring. Could be opportunity and nothing else."

"I'll look into more cases in the surrounding area and to see if this goes beyond state lines. I need to develop a pattern."

"Good luck, I'll do what I can, but without bodies, my say isn't that great. Are there any photos of the injuries the mothers claimed happened during the attack?"

"The evidence log says they're in storage at the main courthouse."

"I'll head down and check them out. I know the evidence clerk from Vega's favorite leather bar. She thinks I'm adorable."

"Who doesn't think my baby is adorable?"

"Daddy, you might just be biased." He smirked as I winked at him.

He stood up and kissed me again in that way that told me he didn't want to stop or leave. "Have your coffee and eat your snacks. Don't forget lunch."

"I promise."

"Good, behave, no trying to replace me with leather lesbians."

"I make no guarantees. She rocks as a Drag King."

He playfully growled as he took the files and left. I sat on my desk staring at the door, and all the indecision I'd worried over that morning disappeared. He wanted this to work, and I wasn't going to complain.

23

STEVENSON

COLD CASE
UNIT

"Hey, Daddy." My baby whispered in my ear, and my cock went instantly to ready. He twined his arms around my neck and buried his face against my shoulder. I'd thought I'd understood what wanting him felt like, but after only a few days of us becoming a couple, I was obsessed. Turning my head, I brushed a kiss to his temple.

"Did you come to say bye?"

"I'm going to miss my coffee and cuddle. You never forget."

"And I didn't today. We talked about me having to go take care of those interviews."

"I know, doesn't mean your baby has to like it." He released me and stood. As soon as he was safely away from my chair, I straightened.

"What if I could still give you your cuddle?" I asked as I stepped forward, and he countered as I herded him toward the back of the unit's office space. I didn't miss a thing about him. The way his lashes lowered. His tongue stroked the full curve of his bottom lip or his quickened breathing that made his chest move quickly under his scrub top.

I grabbed him around the waist and lifted him high on my

chest as I slammed him back against the wall between two particularly full shelves. "Fuck, baby, I gotta go." Even as I whispered the words, I was pushing my mouth to his and shoved my hands down the back of his scrub pants to palm the rounded cheeks of his little ass.

"No, you don't. Your baby needs your time." He sounded so sweet and needy, and I wanted his fucking clothes gone. "I even have easy access scrubs on."

"Company!" Remy's amused voice carried from the front, and I groaned as I rested my forehead on Doc's.

I fisted my hands in his soft hair and kept pressing our lips together as he rubbed his dick against my rounded belly. "Tonight, you and me at your place, no interruptions."

He nodded as he squeezed my sides with his trim legs. I reluctantly lowered him to his feet. His long, thick cock tented the front of his loose pants, and we were going to have a discussion about him not wearing underwear when I wasn't around.

"Stay here and calm down. No one sees that but me anymore."

"Of course, Daddy," he whispered, and I brushed a kiss to his forehead, adjusted myself to his great amusement.

I tugged my sweater over my hard dick and walked out of the space, and then instantly didn't have to worry about my hard-on. Joseph stood there in his tailored suit with his perfectly styled hair. Might as well have tossed ice down my pants. He hadn't changed at all.

"Mr. Chambers." I greeted him as I heard soft footsteps behind me, and I automatically turned to track my baby until he sat on my desk.

"Detective, you made contact with my client to arrange an interview on a twenty-five-year-old case. Mr. Maxwell has no knowledge of what happened to his stepdaughter and son, no more today than he did at the time of the incident."

"That's why I called him in. We found that DNA swabs weren't taken. We have Aiden's mother's on file."

"Because she's a felon, my client has no criminal history."

"We know that doesn't mean shit."

"Still as crude as ever." He huffed at me, and a throat clearing sounded from the other three men in the room.

"This isn't personal. All our samples were degraded from improper storage, and in the hopes of finding John Doe's in the system, we need more than the mother's. Doc?"

"We want to build a DNA profile using Mrs. Barnes and Mr. Maxwell's samples. The case is twenty-five years old, as you pointed out. We have come a long way in our forensic processing procedures. If your client has nothing to hide, what could be the issue in allowing us to take a buccal swab and have a discussion with Mr. Maxwell?"

"And who are you?"

I was about to step in to warn Joseph of his condescending tone. "Oh, Joey, you know exactly who I am. I've handed you your ass thirty-two times. In about a month, it will be thirty-three."

"Baby." I tried to sound stern because I needed cooperation, but also my baby was just being bratty.

"Fine, bodies await me. I'll see you at home for dinner. Bye, Joey."

I kept my attention on Joseph and easily saw the disgust in his expression, and I could understand it. Morgan was his exact opposite. He was everything Joseph couldn't be, and I loved that about my baby.

"Like Doc said, what's the issue?"

"You're not looking at him as a suspect?"

"At this point, no. We need a stronger DNA sample to run against any John Doe cold cases. Doc..."

"That man needs to be censured for his attitude."

"You want to try that? Because I want to see you try to argue against him," Remy said from behind me, and I turned to find him seated on his usual spot on Robert's desk.

"Fine, Monday morning at nine AM. You have one chance to talk to him. Make it count." He turned on the toes of his high-shined shoes and left.

"That was your ex-husband, wasn't it?"

"Yeah, that was him."

"At least your taste has approved. Also, *Daddy*, voices carry." Remy winked at me. "I thought Joey was going to have a stroke the first moan he heard."

"Why do you think we're exes? I've got a long drive ahead of me and need to be back in time for dinner."

"With your baby? You two are extremely cute," Remy said as Robert chuckled, and I picked up my jacket and the files I needed to speak with the three women. Doc had helped me prepare. He'd sat on my lap as he went over every piece of evidence.

If we had a serial kidnapper, the best-case scenario was they were already dead. And worst-case, they were still out there somewhere still in possession of the people who kidnapped them or bought them. I didn't know what to do with either option. I had no evidence to reopen the cases and nowhere near any to prove they were innocent. All I could do was speak with them. I hadn't made outright promises to Mrs. Barnes, but I did say I would do everything I could. And that's what I was going to do.

FARRIER, Marx, and Lowell all stared at me from one side of the table. I'd carried out the individual interviews, and it was speeding toward late afternoon. The suspicion rolled off them in waves, and after decades in prison after being screwed over by their lawyers and the court system, I didn't hope for miracles.

"Have you three met before?" They all nodded. "As I said, I work the Cold Case Unit. One of my current cases I'm taking another look at is the murder of a young woman, Angela Barnes. Do any of you recognize the name, maybe know her?"

"If I remember right, it was on the news. She was killed, and her brother disappeared." Farrier spoke up, but the rest remained silent. She'd been the one from the upper-middle-class neighborhood with absolutely no red flags.

"That's her. She and her brother, Aiden, were walking a few miles from home like they always did. She was found violently attacked. Footprints in blood were found at the scene. A fellow detective brought your three cases to my attention."

"And?" Marx asked as she shifted in her seat.

"I can't say with certainty that you're innocent. I don't have the evidence, which is what I need, but my gut and that of a medical examiner, there isn't a reason they would've convicted you with what the prosecution had."

"You think we're innocent?" Farrier looked at me like I was insane, which wasn't unusual.

"I did individual interviews with all of you. Your stories remained consistent and match what I think happened with Barnes. She was a young woman with a child, but she was a fighter, trained to defend herself. I believe the only reason you three survived was that you had your younger children and babies with you."

"If we'd have fought them, we'd be dead, and all our children would be gone?" Lowell seemed to break a bit as she asked.

"In my opinion, as a twenty-year veteran of law enforcement, I believe I'd be investigating your murders alongside Angela's. Do you remember anyone possibly following you three in the days leading up to or on the day of the kidnappings?"

"I had three children. We were out doing grocery shopping and errands. We were just getting into a routine after my husband died. Most days, I wouldn't have noticed if the world exploded around me." Farrier ran her fingers through her hair. She looked decades older than her almost sixty years.

All of them had aged significantly, but that's what life behind bars got you. Especially when you were innocent, and no one would listen.

"Same, but my ex-husband moved to Alaska to work on a fishing boat. Some midlife crisis or some shit. I hadn't heard from him in two years until the trial, and he arrived to take my remaining children." Lowell snarled her nose.

"What about you, Mrs. Marx?"

"Down on the strip, there's always new faces. It's not weird to see a new crop of sex workers or do-gooders, but someone following us? No. When they attacked us, I just reached for my daughter. She was only three. They had no interest in her. They just wanted Ty."

"Do you three remember anything about the people who attacked?"

"No, just they pulled up in a van, and two men got out. Black clothes and masks, no guns, but they had tasers…no, like those cattle prods. They grabbed my son, and when the side doors flew open, there were two more men inside. It was like minutes but felt like hours." Farrier's voice finally broke, and both women agreed with the setup.

"What's next?"

"I can't promise anything. I didn't when I spoke with Mrs. Barnes, but I'll do all I can. I don't want to give any of you false hope."

"Detective Stevenson, we've been in prison for over twenty years, our children have grown up, graduated, married, and had children. This is our life. At least for me, I've determined I'm going to die in this place. Do you think our children are still alive?"

"Honestly?"

"We'd like to hear something new," Marx said with snark.

"I don't know. Part of me wants to say yes, they're out there somewhere living good lives. But I'm sorry to say, the cop in me thinks we just haven't discovered the remains yet. Would you be willing to give new swabs for DNA testing?" They all agreed. "Thank you for your time and talking to me. I know you have no reason to trust me."

"Detective, why weren't our cases connected?"

"Brutally honest here, Farrier upper-middle class neighborhood, widowed. Marx was from the strip recently separated from an on and off again boyfriend. You, you were at the tail end of a tumultuous divorce from a cheating husband who ran off with his mistress. All different areas of the city, you couldn't be farther from each other in socioeconomic backgrounds. Due to, I believe, is bias and nothing more than conjecture from neighbors and friends, you were bullied into taking the Alford Pleas. I'll arrange for someone to come and get the swabs. Also, if you have any issues or something comes back to you, call me." I handed all three a card. "I'll be in touch to speak with you all again. I hope I can help, but again, I won't placate you and make promises."

The correction officers came back to return the three women to their cells, and I grabbed my jacket and slipped it on. I started the hour ride home to change and then head to Doc's. I needed cuddles from my baby and forget all about the stress.

24

DOC

COLD CASE
UNIT

I checked the time on my phone to see if I had time to finish dinner. He'd texted me when he'd left the prison and again when he got to his apartment. I'd started dinner. All day, I replayed him pressing me up against the wall. I loved his strength and his husky body. Seeing his ex had tempered my happiness a bit. Joseph was tall and lean, handsome. He'd said his husband was an attorney, and with the familiarity between them, I'd known instantly even if he hadn't told me who.

I'd reminded myself that he wanted me. It was in the way he never wanted to let me go. That didn't mean my brain didn't misfire that I wasn't tall or muscular. Yet my Daddy thought I was beautiful. I hated living with all my insecurities. The door rattled with a knock, and then it was being pushed open.

"Honey, I'm home."

A thump of a bag sounded behind me, and I tracked his steps on the floor as he crossed the single room, and then his arms were around me.

"Damn, I missed you today." I tilted my head to give him access to my neck, and my lids closed at the tease of his beard.

His hands slipped under my t-shirt to rub my belly, and I leaned back into him.

"Missed you, too. How was work?"

"No surprises. I don't think they're ready to trust me yet."

"They have no reason to, but I'm sure they'll come around."

"How was your day? Behave yourself?"

"Yes, because you weren't around to misbehave with."

"Good boy."

I smiled like a fool and tried to hide my expression, but he gripped my chin and turned me to look at him. I dropped my gaze to his mouth, and he stroked his thumb across my lower lip.

"What are you thinking about?"

"How beautiful you are and how much of an idiot I was."

"You weren't an idiot." I turned in his arms and squeaked as he lifted me to sit on the counter. He was so handsome and all mine, but I refused to think it would be forever. I knew if he left me or said he just wanted to be friends that he'd destroy me, but I'd waited so many years to have him look at me the way I did him.

"I was. That first night I stayed over to watch over you. I stood beside your bed before I left. You looked so warm and comfortable, and I wanted to have the right to slip in beside you. I went home to jerk off to thoughts of picking you up and shoving you against the wall of my shower. I'm scared I'm not going to give you what you need...not going to be able to keep you happy with me."

I didn't like when he lowered his head so I couldn't see his soft blue eyes. I cupped his chin in my hands and urged him to look at me. "Don't hide from me. I like when you look at me...the way you look at me." I gave him a small smile when his gaze finally met mine. "I'm not going anywhere. I've wanted you since the night I met you. All handsome and burly, a big ol' teddy bear that my Little wanted to cuddle so badly. The man in me wanted you to fuck me against the nearest available surface. But despite that,

I love everything about you. Have you noticed you're here a lot of nights?"

"I may have noticed, but I sleep better with you."

"Me, too. Carter, I want this to work more than anything. I'm scared. I'll admit that. I'm a lot older than you, I'm needy, and I crave my cuddles and affection. That's a lot for some men to take, especially someone who never wanted to be someone's Daddy or Dominant before. We can go as slow or fast as you want because however you want to do it, then I'm going to be ecstatic that you're mine, and I can tell everyone. Especially that asshole, Joey. Him giving up all this, no wonder I didn't like him."

"Have you really gone up against him over thirty times?"

"Yep." I gave Daddy my brattiest grin. "He has a habit. He asks the prosecution witnesses the same question three times, just phrased differently each time. I mean, seriously, he should get a better strategy. He's complained to my supervisor and the District Attorney's office no less than twenty-five times for lack of professionalism, which is bullshit. I purport myself with an abundance of professionalism on the stand. How did you put up with it? Before court one time, I *accidentally* bumped into him and dripped white correction fluid onto his black shoes. You should've seen what happened when he noticed them during his opening statement."

"No wonder he doesn't like you."

"I like him even less now that I know he's your ex-husband. He's gorgeous."

"Maybe, but I got someone even better right now."

"You think so?" I draped my arms over his shoulders and laced my fingers together.

"Very much. I want this to last, Morgan, not just for a few months or a year. I need you, and I just have to ask for you to be patient. I'm not used to someone wanting me back."

"You have me as long as you want me. I know you need time. I know you need to get used to my annoying ways."

"Baby, I don't find you annoying at all. You're perfect." He tweaked my chin with his thumb and index finger. "You need help with dinner?"

"No, you work because I know you brought case files, and you're way too distracting for me." I smiled as he dropped a kiss to my smile and then lifted me off the counter to gently set me on my feet.

"You're really good for my ego."

"Only telling the truth. Work because you have three women to get out of prison."

"So much pressure, baby." He kissed the top of my head, and I watched him as he left the kitchen to grab the file box and set up on my couch and coffee table.

Some people would find his focus on a case offensive, but I loved his passion for his job. That was one of the first things I'd noticed about him. He hadn't allowed the job to turn him bitter, even though it frustrated him on occasion. I shook my head as I finished up dinner and listened to him mutter curses. When I turned around, I found him forcing his fingers through his hair until it stood straight up.

"Come on, Daddy, eat, and give your brain a break for a minute."

He left everything spread out on the coffee table and pushed up. I smiled as he drew near until he could wrap his arms around me. "Thanks for dinner, baby." He pulled out my chair and lowered me onto it.

"You're welcome, nothing fancy, but it's good. I'm a little out of practice on doing anything other than heating up canned soup."

"Better than me, I promise you that."

"Why were you trying to pull your hair out?"

"The pictures aren't good enough or sufficient to let me visualize the scene. That's the worst thing about cold cases. They rarely did enough documentation of the crime scene."

"Then go back to the crime scene, work it like it's a new case."

"What?"

"If you need to visualize the scene, then work it as a fresh scene. Go there, lay it out. You have friends who'd do a little roleplay to help you out. We can get Major to come back. Maybe it'll trigger something being back there. And he's on his meds again. Text our group and arrange to do it...same time as they were reported to have arrived on scene. I know someone at the firehouse that can get us one of their training dummies to use for Angela." I loved the way he smiled at me.

"Why didn't I think of that?"

"Because you're mired in the what-ifs and don't have distance between yourself and the case. Now, the rest of the night, you're going to relax, and then tomorrow night, we reenact the crime scene."

"Monday morning, Joseph is going to bring Mr. Maxwell for an interview and to get a DNA sample. Can you be there?"

"To piss off Joey..." I pretended to think about it. "Definitely."

"Brat."

"You should expect that by now. Eat, I want Daddy cuddles."

"What my baby wants, he gets."

"That's dangerous to say to me, Detective."

"I think I'll chance it." He pinched my chin and pulled me toward him as he leaned in, his mouth brushed mine, and that sense of rightness overwhelmed me.

My brain wanted to misfire and tell me it wouldn't last, that he'd get tired of catering to me, but the softness of his kiss soothed my anxiety. I wouldn't sabotage myself, I'd waited far too long for him to see me, and I wasn't going to ruin that.

STEVENSON

COLD CASE
UNIT

Most of my friends were assholes. It's the way we bonded; by giving each other shit, but when I needed them, they'd always be there even if that was working in a dark alley on a freezing night. We stood in a circle, and we all flinched as the mobile spotlights from the coroner's van clicked on. A few minutes later, Doc was cuddling to my side.

"This is your show, Stevenson. Get to it. I'm freezing off my balls here, man." Graves pulled the collar of his peacoat higher to cover his earlobes exposed by his black beanie.

I sympathized. I was freezing my ass off and wanted to go back to Doc's place to snuggle on the couch with my baby warm on my lap. Waking up that morning, I'd found him draped over my chest, and he tried to get closer if I made any move. I'd get him home soon. First, we had work to do.

"At six-thirty PM, Angela and Aiden entered the alley from the east. At seven PM, a nine-one-one call was made to report a bloody female body, obviously deceased. So we have a thirty-minute window."

"Any reports of vans or SUVs in the area?" Remy asked.

"There was a report of squealing tires, but no one noticed a vehicle."

"Talk it out, Stevenson," Robert said as he backed away.

"Their mother's report said at five PM, Angela and Aiden were having dinner at a Chinese place about a block and half away. Nothing unusual...seems to have been their normal Friday night ritual. They left the restaurant about quarter after six, which is why I estimated about six-thirty." I walked to the east side of the alley. "They'd cut through here to head back to their apartment." I carefully made my way down the narrow alley. "If a vehicle did enter behind them, it would've blocked them in from the east, but Angela was a physically fit woman. I believe she could've easily evaded capture even with Aiden."

Robert looked right and left. "Once you're in here, you only have two ways of escape. What if it was a two-vehicle team?"

"That would block her in, but we have apartments on both sides here. Angela's wounds show that she would've been in extreme pain. No one reported screams of any kind?" Remy asked as he tipped his head back, and I followed to find windows lit up on both sides.

I checked the reports and flipped to witness statements. "The responding officer taped off the area, called in the coroner, and Homicide responded. Uniforms were dispatched to make inquiries to the tenants of the apartments, but they all claimed to hear nothing."

"So we have a woman and child who enter this alley, and in a matter of minutes, she's dead, and the minor is gone. Angela has a set pattern to her movements. Were there any mentions of stalking or suspicious shit in the days or weeks leading up?" Graves approached and took the folder.

"No, but Angela had a girlfriend. I've tried to track her down, but when I asked Boss, he said about a year after the killing, the girlfriend moved away."

"Hate crime?" Doc asked.

"She hadn't come out to Mary, but from all information, they were pretty open and never seemed to have any issues. That wasn't in the original report. It wasn't mentioned anywhere, and I didn't know until I talked to Boss."

"So, let's go with the assumption this was a team in two vehicles. Vehicle one waits outside while Angela and Aiden have dinner. Once they exit, our unknown assailants pull into traffic, and if this is the same route, they walk around the corner." Robert grabs Doc and acts it out. "We have the van pull into block. Angela grew up around here. She's street smart. What I read in the report is she trained nearly every day. She had the means to protect herself."

"She would've told Aiden to run, and she would've stood her ground. From her wounds, the attack was so vicious that she was practically holding in her intestines by the time she dropped." Doc cuddled to Robert's side as he shivered a bit.

"If that's the case, she enters the alley, and a van or large vehicle pulls in behind her. Something happens to trigger her to protect Aiden. She tells him to run." Graves seemed to play it out in his mind. "I agree. Her acting as decoy while Aiden escapes, the only way they could've got them both was if they were working in two teams. This seems awful organized for a one-off. Just listen." We all went silent. The sounds of people and traffic echoed through the alley like a tunnel of sound. "They knew where to hit, even if she screamed, we're so desensitized to sound, especially down here, we block it out."

"Douglas..." I cleared my throat to hide my laugh at the look on Graves's face. "He brought me three case files, all with convictions. The three women had the same story. Van pulled up, grabbed the boy, all of them were between eight and ten years of age. Only difference between those cases and Angela's is they had other younger children with them. They instantly went in to protect the little girls, not thinking they'd take the older boy.

Only reason Angela's dead is she was alone with Aiden, and she fought back."

"What about defensive wounds, fingernail scrapings, or are they all a lost cause?" From Graves's eye roll, I could see he'd already mentally answered his own question.

"All the samples were degraded. Mary allowed me to take a DNA sample even though hers was already on file because of her felony conviction. Any belongings of Angela and Aiden's disappeared long before Mary was released. The only thing she had left was some pictures that friends grabbed before the landlord cleared out the apartment."

"Are you thinking they're all connected? And where does Angela's case fall within the pattern?" Remy had something on his mind—I could already see it. But he usually kept things pretty close to the vest until he was sure.

"Timeframe wise, her murder and Aiden's kidnapping were the last in the obvious pattern. I'm not saying they didn't continue whatever they were doing, but I think they switched MO. Up until that point, they hadn't even left a mark on the mothers. Case files said a dark van pulled up and stopped fast, two men exited through the side door, went right for the oldest male child, and then they were gone, lasted maybe minutes."

"How were the mothers convicted?" Graves frowned.

"I have no idea. Each was convinced to take the Alford Plea. Which basically means they believe they'll be convicted by what the prosecution has, but they won't admit their guilt. I went over the cases and transcripts. I have no idea how they got the agreements. Other than some tiny blood amounts at supposed crime scenes, they took them down with no bodies."

"Victimology?" Remy asked.

"Male children of single, widowed, or recently divorced mothers. Neighbors all claimed the same thing. The mothers seemed overwhelmed. Between eight and ten years of age. They were all different races and socioeconomic backgrounds, and three separate precincts handled the cases. Other than the single mothers and ages, there's really nothing linking them. I went to interview them. They didn't even know each other before they began serving their sentences.

"Sandowski was the lead on Angela and Aiden's case. A Hartman in the same squad handled the Marx case. He's retired and on a houseboat in Florida. He couldn't even remember the case when I called. The other two, the detectives didn't even want to talk at all."

"Sandowski was...is a drunk. Instead of calling all his cases into question, his superiors offered him early retirement with full benefits. I think there was some heat coming down on several of his cases, not only for mishandling of evidence but also excessive force. They went with an out of sight, out of mind strategy." Robert sighed as he gathered up all the files and pulled out the images. He dropped each one to the ground. "What do these four boys have in common?"

"I checked the medical records I could find. Each boy was in perfect health, with no history of anything other than common ailments for children of that age. There were several notes about medical releases for sports, but they didn't play in the same leagues that I could find. Aiden and Marx attended the same school, but the other two didn't."

"Could it be a matter of sex trafficking?" Graves asked.

"Angela was beautiful. They would've taken her and Aiden, I believe. Who runs that now, Graves?" Remy crossed his arms over his chest.

"Dekland Mancini. He's been making a name for himself for about a decade, but he has a certain flavor, blonde and thin, cheerleader types. As far as I know, Organized Crime hasn't gotten any intel on him snatching children, especially male ones. As much as I hate the guy, he doesn't fit for this, but he's very money motivated. I could make contact with a few people from my days there."

"I'd appreciate it."

"Has any DNA turned up, body dumps, skeletons, something?" Robert kept staring at the pictures on the ground.

"No John Does have been found, but Vega is helping out with that. I got her the DNA on all the cases, and she's running them through her system for an organization she works for that specializes in naming skeletal remains. Except for a few drops of blood, it's like these boys never existed. Maxwell is flying in over the weekend, and his lawyer is bringing him in for an interview Monday. I don't want to put this case back on the damn shelf, especially thinking it's a serial kidnapping and three women are going to most likely die in prison."

"I'll call Gladys and see what her schedule looks like for some pro bono work. She'll be able to get us access. We're going to take some heat for this one." Robert lifted his gaze and moved around our tight circle.

Remy snorted. "Daddy, when don't we have heat coming down on us?"

"This is true, baby. We haven't picked up another case yet, so Remy and I are in since it looks like you need the extra help."

"And since someone in Homicide thinks I do shoddy work, I'll volunteer to be errand boy to just stay out of the office."

"I think our Graves has a crush." Remy teased Graves as he flipped Remy off.

"I'm going to go see Mama Sue since you're all mean to me." Graves made a show of throwing a tantrum and stomping out of the alley to get to a nearby diner.

"Since he's gone, who was the DA assigned to the cases?" Robert asked as he bent to pick up the photos, carefully stacking them and putting them back in the folder.

"You know it was his old man. He didn't personally prosecute the cases, but ain't no way he saw them come through his office, and no one got suspicious." Remy and District Attorney Graves had an animosity that caused wars, he had no respect for the

District Attorney or the State's Attorney, and Graves's mom held that position.

"The Attorneys Graves don't care about shit other than their convictions and approval ratings. You think Gladys could get me the transcripts?" I asked as I glanced at Doc and saw my baby needed to get home. He was looking tired.

"All I can do is ask, Stevenson. But you know she'd do anything for us," Robert answered, and I turned my attention to him to find him darting his gaze back and forth between Doc and me.

"Remy, can you talk to Fran and see if any complaints came in on our first three victims? I know there was nothing on Mary or Angela. I checked when I got the case."

"You got it."

"I'll talk to Vega about breaking out her animation software and recreate that night with several options about how it went down."

"Thanks for coming out."

"We're your family, man. All you ever have to do is call. I'm going to get my baby boy home. It's almost time for our daughter's storytime, and I'm not having my youngest mad at me."

Roo had her dads wrapped around her little finger, and she knew it. "Go on, your husband and daughter bat their lashes at you, and you cave."

"I do not."

I rolled my eyes at Robert's protest, but he laced his fingers through Remy's and led him toward the street where they'd parked. Doc packed up the lights, and I stowed the files in my truck to help him.

"You look tired, baby," I whispered as I came up behind him and wrapped my arms around his waist, tugging him back to me.

"I'm always tired. Maybe we can plan a vacation."

"Mountains with no cell reception?"

"Sounds perfect."

"Baby, let's solve this damn case, and I'll take you anywhere you want to go."

"Don't tease, Daddy, because I'll hold you to it."

"I wouldn't tease you, well, not in any way you don't like. Let's go home and cuddle on the couch."

He nodded, and I turned him in my arms, lowered my head until my mouth pressed to his, and once again, that overwhelming sense of belonging hit me. I stroked his smooth cheeks with the backs of my fingers and then tucked his hair behind his ears. I reluctantly released him. I'd follow him back to the coroner's office and then drive us to his place. I waited until he was safely in the driver's seat with the doors locked, and then I walked to my truck.

Since the night of his birthday, I'd broken down and analyzed every interaction I'd had or feeling I'd had toward Morgan in the years after we'd met. I wasn't unaware that Joseph had royally fucked with my head and my self-esteem. Yet I hadn't realized how much I'd kept my baby at arm's length to unconsciously protect myself. No more, he was mine, and I'd make sure he was always happy and safe with me. I just hoped I could do that.

DOC

COLD CASE
UNIT

A s I entered the morgue, I pushed a sigh out and slipped the straps of the backpack from my shoulders. I was dressed in my court clothes since that's where I was going to be forced to go later that day.

"Hey, Doc, I thought you were in court today?" Stuart, my assistant, came out of the storage cooler where we housed our overflow.

"I'm headed there soon, but I needed to pick up some notes. Anything exciting today?"

"No, but a messenger came by earlier and dropped off a package for you. I signed for it and just told them to put it on your desk."

I frowned as I looked at the plain cardboard box and dropped my bag on my desk. The Feds better not be sending me more shit to go over. I was already tired of outlining every fuck up the original coroner had gotten wrong, and the list was long; that didn't bode well for me.

The address on the box was from the strip, but the number was fake, and I stepped back. "Was there anything weird about the delivery person?" I'd gotten suspicious of weird packages. In my years as the medical examiner, I'd received a threat or two.

"No. Speedy Messenger service."

A bike messenger, they delivered just about everything in the city that people didn't want to go through the regular channels. I pulled my phone out of the front pocket of my backpack and called Carter.

"Hey, baby, you okay?"

"I got a weird package. Box isn't that big, but the address on it is the street from the strip, but the number isn't right."

"Baby, I'm going to have Remy call someone to come look at it. I want you to stay on the line, okay?"

"It's probably just a typo."

"Better safe than sorry." *Robert, Doc got a weird package. Call that new guy you know in Bomb Squad.* "Have you picked it up?"

"No, but isn't the Bomb Squad a bit overkill?"

Stuart jerked his head up, and I motioned him to leave. He didn't wait to think twice about that. I hit the biohazard alarm that would lock down the morgue. I'd gone through one other bomb threat, and as much as I tried to play it off, I thought about every person I'd helped put in jail, especially me going head-to-head with Officer Comstock in the murder of his estranged wife. That's when it hit me. I was due to testify before the grand jury in the case against him the following week.

I left the room and stood on the other side of the automatic doors, and just stared at my desk.

"Not when it comes to you, baby. I'd rather overreact about this than you get hurt." I heard Remy's muffled voice talking to Carter. "There's a Commander Dolan Sharp coming your way. He's a new guy. He's bringing his K-9 to check the package and will open it for you. Me and the rest of the guys will be headed your way in a few minutes as soon as I know Sharp is there."

I groaned. I heard about Sharp. He'd already gotten a bit of a reputation for being an asshole. SWAT and Bomb Squad people had a bit of an attitude anyway. "You're incredibly sweet, though."

"Gotta make my baby happy."

"This better not be a bomb or anything. Do you know what would happen to all my samples and residents?"

"Of course you'd be worried about what would happen to the bodies."

"They've already gone through enough trauma."

"Why the fuck is an alarm going off at the morgue?" Douglas's voice boomed, and I grinned.

"I'm going to see your boyfriend." Graves muttered.

"I think Graves has a crush."

"Graves is going to start pouting if we don't stop that."

"He's adorable when he pouts."

"Baby."

"But not as adorable as you, Daddy."

"Uh-huh, nice save." I giggled at the frustration in his voice.

"Doctor Warner?" I turned to glance over my shoulder as a tall, imposing man with a black German shepherd at his side. His black hair shaved on the sides and long on top, he was in his SWAT gear. A black bag held in his left hand.

"Yes, the package is on my desk."

Sharp gave me a stiff nod and entered the morgue. I watched through the glass as I saw his mouth move in silent commands as the dog carefully sniffed around the box. The dog sat down. When Sharp pulled out a knife, I entered to join him.

"Jupiter didn't hit on any explosives."

"Sorry you had to come out, my boyfriend is a bit..."

"Better to have me come in than have a colleague scraping you off the walls."

"Aren't you lovely?"

"Do you have a mask in case we're dealing with a biological threat?"

"Of course." I retrieved my mask as he slipped the straps of his own over his head. I stepped back to allow him to open the box. The sensors would've alerted to any known substances, but if they were sealed, it wouldn't trigger the alarms until they went airborne.

He split the tape and eased back the flaps. "Call crime scene and have them get here now." He eased backward until he was away from my desk. "You have some fucked up friends."

I called in Crime Scene to take over. I was impatient to approach but didn't want to disturb anything until the techs had a chance to take samples and pictures. "What was in there?"

"Four pictures of children covered in what looks like blood."

The automatic doors whooshed open, and the entire Cold Case Unit, along with Douglas, rushed in. I grinned as Carter hugged me tight to his chest. "Are you okay?"

"Let your baby breathe, Jesus fucking Christ," Graves muttered as he passed and headed for my desk, peeking into the box without getting too close.

"Thanks for coming out, Sharp," Robert said and then leaned down to whisper in my ear to ask if I was all right, and I nodded.

"Not a problem, Kauffman. Is there a reason you called?"

"Return address didn't exist," Robert answered.

"Street exists, but the number and apartment don't."

"You have any ideas who would send it?" Douglas went to take a look himself, and Graves instantly moved out of the way. Those two were going to come to blows one of these days, and I really wanted to be around when it happened.

"Comstock popped into my head. His grand jury for capital murder is next week, but he'd be more the type to attack in person."

"Comstock?" Sharp asked.

"Officer Comstock is being tried for the murder of his ex-wife."

"I'm new in the city. I don't know him."

"But to be honest, the list is really long, and I'm doing that project for the Feds. I don't know if that's common knowledge or not beyond Stevenson and the agents who brought me in to review several cases."

The questioning ceased when the crime scene techs arrived and took over. They photographed the scene and bagged everything to see about pulling prints in the lab. I broke away from Carter and went to talk to the senior investigator. I asked him to lay out the pictures in the box.

"We'll do a test to see if it's human blood or not once we get back upstairs. Do you recognize the kids in the photos?" Porter pointed at them with a gloved hand, and I leaned down to get a better look.

"That's Aiden Maxwell. Older but still Aiden."

"What?" Carter said and then was leaning over my shoulder. "Those are the other three kids, the ones from the closed cases. What the fuck is going on?"

"Doc, are you saying those photos are from the cases, but our missing kids look older?" Remy was right there, looking over my other shoulder.

"Yeah, bone structure is the same, but they're gaunter as if they lost their baby fat. Porter, can I get copies of all of this? I'm reexamining some cases, and I want a better look."

"I'll email you a report as soon as we're done."

"Thanks, Porter."

"Not a problem, Doc, we'll get out of your way. We'll get a preliminary report by the end of the day."

"That'll work, thanks."

They gathered up everything they needed, and Sharp didn't bother saying goodbye as he left behind them with his K-9 close at his side.

"Those can't be the same kids, could it?"

"It would explain why we never found bodies or had hits on the DNA for John Doe remains. The Maxwell case is cold but still active. The others…they probably didn't even put those samples in the national database since they got the guilty pleas. Why now, though? Why taunt Doc?"

"Maybe they're tired of not getting recognition for the perfect crimes. They committed four, three scapegoats pled out to get a life with the possibility of parole, and people just stopped looking for Aiden." Douglas leaned back to perch on the edge of my desk, and Graves snarled as he moved out of the way. "It's been over twenty-five years."

"What would make someone come out now?" Graves crossed his arms over his chest.

"Why wouldn't they? We still have no idea who they are. No closer to catching them or whatever their motive was for taking these boys and framing the mothers. Again, perfect, and those don't happen. There's always some fuck-up, and maybe this is his. He's just a few decades late giving himself away." Remy leaned back against Robert's chest where the older man reclined against the wall.

"I think I need to have a serious talk with Gladys. I gave her the information to look into everything, but with this newest development, she can make arrangements to meet with them and ask her own questions."

My phone chirped, signaling I was supposed to be on my way to the courthouse. "Fuck, I have to get to court. Bye, Daddy." I jumped up and kissed Carter's cheek, grabbed my bag, the notes I needed, and then made a run for the doors. Everyone was laughing behind me, and I nearly ran into Sharp outside the door. "Um, is there a reason you're creeping around, Commander?"

"You need protection."

"I'm perfectly capable of taking care of myself. And sorry to say this, Sharp, you're not my type."

"Brat, you ain't mine either."

"My feelings are hurt. You want to walk me out so you can satisfy whatever sense of duty this is you have?"

"Your Daddy doesn't spank you enough."

I let out an offended gasp and walked towards the ambulance bay exit. "How do you know—"

"You throw around Daddy an awful lot, and I've heard rumors that you and that Cold Case Unit are on the weird side. Douglas seemed okay the few times I've met him."

"Douglas is getting corrupted. He was too uptight, and I think he wants to belong to the cool kids club. You looking for membership, Commander?"

"No, I can do without weirdness. I found out what type of vehicle you drove and already had Jupiter clear it for you."

"Ain't you sweet."

"I'm really not. Don't make a habit of my dog having to sniff your mail."

"Too late, Commander, I'm very popular."

"Goodbye, brat." He broke off, and he and his K-9 went in the opposite direction.

People thought we were weird. They were the weird ones. I got in my car to make my way to a long day at the courthouse. I loathed testifying, but it was a part of my job. Hopefully, Porter had a report for me by the time I was done. Why would someone come out of the dark just to fuck with us? Yet, also the horror that the boys were still alive terrified me. Because if they were, what the hell had they endured for almost three decades.

STEVENSON

COLD CASE
UNIT

I'd held it together for Morgan but whoever the bastard was who snatched the kids showed up a little too close for comfort. The talk with the messenger service didn't go anywhere. All they said was the guy paid cash, average height and weight, plain brown hair and eyes; there was absolutely nothing extraordinary or noteworthy about him. What made matters worse was I had Vega on my ass for a threat to her precious Doc. At that moment, he was working. They'd called him in because the usual ME was sick, and while he took care of that, I needed to get ahead on this fucking case. I was tired of being in the dark.

I laid out copies of the four photos on my desk and stared at them. The next day I had that interview with Maxwell. I needed something to push him but keep Joseph from shutting Maxwell down.

"Do you love me, Stevenson?"

I jerked my head up and glanced over my shoulder to find Vega framed in the doorway, holding up a letter-sized envelope. "That depends on what you got to offer me."

She entered and came to hop up on my desk—her and Doc's favorite ways to sit. "I did age progression on your four missing boys. I used the photos from their case files and the ones delivered to Doc as reference."

I took the envelope, bent the clasps to open it, and slipped the four images out. I was amazed at the detail. "These are great." I noticed her slight shrug. She and Morgan were the same about compliments. "Did you run them through the facial recognition?"

"As we speak, but I lowered the percentage for matches, and doing a manual comparison. It might take a bit longer since its flagging a bunch. But I also had an idea. Something hit me last night while I was inputting the markers for the faces into my programs. It may be a little out there."

I let out a bitter chuckle and followed it with a heavy sigh. "I'm willing to listen to whatever theory…I seriously don't care about how crazy." I stared at the age progression images along with the ones in the package delivered to Morgan. If they were actually alive several years after being taken, what the hell did the people who kept them do to them all that time? The photos from the box didn't show any obvious physical trauma, while they were skinnier, that could be attributed to aging and reaching the start of puberty.

"It's sort of theory mixed with a bit of urban legend."

"Boss mentioned something about urban legends when I went to talk to him about Angela and Aiden's case."

"Back in the sixties, seventies, and some of the eighties, there was a host of groups coming in, religion and spirituality. A lot of street-corner preachers, and the end is nigh-type shit. Cult type stuff. Disenfranchised runaway youth seduced by the promise of something better. We still have a few Christian Outreaches coming onto the strip, but Boss has a bit of a monopoly, and we're open to everyone."

"What struck you?" I asked as I let her process. Her and Morgan's brains worked similarly, and I knew just to sit back. She'd talk it out.

"There was a group just called Transcendence. I called some

of the old-timers to get specifics to see if it held any weight... again, urban legend. They had a thing for bringing single mothers into the fold. They were attempting to build this great army and needed children to do so. As far as anyone knows, they disbanded in the mid-eighties, one day there, the next gone. They had an old hardware storefront on the edge of the strip."

"What was the point of the children?"

"They got them young, easier to mold to the group's cause. They ran a free childcare program for two decades. Child protective services were brought in a few times, but nothing came of the reports. The children weren't showing signs of abuse or neglect. Transcendence flew pretty low on the radar. They weren't flashy. Not a lot of money being thrown around. They did just enough to skirt the line that no one really talked about them. Most thought it was just an organization for unwed or single mothers to tap into help."

"What made you think it could be a group like that?"

"At first, you look at those images, classic proof of life pics for a ransom. There's newspapers with dates. These aren't kids with families that have the means to pay a ransom. It seems cruel in a way, taking an image every year. Check the dates."

I leaned down close. Oh shit. "It's the anniversary of the grab."

"It's progression, like before and after. It's an experiment... data for an eventual hypothesis."

"Why, though? I get the mentality of a kidnapper...someone taking children for a purpose, whether that's monetary or to sexualize them for either trafficking or for private use. I've been around, I've seen all kinds of shit. This just seems over the top, and to pop up with this after decades even crueler to me."

"What do offenders usually do right before they escalate?"

"They get impatient, but almost thirty years is a bit long to suddenly lose patience."

"No one was looking before. You and Doc are asking questions. Inquiries are being made by others. An entire production at the Barnes-Maxwell crime scene. Rumors spread. It got back to our unknown suspect."

"So, we may be looking at a group with ulterior motives. Some long-term sociological experiment?" Just what I needed, some cult or whatever, that just meant more cases, random snatches from around the world, depending on how far the group traveled or where their leader resided. As much as I wanted anything to look into, cults weren't something I wanted to have to deal with.

"Why not? Crazier things have happened in this city. You wanted a theory, and every urban legend has some hint of truth."

"Anyone I can talk to to learn more? Maybe Boss?" I leaned back in my chair, lifted my arms, and wrapped my hands around the back of my neck. The stiffness and posture were making my neck and shoulders ache. It didn't help that I felt a headache coming on.

"Boss, no. It was before his time as a community activist. He was around but not immersed yet. There's a street historian, a preceptor if you will. Prof. Kinda weird. Total burnout, but he knows all the history of the strip, good, bad, and horrific."

"Do I need an intro?"

"He's not a fan of Remy, so avoid that backup. He runs an unofficial Strip Museum of sorts. He loves Doc, so mention his name."

"Most people love Remy."

She shook her head. "Most people either love or hate Remy. There's no in-between. Prof and him had a beef. I don't know what it was about. Sometimes best not to ask questions when it comes to Remy's past. Prof can definitely tell you about the groups operating on the strip."

"Got an address for me?" She gave it to me, and I put the address in to get directions.

"Just be careful. He'll only give you so much. Don't treat it like an interrogation."

"Would it be an issue to take Doc?"

"May work in your favor. How's my Doc doing?"

"He's not acting like he's freaked out…maybe he isn't, but until further notice, he goes nowhere without me or someone else. He didn't fight me."

"Of course he didn't. Daddy knows best. How are you doing with all that? I know you fought it."

"I guess…I only fought it because I didn't think I could give him what he needed to be happy. That's all I cared about."

"Which is the reason you're the person for him. Even if there were no titles shared, you still do everything he needs. Cash told me she talked to you the night of his birthday, and if I'm not mistaken, that's the night you claimed him."

"She said some things I needed to hear. The attraction was always there, but my insecurities got the better of me."

"We all have them, even someone as perfect as I am."

"Your ego is too big for self-doubt."

"No, it's not. In the world, there are these preconceived notions of what a Dominant or caregiver should look like. It's in the media and books. I never saw a Dominant who looked like me until I was well into my twenties. I'm a short, adorable computer geek with a tall, gorgeous, and butch babygirl. We can't worry so much about what the outside world deems is appropriate or acceptable. Doc is a Little and Submissive in his fifties. Power exchange has nothing to do with outward appearance. Everything is a state of mind. You don't have to run scenes or go to some club. How two consenting adults, or more, choose to love each other is up to them."

"Thanks."

"You're committed to my best friend. You're stuck with me now. Best to be friends because, Stevenson"—she leaned in close —"you don't want me as an enemy."

"How can you be adorable and terrifying at the same time?"

"It's a gift. Okay, I got to do lunch with my babygirl. She's working through dinnertime. Seems everyone was called into a work emergency on a Sunday."

"I really do appreciate all this. Graves and I are the new kids to the club. You, Remy, and Doc, even Robert have always been this cohesive unit from the time I met you. Y'all don't have a lot of reason to trust. I'm not speaking for Graves, but thanks. We definitely get avenues of intel we weren't privy to before."

"You're welcome, and don't tell him, but I like Graves. He's easy to ruffle, and his pout definitely sets off my Mami side."

"I think I'll keep that one to myself."

"Appreciate it, don't want him to get too freaked out. He's actually starting to loosen up." She winked at me as she jumped off my desk and headed for the door.

As I was left alone, I once again looked at the photos lined them up from their missing person reports to the *proof of life* images, and the ones Vega dropped off. These kids could be men in their thirties. I'd tried not to think about what would happen if they'd survived somehow. Didn't even know they were missing. Living life believing whatever their kidnappers told them. Yet there was the other side, decades of abuse, torture, them doing whatever to survive. It would be a miracle to bring them home, to free three women falsely convicted.

So many lives ruined, and for what? A belief or psychological warfare. I needed to see my baby and then ask if he wanted to go talk to Prof with me before going to have dinner. Not exactly the date night I wanted. Maybe when this case was solved or cold again, I could actually do this relationship with Morgan right.

28

DOC

COLD CASE
UNIT

I bounced on my toes outside Prof's brownstone. I knew it looked like something out of a Gothic horror, but it was amazing. No one knew much about the man other than he was an ancient elder, a fixture on the strip before there was even a district. He knew everything, and he was a wealth of knowledge. I remembered meeting him at one of my clinics. He'd come in to see what I was up to and invited me for tea afterward. He was an odd recluse. He never left the strip area. If he couldn't find it there, he said he never needed it.

"Should I be insecure that you're so excited?"

"Aw, Daddy, don't be jealous. You'll understand after you meet him."

"What's this feud between him and Remy?"

"No one really knows, some rumors say it was because he became a cop and others say he slept with a former lover of Prof's. We don't really ask."

"You can ring the bell," he said, and I jumped at turning the old-fashioned bell that gave a tinny sound on the other side of the door.

I cuddled to his side as we waited, and I smiled as the door opened to the majestic sight of an elderly man in a tie-dyed caftan with his long silver hair in two braids over his shoulders. I didn't know what the man did, but there was no way he was coming up on eighty.

"Morgan, my sweet, you brought me a guest."

"Hi, Prof, this is Carter Stevenson. He wanted to learn more about the strip."

"He came to the right place. Please come in." He stepped back and motioned Daddy and I inside. "Please hang up your jackets and remove your shoes. I just started a pot of tea."

"Thank you, Vega gave me your name," Stevenson spoke as he helped me off with my jacket, hung it up, and then removed his as I kicked off my shoes.

"How is our Vega?"

"Good, scary as ever," Stevenson answered with a smile.

"Somethings truly don't change."

We followed Prof, and every square inch of wall and available floor space contained some history of the strip. Neon signs from long-closed establishments. Photos, some even dating back to the twenties. That's why we treated the strip as a separate entity, a closed community within a city, a part of the history yet still separate.

"Morgan and Vega said you were a historian."

"Not so much, I'm just an old storyteller, and this place has always held a bit of fantasy and mystery. An almost private community for the unique amongst us." Prof motioned for us into his office. "Wait in here, and I'll be right back with tea."

He continued on as Stevenson and I took a seat on the antique couch in a deep blood red velvet. We sat close together. A fire warmed the room and set off flickers of light against the dark paneling and furniture.

"He wasn't what I expected but also what I expected."

"Prof said old Queens don't give a shit about much once they reach a certain age. He's lived in this house since he was born in the forties. It should be a historical landmark."

Stevenson was about to speak when Prof entered the office and placed a tray with three cups and a teapot, along with some cookies, onto the battered coffee table. Once Prof took a seat, I poured the tea.

"Any particular part of history you'd like to know about?" He smiled his thanks at me as I handed him a cup and saucer and then passed one to Stevenson.

"He's working on a case, Barnes and Maxwell," I answered and checked for any sign of irritation that I brought a cop into his home, but there's wasn't.

"That poor girl, a lovely woman. Her and her girlfriend used to come by for tea and stories. Di, that was the young lady she was dating. She helped with my collection. She worked at the university as a student curator and helped me catalog"—he sighed and waved his hands around—"all this after I truly realized what I'd amassed. My mother was a collector of sorts, every piece a story she'd tell. It became a habit, but if I'm not mistaken, wasn't that case closed?"

"It went cold. I work in the permanent Cold Case Unit. We have four full-time detectives and Vega working through cases. Vega's mostly gathering any DNA evidence to do a genealogical profile to look for new leads. A few months ago, I chose the Barnes-Maxwell case at random. I met with Mary, and I'd love to give her closure."

"Very compassionate of you. Historically speaking, cops haven't cared much for what happened in our community. As much as I believed Boss to be a do-gooder outsider at the beginning, I must admit he's done well with fostering *some* goodwill between us and law enforcement. And also done amazing things community-wise. His passion is admirable." He took a sip of his tea. "Unfortunately, I don't know what I can do to help with your case."

"Vega brought up an interesting theory earlier, and she said if anyone would know you would."

"I'll do what I can, and afterward, I'll take you on a tour. Plenty of your Morgan is in this house."

I lowered my chin after Prof winked at me. A lot of memories existed and were cared for in this house. Love and passion kept them alive, and it was sad that one day it would end.

"Thank you, um, Vega mentioned a group called Transcendence. She used that one as an example of the types of groups in between the sixties and eighties that migrated to the strip."

"Transcendence Through the Elder Prophecy, just Transcendence on the street, though. They were an organization that popped up in the sixties, a bit of new-age fluff mixed with fundamentalism. Prophesy makes it sound so end-of-the-world and cool. There was a rise in cults, *Children of God, The Family, Jonestown,* and many others. Those are just the most notable and newsworthy. Most cults aren't even known until something goes wrong...some scandal brings them to public light."

"What particularly did Transcendence believe in?" Stevenson asked as he hugged me to his side and kissed my temple. I caught Prof's small smile. He'd listened to me complain a lot over tea.

"It was a strange mix of health, religion, and spirituality, and some good old-fashioned doomsday thrown in. They believed in saving souls for an army that would eventually be called to assist in a war of good against evil. All rather cliché. You'd think cults would have a bit more creativity. Doctor Gordon Platt. That was the leader of Transcendence. He had some success with the health and training portions of his programming."

"In what way?"

"Follow me. It would be better to show than tell." He stood, and we followed him to a room all the way in the back.

I laughed at the Strip Oddities burned into a splintered plank.

"This is where the oddest history is kept." Prof approached an aged group photo. "Gordon." He pointed to the distinguished man in the center. He was dressed in a well-fitted suit. I'd expected something else. "His two sons on either side, Isiah and Ezekiel. They were noted as his first successes. Mother, or mothers, unknown. Rumors were of *adoption*, but no one really questioned. Back in the day, it wasn't all tech and computer records. Forging documents was a lot easier before barcodes and chips." He lifted the picture down to let Stevenson have a closer look. "The children were programmed with the scripture of the group, indoctrinated by repetition and psychological conditioning. It was classic torture used in war and brainwashing groups, break down the psyche enough to be able to rewrite the code with your own."

"What about the training part?" Stevenson asked as he started to circle the room checking everything out.

"It was about spiritual and physical health, to be prepared when the great prophecy comes to fruition."

"Were they a certain age when the mothers were taken into the group?"

"They liked to get them young for the first phase, which was the teaching of the preceptor. They were allegedly written by Platt's teacher, the one who passed on the knowledge of the prophecy. Second phase was turning them into warriors. Trained in everything from firearms to hand-to-hand combat. They owned property outside the city, and they built a compound. It's believed that when they supposedly disbanded, that's where they went."

"Why did they suddenly disappear?" I asked as Prof followed Stevenson with his gaze.

"A young reporter, I don't remember his name, blame my age, but he infiltrated the group. Wrote some scathing articles…first one to publicly throw out the word cult. Come to find out, no teacher existed. Gordon Platt came from old money. He'd never worked a day in his life. When his parents passed away, he sold everything, moved across the country and rewrote his own history. There was one follow-up article that the compound was abandoned and the land sold when it went into foreclosure. It seemed everyone disappeared. No other mentions. And it became the quintessential urban legend. Why the questions?"

"As you know, Angie was murdered, and her eight-year-old brother disappeared. No body was ever found. At first, I thought it was a paternal kidnapping case, but from what I learned, I don't think Maxwell cared enough about his son to give a damn. Angie was Aiden's primary caregiver. Boss told me that she was interested in adopting him to raise with Di. Then a homicide detective threw a twist in I didn't expect. There were three other kidnappings with the same MO. In those cases, though, the mothers were convicted of murder. All the male children taken were between the ages of eight and ten. Again, no bodies or crime scene other than the grab location."

"So you're thinking a group, maybe a cult took them?" Prof asked.

"It was something Vega brought up. Yesterday, Doc received a package with four pictures. It appeared to be the boys several years later. They were all holding newspapers, like proof of life, and they were taken on the anniversary of the kidnappings. They didn't appear to be injured, relatively good health that we could tell."

"All in the nineties?"

"Yes. I'm not sure about the cult angle, I mean, I've seen some weird stuff in my years as a cop, but my gut says no."

"Then what *does* your gut say?"

"The word experiment came up, and if that's the case, then they could've used Transcendence as the baseline."

"What do you say, Morgan?"

"It's a novel idea. The scientist in me sees the validity in the claim. It's not like there wouldn't be a demand for a perfect malleable soldier, and they could be sold or hired out to anyone.

Platt devised the perfect parameters to take it to the next stage. Yet, who inside the group would be so familiar with its practices? Also, Platt went underground, and age-wise, he'd most likely be dead or close to it by now, no matter how healthy he kept himself."

"The sons?"

"Give me a second." I pulled out my phone and called Vega.

"Hello, Doc."

"Could you do a search on a Gordon Platt and his sons, Isiah and Ezekiel? Cross-reference with Transcendence."

"Can do. Anything in particular I should keep an eye out for?"

"Just a theory."

"Give me a few hours to do an initial search, and I'll check-in."

"Thanks, Vega."

"No problem. Breaks up the monotony of my days. And my babygirl is working. I think that singer has a crush on my girl."

"Like she would even look at anyone else. Do the work to distract yourself." She growled, and I giggled as I disconnected the call. "Vega said she'd call in a few hours with any information."

"I may have something that will help." Prof went over to a series of wooden file cabinets. "I used to collect pamphlets. There were always groups handing out the literature. I knew it was in here somewhere. I have pamphlets, and you lucked out, I have one of their initiate bibles. Pure propaganda."

"Can I take them to look over and return them later?" Stevenson took the stack.

"Of course. Just return them when you're done."

An idea hit me, and I looked at Prof. "Prof, if we're talking about a religious sect, were girls ever used or trained as warriors?"

"I can't be sure, but female members were usually support or caregivers. Mainly I think they were used as breeders. You know, strength in numbers. Maybe the kidnappings were to rebuild the ranks again."

"Or they were just used as experiments. If they were used as subjects, then the images may just be for a file to show physical progress. And we might have more than just four missing boys."

"I'll see about expanding our search with the new parameters. You have anything else, Prof."

"No, I'll look around to see if I can find more information... maybe talk with a few people who might know where to locate some of the former members. Best way to learn about a group or person is to talk to the people they betrayed."

"I really appreciate all your time and information."

"You're more than welcome. Now, why don't I tell you some embarrassing stories about your little man there."

"No, no, that's okay, we really need to be—" I squeaked as Stevenson wrapped his arms around me and pulled me to his chest.

"I want to know everything."

"You're so mean, Daddy."

He gripped my chin and turned my head until I could meet his gaze. "I want to know all those stories that made you...you. All your selflessness and quirks. You know I'd never shame or look down on you. You're perfect. Yet, you're also adorable when you blush."

"Fine, Daddy, but don't laugh too much at my expense." The corners of my mouth curved upward as his lips came down on mine.

"I'd never laugh at you. I'd never make you insecure like that. I inadvertently did it once, and I won't repeat that mistake."

"Thank you."

"No need for thanks, let's have some fun, and then we'll go home. I know you want to be there to annoy *Joey* tomorrow."

I laughed as he gave me a tight hug before he released me. We spent the rest of the evening with Prof showing off all the treasures with stories with me mixed in. There was a moment of respite from the stress of the case, four missing children, three falsely imprisoned mothers, and why whoever they were deemed me worthy of a threat. I didn't want to believe I needed to constantly look over my shoulder. I'd already spent too many years doing that.

29

STEVENSON

COLD CASE
UNIT

The seconds counted down to the moment Maxwell and Joseph would show up, and I wasn't in the mood. I'd stayed up too late reading that lovely piece of propaganda bullshit Prof had given me. The only thing that had made it bearable was my baby curled up on my lap—his head tucked under my chin as he snuggled with the doll I'd given him. He'd barely lasted an hour after we'd gotten home. We'd gone through a drive-thru to grab dinner, so at least he'd eaten something before he'd passed out.

He needed all the sleep he could get. Something I'd learned since our relationship started was that he put in a lot more hours than I'd first thought. And that was just as an ME, that didn't count the hours of volunteer work and the time he put in as a board member at the Outreach. He pushed himself too much, yet he didn't complain or fight me when I tried to get him to slow down. My baby liked to be taken care of, to be made to take a moment to breathe.

"Am I late? Tell me I didn't miss it?" Vega's voice echoed through the halls, punctuated by the heavy pounding of her boots on the cement floors.

I groaned as Remy, Robert and Graves busted out laughing,

and I flipped them off as I turned my head to look over my shoulder to find Vega and Morgan rushing through the door.

"Hey, baby." I held out my arm, and he let go of Vega's arm to give me a kiss.

"Hey, Daddy. I swear I tried to talk her out of it." He straightened and slipped onto my desk in front of me.

"I think that was kinda useless. She's nosy."

"Dude, it's your ex. I have to meet this piece of work." She squealed as she hopped up on my desk and turned to offer her cheek to Graves. "Simon, looking awful pretty today. Is that big, handsome detective supposed to visit?"

"Don't call me Simon." Graves growled and blew a raspberry on Vega's cheek. "And you're not funny," he said as Vega batted her lashes at him.

"We have an overly full house today. We planning on performing an inquisition?" Robert's voice clearly broadcasted his amusement.

"No, we're just here for moral support and see the fireworks. They're gonna be amazing since Doc has shown up." Remy seated himself on his usual spot on the corner of Robert's desk. "I think Joey might be jealous."

I rolled my eyes at Remy. Joseph wouldn't be jealous over me if I lost forty pounds, waxed from head to toe, and started rocking a six-pack. He hadn't changed any since our divorce. The only reason he was pissed was he couldn't bully Morgan into worshipping at his high-polished shoes. Joseph was going to hate the entire Cold Case Unit, that is if he didn't already.

"We have a perfectly good excuse for being here." Vega pouted. "Doc is getting the swabs, I'm taking them to the lab, and once they process the profile, it's getting sent to my lab. I don't trust Coleman, so I'm going to ride the tech's ass until he runs it. Coleman has been pushing back with the number of samples I'm demanding. Little does he know, I have an almost unlimited amount of grant money."

"Please behave...at least a bit."

"For you, Stevenson, I'll make an effort, but I make no guarantees if he makes digs at our Doc."

That was as close to a promise as I'd get. I was about to say yes when everyone turned to the door, and I spun my chair. Joseph was as put together as always. Not a hair out of place. His suit pristine.

"Mr. Chambers, Mr. Maxwell." I pushed up from my chair and extended my hand to Maxwell. I didn't even bother with Joseph. Maxwell's hand was cool and slightly clammy, and I forced myself not to cringe as I released his weak grip. "Please, have a seat." I motioned towards the couch, took the small notepad and pen Morgan held out to me, and rolled my chair closer as I waited for them to sit. "Would you like some coffee, tea, or bottled water?"

"No, just ask your questions so that we can be done with this." Joseph's cool tone didn't faze me, and he dug into his satchel and pulled out a legal pad and pen.

"Well, first, let me thank you for coming in to speak with us." I lowered into the chair. "We just want to clarify a few things since the original report lacked a lot of details."

"Whatever I can do to help," Maxwell spoke as he rubbed his palms on his knees.

"When were you informed that Aiden was missing and your stepdaughter was murdered?"

"A few days afterward. They didn't even know he was missing until someone tried to file a missing person's report. I think someone named Di went and reported Aiden missing. I think she was Angie's roommate."

"What was your son like?" I asked the question specifically to see if he knew his son at all.

"Quiet boy. Not too social. A bit odd. He spent too much time with Angie. I don't think she was a good...role model for him."

I tried not to frown. The story I'd heard was that he was a

bright boy and caring, and Angie took excellent care of Aiden. "If you didn't think she raised him well enough, why didn't you take custody when your ex-wife went to prison?"

He cleared his throat. "I was living with my new girlfriend, and we already had a full house with her three children. My job was demanding, and he said he wanted to live with Angie."

I made notes and glanced up to find Joseph glaring at my friends and my baby. "After his disappearance, did you receive any strange calls, letters…maybe something that could've alluded to a possible kidnapping?"

"No, nothing. The only people who called me was the detectives…I don't remember their names. After a few weeks, there were no calls at all, and my girlfriend and I moved away, a better position came up with my company. The longer he was missing, the more I just figured whoever killed Angie did the same to Aiden and disposed of his body elsewhere."

"Did you ever check in…"

"My client was not required to do the jobs of the cops. He trusted them to do their job. Let's move on."

"A young woman was disemboweled as she fought to protect your client's son. Some compassion and courtesy would've been expected to check in on the case. I didn't ask him to investigate. Although, Ms. Barnes did a great job of doing that herself once she was released."

"Carter…"

"Detective Stevenson, Mr. Chambers. Where was your client on the day of the murder and abduction?" I watched them exchange glances, and Joseph nodded.

"I was away with my girlfriend. We'd had a long weekend planned for some time alone without the kids. The following Monday, there was a message on our answering machine asking me to call."

"Excuse me, Stevenson, Mr. Maxwell, when was the last time you'd seen your son?" Robert asked.

"Um." Another throat clearing. "I don't remember, maybe a few weeks before he went missing."

"When you did see him, did he mention anything strange? A stranger to him hanging around...talking to him? Maybe a new *friend?*" Graves's voice went cold, a tone I hadn't heard since our days working Homicide and the Fellows' case.

"No, nothing. Like I said, he didn't talk much, just had his nose in some book...comics that Angie bought him. Any time he visited, he didn't interact with us that much. I always invited him outside to play catch or whatever with the other boys...he wasn't interested."

"Did you speak to him at all, Mr. Maxwell?" Remy piped up, and I realized what they were doing. They were going to push. They were bad cops to my good cop. It was a game we rarely played.

"I loved my son..."

He hadn't given a shit, and I knew it in my gut. It would only be a matter of time before his acting disappeared. We just had to wait him out. "We didn't ask if you loved your son. We asked if you talked to him at all."

"I think that's enough. We didn't come here for an interrogation. My client came here as a courtesy."

"This is what Aiden would look like today at the age of thirty-three." Vega held up the aged picture of a handsome man, and looked like anybody you'd pass on the street. And if he was alive, he may be walking in plain sight. "He was eight, walking home after dinner with his big sister, and he had to watch as she was butchered, and you haven't even flinched or shed a tear."

"Vega."

"I didn't guarantee anything, Stevenson."

"If this is the way this conversation is going to go, I think it's time—"

"Mr. Chambers, I'm dealing with a case that's twenty-five years old that was barely investigated because the cops thought one thing when they saw a pretty, Latina girl dead in an alley. And an abduction that was already cold by the time someone cared to report Aiden missing. So forgive us if we're not being polite enough in trying to solve this crime to give Angie and Aiden's mother closure."

"If she had acted right, she wouldn't…"

Remy's laugh behind me was sharp and angry. "Mr. Maxwell, before you even try that, I have several sources who would gladly swear under oath that even if Ms. Barnes made a mistake, you did too. You just didn't get caught. The people on the strip have long memories. Doctor Warner and I sat with Mary for years as she came in to identify every John Doe, cried with her when she realized it wasn't Aiden. So, what my colleague is trying to do is make sure that even if your son isn't alive, that we make as much effort as possible to find a body so that she'll know what happened to him."

"I can't help you." The veneer Maxwell wore of a respectable man disappeared. In his place was a cold, smirking man. "I didn't want the kid. Mary was a bit of fun, slumming. But no one I was going to take home or would meet my friends or colleagues. Aiden came, stayed for a day, and I took him home. I was happy to have Angie take over."

"Morgan, take the sample, please." I didn't look away from Maxwell as Doc removed a swab and told Maxwell to open his mouth. Doc took the sample and then sealed it in a tube.

"Vega and I will take this to the lab."

"I'll see you at home," I told Morgan and watched him and Vega leave. I stood and returned my chair to my desk.

From the corner of my eye, I saw Joseph whisper to Maxwell, and then the man left. I glanced around at my friends. Graves looked slightly pissed. Robert and Remy spoke quietly as they darted glances at Joseph.

"Is there a reason you're still here?" I asked.

"You got everything you needed from my client, are we done?"

"Your client's an entitled bastard, but he didn't give enough of a damn to do anything to Angie or Aiden. So we're done."

"You'll see him at home?"

"You got an issue, Joey?" The question slipped out, and three choked-off snorts almost made me smile.

"Figured you had better taste."

"It's been pointed out by good friends that my taste has greatly improved."

"We all said his taste improved so much." Remy smiled sweetly as Joseph sent him a dirty look.

My ex brought his attention back to me, and for the first time, I saw true emotion in his eyes—hate. What the fuck had I done so wrong in my former husband's opinion? Yet I knew that no matter what I'd done back then wouldn't have changed the outcome, and I'd tortured myself for so many years for nothing.

"I'll destroy him on the stand next time."

"You don't have a chance. My baby boy will laugh at any attempt to trip him up. I may have to take a day off just to watch." I winked at him and waited for him to respond, but he disappointed me when all he did was storm out.

"Truly, Stevenson, whatever did you see in that man? Even if he's hot…" Graves held up his hand before Remy could comment. "I'm around gay and bi men *all* the time, my masculinity isn't fragile, he's hot, anyone would think so. But I digress. He's got an extremely bitter ex vibe."

"I don't know what he'd be bitter about. He's the one who asked for the damn divorce."

"Daddy." Morgan's voice came from behind me, and I turned to find him leaning in the doorway.

"Baby, I thought you'd left."

"I wanted to see you before I did. Vega's waiting in the car."

"Come here. Daddy needs a hug." I grinned as he rushed into

my open arms and hugged my waist tight. I held him close as I lowered my lips to the top of his soft hair. "I'll see you at home. Are you going to work late?"

"Unless they need me for some emergency, I should actually get out of the office on time."

"Then I'll see you then. Be good, and don't you and Vega have too much fun torturing Coleman."

"Now, don't ruin our fun." He tipped his head back, cupped his smooth cheeks, and lowered my head enough to brush my lips to his.

"Go on, brat." I reluctantly released him and felt a sense of loss when he backed up; I instantly missed his warmth.

"Bye." He waved, and I didn't look away until he disappeared.

"When are you going to tell that boy you love him?" I jerked my head around to stare at Robert. "Don't even start trying to deny it because anyone can see you do."

I didn't open my mouth to deny it, but I couldn't do that. To lie and say I didn't just disrespected Morgan. "I'm still processing."

"What's there to process? You've known each other for years. If I'm not mistaken, you're at his place more than yours, so can we say practically living together? Like I said, what do you have to think about?" Graves innocently smiled at me, and I didn't buy it.

"We've only been dating a few months."

"Being friends first cuts down on the time. I fell in love with Remy and didn't even recognize what it was until it was almost too late. And don't try the Joey bullshit because Doc and him are as different as night and day. And your boy may be a bit obsessed with you, but he knew his Daddy needed a hug."

"I just wanted to get this case…"

Graves threw a pen at me. "Stevenson, what does being done with the case have to do with anything? What do we learn from this job? That it can all end with no warning, and you didn't get to say what mattered."

"When did you become a romantic, Graves? Turning over a new leaf? Someone—"

"Don't even. I'm not dealing with that shit from you. Vega's bad enough. Just think about it, man, okay. You don't have to say it, but at least think about it. You can't do better than Doc."

"You got intentions toward my boy?" I snorted as Graves rolled his eyes.

"Jealousy doesn't become you. Now finish work so you can go home to Doc and romance him. I may not want him, but I bet he's got a long list of admirers."

I cursed and didn't appreciate the laughter from my so-called friends. I'd tried not to acknowledge my feelings toward Morgan. Joseph still fucked with my head all these years later. But I knew myself. I wouldn't have started anything with Morgan if I didn't want permanent; I wasn't made for casual. Was I brave enough to put myself out there?

"Stevenson, don't worry so much. Our Doc will be thrilled when you tell him if that's tonight or when you close this case." Remy nudged me with his shoulder, and I nodded.

Enough time to think about it later, I needed to figure out my next step, and I had to close this case. I didn't have any other choice.

30

DOC

COLD CASE
UNIT

I threw another file in the done box, and I only had one more to go through. The Feds had a shitstorm on their hands. The coroner had done the bare minimum on the cases. Not only had he put his entire career in jeopardy, but hundreds of guilty verdicts. That meant I was going to get even more cases to reexamine. I rubbed my tired eyes with the heels of my hands and then glanced at the clock on the mantle. It was already eight, but Carter should be there at any time. He'd called to say he was stopping at his place to pick up clothes.

That morning kept running through my head. Maxwell had acted like the concerned father there for a bit, played up the nervousness, but it had been easy to see the mask slowly crack. As much as I disliked the man, he hadn't had anything to do with what happened with Angie and Aiden.

I was experiencing secondhand frustration for Carter. He was working so hard to solve a case that started with just two victims and morphed into four missing kids, one murder, and the probably wrongful conviction of three women. I wanted to take some of the weight off his shoulders. Yet I didn't know how much help I could offer.

The second I heard footsteps on the single step, I jumped up and went to get the door. I opened it. Carter stood there with an overnight bag and paper to-go bag from a fast-food place.

"Hey, baby." He stepped inside and paused as I tipped my head back. His mouth brushed mine.

"Hey, I would've made you dinner, Daddy." I liked taking care of him. Making dinner. Rubbing his shoulders. Easing some of his stress. I lifted the door to get it to close and slid the lock into place.

"I know, but you said you already ate, and I wanted you to relax. I know the Feds thing has turned into a bigger project than anticipated. Did you relax?" he asked as I turned around to find him tossing his bag in front of my armoire.

I chuckled as he glanced at me as his brow arched. "No, I marked another case off the list, and I have one more. I wanted it done before you got here so I could have quality time with my Daddy."

"And I plan to spend all my time cuddling you. No work tonight. No mention of cases. How does that sound?"

"Well, Daddy…" I closed the distance between us and lifted my arms to lace my fingers at the back of his neck. "Work has been taking up a lot of our time."

"It has," he whispered as he tucked my hair behind my ears and then stroked his thumbs across my cheeks. "Do you feel neglected?" He had a hint of insecurity in his voice.

"Absolutely not. I enjoy every second we spend together, even if that's just us so exhausted we fall asleep on the couch or in bed. Daddy, my job doesn't allow for regular hours, and I've been around law enforcement for over three decades. I know how it works." We'd gotten each other off a lot in the past few months, but it was mostly blowjobs or mutual masturbation, and some nights it was just us talking and cuddling. I had no complaints about our relationship. "I'm not him."

"I know you're not, but you…what's going on is important to me. I don't want you insecure. I think I did that to you enough."

"Quit with the guilt. Have your dinner and then you're all mine." I squeaked as he bent his knees, palmed my ass, and lifted me until my legs circled his waist. His left hand stroked up my back to finally tangle in my hair. The second his mouth came down on mine, my eyes closed. Kissing him was always like coming home; he made everything right. I giggled as he eased the kiss but kept pressing his lips to mine as if he couldn't bear to pull away.

"I just wanted you to know that I'd never take you for granted."

"You're very sweet, Detective."

"I try. Grab my food. I'm not ready to put you down yet. I'm gonna eat and jump in the shower, and you can pick a movie for us to watch."

I leaned to the side and grabbed the bag he'd set on the bed and then straightened. "Anything?" I nibbled at my lower lip and batted my lashes at him. He had a weakness for the cute, innocent thing, and I could work that to my advantage.

"Yes, anything."

"And you didn't think you'd be a good Daddy for me." I tightened my legs and left arm around him as he walked toward the couch.

"You get away with everything."

"There's always more spankings," I suggested.

"You like them too much." He growled, and I pouted. "I may take a page out of Vega's book and punish you with corner time."

As he lowered to sit down, I moved my legs to place my feet on the cushion next to his hips. "Now, don't be mean, Daddy." I fell to the side and rolled over, and stretched my legs over his lap. He rested the warm bag on my calves. "You need a drink? What do you—"

"You stay right there. I'm not lucky like Robert and can have you sitting on my desk all day."

"They *are* sickeningly sweet, aren't they?"

"They always were. I noticed as soon as they became partners. I'm surprised Robert didn't see it." He slowly ate as he draped his left arm across my lap and drew soothing circles on my hip.

I loved his unconscious affection. He didn't even realize the touches—a natural inclination. All of that was mine and only mine. The past month I'd found myself fighting an inner battle not to blurt out that I loved him. A few short months was too soon, but I still feared in some ways that what we had couldn't last. I pushed the dark thoughts away and focused on just him and our time together.

"Remy deserved someone good."

"What was teenaged Remy like?"

I grinned. "Tragically beautiful. His childhood should've destroyed him, but he was always the first to offer to help...to give food even if he went hungry."

"Seems all of you have that selflessness in common."

"We're nowhere near sainthood. God." I breathed out a heavy sigh and then chuckled. "We were a force back in the day. Remy, Boss, Shine, Davian, Vega, hell, the entire crew, most of us should be in jail by now."

"Should I be worried?"

"No, Daddy, we were all stronger together. There were several years there that I kept something from them, I still do."

He packed all his trash into his bag, leaned forward to set it on the table, and then turned slightly to look at me. "What do you mean?"

"I dated this guy, Leif, and I told no one about him, never did."

"Why?"

"He was different. He worked in research and development at a pharmaceutical company. We didn't talk about death or my double life on the strip. With him, I was just...Morgan. Don't get me wrong, he asked about my day, but he didn't demand details. It was all perfect, romance with flowers and dates...all the adoration I could ask for."

"I hear a but, though," he said as he grabbed my hand and tugged me up until I straddled his thick thighs.

"We were together for three years. The first two were idyllic. Then he asked me to marry him. It wasn't legal, but he wanted me to have the ceremony. I counsel people to leave abusive situations, but I didn't leave. Not until the night he tried to kill me."

The back of his hand rubbed my scars through my t-shirt and hoodie. "Did he give you these?"

"Yes. I pressed a towel to my stomach and escaped. I went to the morgue, and"—as I tried to lower my chin, he slipped his fingertips under it, lifting it back up—"I sewed myself up. Took a week of vacation. I thought we'd...Daddy, I thought it was my happily ever after. He wasn't a Daddy or a Dominant, but he had the personality for it, so I never pushed. I figured out too late that I was just like the ones I'd helped in groups."

"And you were ashamed of not seeing the signs. My sweet baby, we rarely ever see it when we're on the inside. Just like you're not Joseph, I'm not him. I'd never put my hands on you in anger. I wouldn't hurt you on purpose for anything in the world. In some ways, I already have, but I'm so sorry for that, baby."

"Carter." I raised my hands to cup his bearded jaw. The sadness and regret in his eyes killed me. "You'd never intentionally hurt me. Fighting is normal. Disagreements. Nights on the couch or in a motel room, those things happen. You'd never leave bruises because they make you feel more like a man. You'd never verbally break me because you relished the pain those words caused. That's not you. That's why I'm so happy to be right here...sitting on my Daddy's lap and knowing that I'm always safe with you."

"You have so much faith in me, and I don't know what I did to instill it."

"You were just you. Now, I'm going to throw that trash away, and you're going to take a shower, don't put on any clothes..." I paused as I leaned in to press my lips to his, never taking my gaze from his. "Because I have plans for you."

"You going to tell me what they are?"

"No, Daddy, because it's a surprise." I slid off his lap and stood, and then I leaned in close. "The best thing about you being here, I get to see you naked all the time. So get to making your baby happy, and return without apparel."

"Your obsession with me being naked is highly ego-stroking behavior."

"Whatever works. Have I mentioned what a shame it is you have to wear clothes at all, Detective?" I winked as he chuckled. He stood and then lowered his mouth to mine.

"Does my baby want to wash Daddies back?"

"No tempting me, when it comes to you, I'm weak."

He shrugged his broad shoulders. "I do love that you find me tempting."

"If someone doesn't, they have no idea what they're missing out on." Daddies needed comfort and praise, too. That was something a lot of people didn't get. As much as he didn't want me to think he didn't take me for granted; I needed the same thing for him.

"I'll be out in a few minutes." He stroked my cheek again and brushed his lips to my forehead. My eyes closed at the peace I felt when he did that.

I didn't move until he walked away, and I bent to straighten the coffee table and put away my work I'd brought home. That night he would get my undivided attention. He catered to me. All the affections and cuddles, and never demanding anything for himself. Yes, submitting to his dominance was my place of peace, but physical affection and service to my partner were my love languages. And since I wasn't quite ready to let the L-word slip free; I could at least show him.

I stoked the fire and added more logs to make sure the cottage stayed warm the rest of the night. I nibbled at my bottom lip, except for fingers we hadn't had penetrative sex, and for me, that was fine. Yet I wanted that connection with Carter. So much time had passed since I'd felt anything inside me but my toys and fingers. I heard the metal rings on the shower curtain rattle as he opened and closed it, and I got to work.

I turned all the lights off and switched on one of the lamps on the nightstand. I pulled the covers back, and then I removed the new box of condoms and lube from the drawer. Nerves danced in my belly as I anticipated the night ahead.

My hands shook as I stripped beside the bed and threw my clothes toward the hamper that held a mix of our clothes. He slept there more often than not. As an adult, I hadn't lived with anyone other than the bastard who wouldn't be named right then. I heard the sound of the shower turning off, and the curtain rattled again. I quickly looked down at myself and then did another glance around the room. I counted my breaths, focused on making them even so I wouldn't hyperventilate. Why was I so nervous? Like it was our first night together.

The door hinges squeaked, and I jerked my head, and my breath caught in my lungs at the sight of him naked and drying his hair. Water beaded on the fur covering his chest and stomach.

"Hey, Daddy," I said as I crawled onto the bed and across it to kneel on the opposite side to wait for him to approach.

"Is my baby ready for bed?" He hung the towel up on a hook beside the bathroom door, and then he slowly walked the short distance from the doorway to our bed.

I nodded as he pressed his burly body against mine. All my nervousness fled the second he had his hands on me. "I want you to fuck me."

"What do you say when you want something, baby?"

"Please, Daddy."

"Good boy. Lay down for me," he ordered, and I obeyed. I stretched out with my head on the pillows. "Spread your legs and show Daddy that sweet, little hole."

I bent my knees and let them fall to the side. I cupped my hairless sac and stroked upward along my hard cock. Just seeing him turned me on, throw in the gruff voice with that edge of Daddy, and I was helpless. I'd submit to anything he ordered me to do, and I'd never worry because I always knew he'd keep me safe.

"Such a pretty baby. Who do you belong to, Morgan?" he asked as he crawled across the mattress until he knelt between my spread thighs. His big hands curled around my inner thighs, massaging the muscles, and he didn't stop there. He stroked upward over my hips. He teased me by ignoring the part of me that needed his touch the most. "I believe I asked you a question."

"You, Daddy, I only belong to you."

"And do you want me to love on you?" I nodded because he moved his hands to the mattress on either side of my ribs and lowered.

My back arched painfully as his hairy skin met my smooth chest and stomach. "Daddy."

"Shh, baby, I know what you need." He rested his weight on me, his stomach hair teasing my cock, and my hips lifted, rutting against the soft curve.

His mouth pressed to mine, his tongue tracing the seam of my lips, and I opened. I could kiss him all night and be happy. I spread my thighs wider and gripped his sides. Time slowed down as we touched and kissed, my body writhing against his as he shifted and lined up our dicks. His movements were slow and sensuous, unhurried. We savored the connection. I opened my eyes as he moved his lips from mine.

"Just lay back and let me take care of you," he whispered, and then his hands and mouth were everywhere, teasing my neck, sucking lightly, and lower. He paused on the slow journey until he lifted my cock, to kiss the smooth skin of my groin. "Do you want Daddy to suck you?"

"Yes, please." My body jerked as he jacked my dick in firm, confident strokes, until he placed the head to his lips, tongued my slit, and his smirk was barely a warning as he sucked me to the back of his throat.

He gave me head as I cried and called his name, grabbed the backs of my knees to open myself wider for him. The sloppy blowjob and the loud suckling sounds drove my ecstasy higher. I was so close to my release, but I bit my lip to hold in my begging for him to just finish me off. I wanted him inside me when I got off.

I whimpered as he pulled off of my cock, and I stared at him as he lowered to his belly, palmed the rounded curves of my ass, and spread them wider. My neck arched at the first swipe of his tongue over my hole. He growled as he buried his face in my crease and tortured my ass.

"Daddy," I screamed as the tip of his tongue breached me, and I grabbed his hair with both hands.

He grabbed my hips, and with rough thrusts and strokes, he loved on my hole I wanted him to own.

"Lube." His voice was muffled, but I frantically grabbed the lube and condom and thrust them in his direction.

My breath hitched as he chuckled and took the items, and just like always, as he pressed lube-covered fingers to my wrinkled hole, he was gentle as he prepared me. Always taking time to make sure I never experienced a moment of pain.

"You think Daddy is going to fit? It's so tiny and delicate." He got to his knees and straightened—his gaze locked on where his fingers were buried.

I grabbed my cheeks and pulled them apart. "I'm ready, no more teasing. I was good."

"Oh, you're a very good boy." He slipped his two fingers from me, tore the condom wrapper, and sheathed his hard cock. He stroked it several times, and then he was back where he belonged, laid between my thighs. "Just breathe," he whispered before he took my mouth in a tender kiss, and I felt the broad head pushed against me. I grimaced as he nudged his hips. "Are you okay?"

"Been a long time, Daddy." I pushed out and relaxed, and he easily slid inside. His deep groan and my soft sigh blended as he buried himself to the hilt.

"Baby, god, you're so hot and tight." His hand that had held his cock grabbed my outer thigh as he began a gentle rhythm. "Shit, Morgan, I didn't think you could feel better."

My lips fell open as he stroked over my prostate, and he focused on that same spot. His body undulated as he loved on me. I stared at his face, the strain as pleasure tightened his features, and he gritted his teeth. I cupped his bearded jaw in my hands, and his eyes opened. They met mine.

"You're so beautiful...how can you..." He shook his head as he braced his right hand on the bed and lifted his upper body.

"I want it, Daddy, love me." My tone couldn't be mistaken for anything but begging, but he didn't just fuck me. His pace increased until the power behind his thrusts rocked me and the bed. I fisted my hands in the pillow as I tilted my hips and submitted to him.

The fucking was brutal and perfect. I wanted to jack my cock, but I wouldn't unless he gave me permission, but I was so close. I could come with just him stretching me just right with his thick dick. Sweat over his body and mine, drops were trickling down his temples and falling to my chest.

He was grunting and groaning, our slick skin slapping together, and I was trembling, trapped under his gorgeous, burly body. "Daddy, Carter, I..."

"Do it, baby, I'm not going to last, fuck, this ass was made just for my thick cock."

My right hand wrapped around my dick, and I jacked off to the pace he set. He braced both hands, and I knew the minute he lost all control—all rational thought—and he fucked me. No gentle urgings for me to get off.

I focused on my sensitive head, and I had no warning. My orgasm hit me, and my release covered my belly. His curses were barely heard over the rushing of blood in my ears. He slammed in one last time. The powerful jab forced my hips higher, bowing my back. He collapsed, and he tenderly pressed kisses to my lips as his hips moved in soft circles riding out his own pleasure.

His weight forced me into the soft mattress, and I savored it. I loved when he gave me that comforting pressure.

"I'm probably crushing you." His voice broke.

"No, Daddy, you can lay on me anytime you want. I love how burly and hairy you are." I pouted as he slipped free, and I stroked my hands from his sides and along his sweaty back, pausing to linger on the small patch of hair at the base of his spine, and to his fuzzy, muscled ass.

"How did I get so lucky?" He brushed his lips to mine even as he smiled.

"I think that's the other way around. I'm gonna want this a lot, Daddy, and I mean a lot."

"And you know what I'll say…whatever my baby wants. I'm going to get up and get something to clean us up."

I reluctantly released him and laid there satisfied and ready for sleep. I stroked over my skin that was pinkened by his body hair. I could get used to this, him there every night, him loving on me and then holding me as he slept. There was nothing in the world I wanted more than him, I wanted to be selfish, and no one had ever made me feel that way.

"Don't sleep yet. Let me clean you up," he said as he braced his forearm under my knees and pushed them back to expose my bottom. He reached between my thighs to wipe off my soft belly, gently cleaned my soft cock, and then tenderly cleaned my bottom.

Once he was satisfied, he left me to throw the rag into the bathroom and returned. He laid down and instantly pulled me into his arms. I cuddled to his chest.

"Get some rest, baby. I'm not done with you yet."

I smirked and bit my lip as I stroked my cheeks over his hairy chest and couldn't wait for him to wake me up for round two and more.

31

STEVENSON

COLD CASE
UNIT

We were going through all the cold cases dealing with abductions that happened a few years before and after Angie's case. We already had the three for Marx, Farrier, and Lowell in a pile. Nothing was adding up, though. I really didn't want to go farther back. That was hundreds of cases that hadn't even made it near being entered into the database. Douglas had brought his ass down from Homicide to help, which meant Graves was back to his pre-Cold Case Unit days and was surly as fuck. I wouldn't admit it out loud, but I was a bit amused by that.

"Hey, man, you got a minute," Vega asked from behind me, and I turned to find her looking nervous with a file in her hand.

"Sure, what's up?" I asked as I stood.

"In private?"

"Okay, why don't we go down to the locker room?" She only nodded and turned.

Vega was never nervous or cagey about anything; she was too balls-to-the-wall. I followed her through the locker room door.

"Um, I don't know how to say this…"

"Vega, just say it."

"You know Doc asked me to run a check on the Platts."

"Yeah, I was there when he called. Did you find something?"

"I did, but we got a problem...a big one."

"Are we looking at police corruption, a high-profile murderer, what?"

"Doc's ex."

"What?"

"Okay, hear me out. Doc had an ex. He was an asshole. Doc thinks he kept it from us, but he didn't...we just let him think he did. That was a lesson he had to learn on his own, and we respected his privacy. If he didn't want the guy to know, fine. We weren't exactly sure that he was putting his hands on Doc until it was already too late."

"He told me about Leif. It's how he got the scars on his belly. You've bathed him so you had to see them."

"We did. It's why some of us became a little more protective than we were before."

"What's this have to do with the Platts?"

"I ran Gordon Platt, he died about a decade ago, Isiah is in prison, has been since the group dissolved, four counts of rape and kidnapping-trafficking, the girls were minors. It happened in Texas. He's there for the rest of his life. It was a federal charge cause he took the girls over state lines. Ezekiel disappeared right before the first kidnapping of the Marx boy...no credit cards, no tax returns. He just ceased to exist."

"What's that gotta do with my baby?"

"The thing is someone can steal a social security number, file for a birth certificate, identity theft is pretty easy nowadays. If you have a social security card and certificate, you can get an ID. Back then, it was a lot easier because things didn't rely on digital records so much. So I did a cross-reference of death certificates of male children born around the same time as Ezekiel, give or take a few years. And then ran those against person or persons with the same name and birthdate. I went after it for a week and was about to give up."

She handed over the file, and I took it, flipping it open to see the picture inside. The picture was of a handsome man with dirty blond hair, cold brown eyes, and wearing a lab coat. Other than the eyes, nothing seemed off about him.

"Is this him?

"Dr. Leif Gerrickson was born from the Platt's ashes. I found an image of Ezekiel and one of Leif. Leif definitely had some work done, so I looked for medical records, and Leif had a nose job, chin implant, and a minor facelift. I may or may not have hacked into their system to get a before picture. Luckily, they scanned all their records, and Leif comes in every one or two years for a freshening up."

"So you're telling me, you're certain Platt and Gerrickson are the same person?"

"Unless I run a DNA test of which we don't have any samples except for Isiah's in the system because of his felonies. Since Gerrickson has a completely clean slate, and by all intents and purposes, he's a boy scout, I have nothing to compare Isiah's DNA to. The thing that hit me was that by my calculations Doc met and started dating Leif right before the snatches happened."

"Like he wanted intel?"

"That would be my guess."

"But he told me Leif never asked about specifics just how Doc's day was."

"Angie's murder and Aiden's disappearance coincided with the breakup, a few months after actually, and then it all stopped. I think Leif was more than aware of Doc's life and pushed his way in. Doc was the medical examiner. He was friends with cops and the people on the streets. I think Doc was a tool for him to use. His father ran a cult. He'd know how to manipulate people. Doc's always been a bit insecure about his submissiveness even if being submissive made him happy."

"What do you have on Leif, though?"

"Supposedly works for research and development for a

pharmaceutical company. The board members are ghosts. They don't exist except on paper. The company was founded under a dummy cooperation. But when I followed the paperwork and money transfers, it's connected to a company on a non-extradition island in the Caribbean. Seems to be a tax haven for the rich and famous. Transcendence Corporation was founded in the early seventies, right? When the *church* popped up. Lots of money flowing in, but I could only get so far before setting off red flags and alarms, and I didn't want to jeopardize your case. If I'm right, fuck, Stevenson, I don't want to be right with this one."

"I'm there with you. This will bring up so much shit with Morgan."

"I know. That's why I came to you first. He needs a warning before this breaks. Couldn't you have chosen another damn case?"

"My luck, I chose a case that links to my baby's past, but he's been a medical examiner for over thirty years in this city. Not much wouldn't connect back to him."

"True, but if Leif is the person we're looking for, we need someone without bias to connect it. You and me, we're already compromised by our relationship with Doc."

"Douglas?"

She groaned, and I had to chuckle. "Why do you gotta bring in the rules and regs man? He's so stiff."

"It would drive Graves crazy."

"Oh, that is a bonus, my friend, definite bonus."

"True. But what I don't get is why the kidnappings? What's the purpose?"

"I did what I could. If it was an actual pharma company, I'd say drug research of some kind, guinea pigs to bypass the strict human trials. Yet if they were doing trials, they'd need more subjects, and as fucked up as it is, paying some homeless people to take part would be a lot less noticeable."

"But you don't think that's it, though."

"No, I checked patent and FDA records, and there's been nothing that's come out of his company, and I mean nothing. I mean, he could be running drugs, using his company as a front to mass-produce. That would definitely bring in the numbers I see funneled into his accounts. You have to get me a DNA sample, something I can compare to Isiah's profile. If we can find out it's him, I have more sneaky avenues to take if need be. The work he had done and what he did to remake himself was a little extreme just for being connected to a cult...one that no one would really remember."

"I guess I could follow him around and see if he discards anything. It's the only way we're going to get a sample. I can't take this to a judge. I don't think even Remy could get me a warrant for his DNA."

"Not a chance, that shit right there, isn't even circumstantial. It's speculation and weak speculation at that."

"Thanks, Vega."

"Sorry you have to be the bearer of bad news."

"I'd rather do it. This is going to hit him hard. He's already dealing with the bullshit Platt or Gerrickson did to him. We're just throwing this on top of it."

"Good luck."

"Appreciate it, and as always, you went above and beyond your forensic genealogist job title."

"Don't sweat it. If all I did was family trees, I'd get bored out of my mind. But the other services I offer you are handled through my company. A company that's extremely well-funded because of what I know. Whatever you or the rest of the unit need, it's yours."

She walked around me, but I stayed in the locker room and reopened the file. I stared at the photo of Gerrickson, possibly Platt, and that was the man who'd tried to kill Morgan. A man that wouldn't hurt anyone, and Gerrickson attempted to break my baby—almost succeeded.

Yes, I wasn't ready to have that talk with Morgan, but it needed done. Maybe Morgan had some information on him, something he hadn't told me or hadn't seemed important. Sending the photos to Morgan, was that a warning? A way of saying that Gerrickson could get to him at any time. Why, though? There were so many unanswered questions. The information Vega found for me could have nothing to do with my case. We'd just stumbled onto another case by following a lead. That wouldn't be the first time.

I closed the folder again, exited the room, and headed back to our squad room.

"Douglas, take a walk." I grabbed my jacket and left as I caught Douglas grabbing his own jacket.

He quickly caught up to me. We walked shoulder to shoulder until we reached the basement door.

"What's up?" Douglas asked as we crossed the parking lot, and I stopped to lean back against my truck.

"Vega brought me this." I handed it over and gave him a quick rundown of what Vega had told me.

"What do you need?"

"I have to assume that if that's Platt with a stolen identity, he knows the players, hence me and Doc, and the other Cold Case guys. You're an unknown. Would you be willing to help me get a DNA sample?"

"We going to trail him until he discards something? Because this"—he waved the folder—"isn't getting you a warrant."

"Yeah, you're just pointing out the obvious. The plan is I'll stay in the car. You'll follow him on the street."

"When do you want to start?" I retook the file and tucked it under my arm.

"I have to have a talk with Doc first. I don't want this to blindside him."

"You got my number. Give me a call when you're ready. You want me to tell everyone you're going to see Doc?"

"Appreciate it, and I'll fill everyone in after I talk to him." He patted my shoulder as he passed me and headed back to the building, and I got in my truck. Hurting my baby or bringing up his past wasn't in my life of things to do that day, but I had to tell him. If he found out about the information from someone else, maybe he'd feel betrayed, and I couldn't have that. I took a deep breath and prepared and planned what to say on the short drive to see Morgan.

DOC

COLD CASE
UNIT

The look of pain and regret in Carter's eyes was too much to take as he shared the information Vega gave him earlier that day. He'd shown up at my work and asked me to go somewhere quiet for dinner. I'd had a moment of panic that he was done with what we'd started to build. Yet all it had taken was one stroke of his fingertips along the indent of my spine to bring me back from those darker thoughts. And then I'd found out it was so much worse.

I tried to calculate the odds that Leif would show back up after twenty-five years, and it was astronomical but still my supreme bad luck. It all made sense, though. He may not have asked about details from my job. Yet, as I looked back, he wanted to know more on certain days. I was just a tool, a thing he used to cover whatever he was doing. To think that he'd designed an entire life, fabricated a company and co-workers, and I hadn't been none the wiser.

So much for believing I was a genius because I felt stupid and used, even more so than the night he'd attacked me the final time or the months and years I'd kept looking over my shoulder. Terrified he'd come back, and apparently, I'd manifested my future because there he was. The boogeyman in the shadows, and maybe ready to finish what he'd started.

A knock sounded at the door, and I glanced over my shoulder in time to see Carter answer. Gladys was on the other side.

"I hate to interrupt, but Robert and Remy said you were here with Doc."

I knew she'd planned to meet with the ladies at the prison and hoped to get the evidence to maybe reopen the cases since Farrier, Lowell, and Marx never considered an appeal. With being fucked over by their public defenders, they weren't interested in trusting anyone in the system. We'd hoped they'd talk to Gladys.

"Baby, is it okay if she comes in?"

I needed the distraction. I could worry about Leif's or Platt's plans for me later. "Of course. Do you have news?"

"I finally got them to agree to meet me. They were a little more open once I mentioned Stevenson's name and that he'd sent me. They were also extremely leery over the fact I took their cases pro bono for the long haul. Skeptical when I said family helps family. Mary went with me."

"That must've been horrible for her," I said as Gladys removed her trench coat and draped it over the back of my couch.

"That's an understatement. I took her an hour earlier than the meeting so we could build up to it. She did great, though. Having her there helped a lot. I have a ton of details to go over. I made up questionnaires to fill out on their own, tell their story like a written statement."

"Written cuts down on bias, and sometimes written statements have more details since they have to picture it."

"Exactly. I *am* rather good at my job, Doc."

"I didn't say you weren't, Gladys."

"I filed petitions for their case files and court transcripts. I'll be going head-to-head with DA Graves, but that's nothing new for me. I wondered if I could get Mary's case file and materials?"

"Yeah, I've gone through it as many times as I can. What do you think the chances are?" Stevenson asked as he went to grab the box he tucked into the corner with the work I'd brought home.

"I'm unsure. I need to see all the materials, talk with witnesses, and that's if I can even find them after so many years. I just told them I'd do my best. If I can get something for leverage, I'm hoping to at least get them out until their retrials. What's the latest on the case?"

He placed the file box on the end table next to where Gladys had laid her coat. "We have a lead. Douglas and me are going to try to get a discarded sample to test DNA. Vega thinks one of, well, our only suspect, stole an identity. His brother's DNA is in the system. We need a sample from Gerrickson to compare."

Her smile crinkled the corners of her eyes. "Douglas? How's our Graves handling y'all being buddy-buddy with the enemy?"

"Graves is cranky on a good day. He'll get over it. We're just not the most social people outside our unit and family. A few allies wouldn't hurt us any, especially in Homicide. Captain Tyson's still pissy we won't come back."

"You four. Running your own unit. A Law unto yourselves. Like you'd give up that power to work for someone other than Robert and Remy. You already run the strip with Boss."

"There are definite perks."

I giggled as he winked at her, and he lowered to rest on the back of the couch and held his hand out to me. As much as I was hiding my meltdown, he knew when I needed extra. I went to him and turned to rest against his chest.

"How are you doing, Doc? Remy filled me in a bit on what's going on. He didn't have many details."

"Carter wanted to talk to me first before he explained everything. Vega made the connection and thought I needed Daddy to tell me first."

"Of course, it's what an amazing partner does. But that didn't answer my question."

"I'm okay. After two decades, you think you'll never hear an exes name again...I was wrong."

"If you need anything handled by a lawyer, you know you can always call. I adore every one of you as much as I do Robert and Remy. As I said, family takes care of family."

"We appreciate that, Gladys. I think Morgan's in the processing stage." He gently squeezed me and kissed the top of my head, sometimes it was odd what someone found comforting.

"I'm sure it's a lot to take in. Just remember, you have a lawyer who works cheap for the people I love."

"You're going to get disbarred one of these days."

"I make my firm way too much money to have them think about firing me or allowing me to get into trouble. Besides, working for y'all could be a full-time job. I could leave that stuffy old firm. Boss could definitely use an on-staff attorney at the Outreach."

"He's mentioned trying to seduce you into leaving a time or two."

"As adorable as the bruiser is, not my type, and I'm sure not his. And dating hasn't been working out for me since the divorce. Shine is going to get tired of being a shoulder to cry on."

"I heard this rumor Shine has moved in with you full-time. She's not even looking at new apartments."

"She has, and she isn't. I told her she could stay as long as she wanted." Gladys's tone dropped a few degrees.

"Oh, that's a tone that implies that we should shut up."

"I thought I was doing this good thing, you know, give her a new place to live...a place to kinda heal outside the environment, but—"

"She's beautiful, and you're extremely confused."

She snorted. "I'm not confused, well, not much, I mean watching my ex-husband fall in love with another man, attraction is fluid, you can love a person and not care about their gender. She's doing so good. She has a job at the bank she enjoys. The shadows have pretty much left her eyes. Other than Robert, I never had a best friend, and I don't want to ruin this friendship, this trust I have with Shine."

"Who says it'll ruin it?" I asked.

"My fifty-seven-year-old insecure postmenopausal brain."

"I'm fifty-six, and Carter likes me just fine. Robert was fifty-five, and we know how much Remy loves Robert. It's obsession. Think about it. Friends to lovers isn't that big of a leap sometimes."

"I know, and the longer she lives with me, the more I like it and her. She said a customer gave her his number last week."

"I sense jealousy." Stevenson chuckled as she gave him a dirty look.

"Maybe a little bit. I know she's bi, and I'm well aware of her past, her traumas, and I don't want to ruin the safe space she's found with me."

"You'll do what's right."

"We'll see, Doc. I need to get going. I'm already later than I told Shine I'd be. She told me she was making dinner tonight."

"Ain't you two so cute."

"Doc, you're a brat."

"We all have our burden to bear." I smirked as she approached, leaned down to brush her lips to my cheek, and straightened to repeat the caress on Carter's cheek. My face became buried in her cleavage. "You're suffocating me." She wore a light, slightly sweet perfume, unlike Vega's usually incense-infused skin, hair, and clothes. I found scents comforting, and Gladys kind of scented of what I would consider home.

"You'd be so lucky. Behave." She pinched my chin and took a few steps back. "Thanks for the information." She pointed toward the box.

"Just keep it safe. Mary wants it back when the case is over."

"It won't leave my sight. I know how much this means to her. It's the last connection she has to Aiden and Angie. Except for a few things friends kept safe, she lost everything."

"Gladys, I'll carry it to your car. Did you park at the main house?"

"Yes, there's no light back here. Remy kept telling me about a dirt road, but I missed it."

"It's easy to drive past," he said as he picked up the box as Gladys put her jacket back on.

Goodbyes were exchanged, and I was left to the quiet of my cottage to wait for Daddy to come back. I walked to the bookshelf next to the fireplace and crouched down to grab a photo album I hadn't looked at in decades. I never had to. I knew the face inside it as well as my own. I straightened and rested it on one hand, flipping open the cover with my free one. It was an account of three years, two happy ones, and the year I pretended everything was okay. I comforted others because that's what I'd done most of my life. Kept the peace, we all had at least one toxic trait, and I'd figured out mine was neediness.

"What's that?" Carter's voice came from too close, and then his arms twined around me to tuck me closer to his big body. I relished the softness and strength that was Carter.

"I've documented my life. I always liked taking pictures. This was my first date where he came and picked me up, took me to a fancy restaurant. The consummate gentleman. At the end of the night, he dropped me off at my door with just a kiss to my cheek. He even declined my invite to come in. Said there was no rush."

"You looked happy, baby."

"I was, and I also felt guilty for having something for myself."

"There's nothing wrong with that. I know Remy and the rest. I've met most of them. I know how protective they get. You didn't want to run off the nice guy."

"In hindsight, he was too nice. We dated for six months before we had an overnight. After it all ended, I analyzed every action and expression. The sex…"

"We both have pasts, tell me."

"It was good, great even, but I didn't really see anything wrong, he had a stressful job, and mine is nowhere near nine-to-five, so the lack of regular sex didn't bother me. I loved the cuddling and intimacy. They say you can find a fuck if you know where to look." I sighed as he turned pages, stopping to ask me about each one, told me to tell him one good thing about the image—about the memory.

"Doesn't sound all bad, baby."

"It wasn't until it was. It was like night and day. It was blissfully normal."

"Normal isn't always a good thing."

"True. I never wanted to disappoint anyone. I found my place on the strip, with the freaks and weirdos. People who were unapologetically themselves, no matter what society had to say about it, and I fell for someone so far outside my chosen family I lived a double life."

"Did you not let them meet him because you knew in your gut they wouldn't approve?"

"They would've accepted him because I liked him…that I saw a future with him."

"They would've given him shit to welcome him into the fold. That's just their way."

"It is." I turned the page and froze. It was a picture right after the first hit.

"What's wrong? Talk it out."

"He'd hit me for the first time the night before."

"You were unhappy before that, though. The change was in your eyes…you held yourself a little stiffer next to him. As if you sensed it coming?"

"He'd become more controlling. He suddenly didn't like when I was away from him…getting angry when I got emergency calls from Boss about someone needing help. Accusations that I was cheating. I should've seen it."

"Honey, we don't always see it when we're in the middle. We can't objectively compare before and after until we're out of it and have a safe distance between us and what or who is trying to hurt us. It was that way with Joseph. He was never overly affectionate or prone to public displays. I knew his image meant everything to him. Again, we don't see the signs until it's too late, and you have nothing to be ashamed of."

"I know, and I'll get it, but not just yet. Like you said, I'm still processing. After two decades, you're pretty sure you won't ever see them again, and what if he was behind the kidnappings and Angie's murder, and I didn't see it?"

"Killers have lived normal family lives. Spouses, parents, and kids were never even aware. We don't want to believe the worst in someone, especially someone we love."

"I know, my stupidity just came back to bite me."

"It happens, and for someone who rarely forgets anything, that's gotta be even harder. Why don't we have an early night? I'm going to meet up with Douglas early to see about getting a sample for Vega to run. But for tonight, what does my baby want to do?" he asked as he closed and removed the album, tossed it aside, and turned me to face him. "You can have anything you want."

"Anything?"

"Anything, as long as it won't endanger you, it's yours."

I hummed and lifted my arms to lace my fingers at his nape. "That's awful tempting, Detective Stevenson."

"It's supposed to be, Doctor Warner. But do you know what I prefer that you call me?"

"What's that?" He gripped my hips and lifted me off my feet.

"I prefer when my beautiful baby calls me Daddy."

"Is that right? Because if I remember correctly, Daddy, you

didn't wa—" His mouth slammed down on mine, and I pushed closer as I parted my lips to let him inside.

His tongue teased mine as I eased into the rhythmic sway of his body as he carried me toward the bed. I let go as he lifted his left knee onto the bed, and I bounced to stare up at him. My cock ached, and my heart beat frantically in my chest. His fists sank into the mattress beside my shoulders, and he lowered until he kissed me with those gentle presses, the ones that made me feel as if he never wanted the contact to end.

I knew I didn't. I wanted him right there for the rest of my life, and I sensed he wanted the same. My patience grew thin, but I knew that wanting me was a leap of faith he'd never anticipated taking. He needed to be ready to make himself completely vulnerable with me, and until that moment, I savored every second we had.

"What's going on in your head, baby?"

"How lucky I am. I'd never dreamed you'd want me back."

"I'll make that up to you, I promise. Now, you going to let Daddy love on you?"

"You're the only person I ever want loving on me."

"Good, that's just what I want to hear. And for tonight, no one else exists but you and me in this bed. Tomorrow is soon enough to invite trouble."

"Carter." I nudged his nose with mine. "I'll never take you for granted."

"I won't ever take you for granted either. I didn't even know I was waiting all these years for just you."

33

STEVENSON

COLD CASE
UNIT

Douglas and I were on hour four of the stakeout. So far, Gerrickson arrived for work and hadn't left yet. Television and movies made law enforcement look so glamorous, and it was anything but. I loved stakeouts, nothing but quiet and time to observe. The only thing I hated was I'd had to drop my baby off at Vega's for a sleepover for the night. I didn't want him without someone, whether that was home or at work, until we knew for sure if Gerrickson was just a coincidence or had a more sinister purpose. If we had to follow Gerrickson until late, I didn't want him unprotected, and I trusted Vega to act as caregiver if my baby needed.

"You're a pig." Douglas shoved another wrapper in a plastic shopping bag, and I nearly choked on my coffee.

"You sound like Graves now. He doesn't like working stakeouts with me either."

"No need for insults. What's Graves's deal anyway? He doesn't really seem to fit with the rest of you."

"Graves is...Graves. He was a bit of a surprise when he became part of the Fellows' case. We didn't spend too much time together, worked as partners occasionally, great cop, personality leaves a lot to be desired. Probably doesn't help that he's the son of high-profile parents from old money that don't seem to accept anything less than perfection. What's your issue with Graves?"

"No issue really, I don't know the man. His antagonism grates on me. How's Doc doing?"

I covered my smile with a sip of my coffee and let him change the subject. I didn't know whether Douglas was gay, bi, or whatever. If he was, Graves had the type of looks that made most men lose their cool a bit. "He didn't need his past coming back, but we don't always have a choice."

"Do you think this guy, Gerrickson, is really behind the missing kids and the homicide?"

"I don't know. We've got a guy with a possible stolen identity, a drug company that doesn't put out drugs, and bank accounts that would make multi-millionaires envious. The fact that he had a relationship with a medical examiner in the same time frame as the kidnappings, a ME that he abused and tried to kill a few months before Aiden's disappearance and Angie's brutal murder…makes me need answers."

"He tried to kill Doc?"

"Yeah. Morgan pressed a towel to his stomach until he could get away and sewed himself up. He never looked back. My baby was too ashamed he let something happen to him that he'd helped other people escape."

"Abusers know how to break their victims, Stevenson. I hope you told him that."

"I told him, but he feels stupid. Yet if Gerrickson is Platt, then he had a very unique education. His father was the founder of a cult."

"He has that look about him, arrogant, probably not used to hearing the word no. So on the off-chance he's our guy, what was the motive?"

"Vega mentioned the possibility he used the kids to bypass human trial protocol for research, but with no drugs being produced, that seems a no. There's been mention of conditioning, creating the perfect soldier, which isn't that farfetched if you think about it. A person with a conscience or empathy can refuse to follow orders. But one brainwashed and conditioned to be a mindless drone? Hell, that doesn't even have to be used for legal purposes? Lots of people pay good money for mercenaries."

"What makes you think the brainwashing angle?"

"I read the Transcendence propaganda, what would be considered their bible. Physical training began as early as eight. They were given physical laws such as how much to eat, drink, how many hours of physical training to do a day. There were rumors of psychological torture. A source sent us a few things. They'd be locked inside a metal crate for days, screams, music, sounds of abuse would be piped in, and the lights were never off."

"Sleep deprivation, overloading the senses. Eventually, your will gets broken down."

"Yeah, and then after their will was broken, they'd play an endless loop of rules and regs. By the time they were freed, their minds had broken, completely susceptible to whatever the elders told them to do."

"Did Platt do it to his sons?"

"The few survivors said that Platt spoiled his sons. Whatever they wanted, they got. The sons treated the group members as servants."

"Sexual abuse within the organization?"

"No allegations of sexual abuse, but procreation was highly encouraged. Yet Isiah is currently serving consecutive life sentences for kidnapping and rape. No one goes from upstanding citizen to kidnapper and violent rapist overnight. There's usually an escalation. Once the group disbanded, though, everyone scattered. They had thousands of names in their files."

"I get how it can happen. I understand a need to belong to a community, but the complete submission? That I don't get."

"To be honest, what I read, it was classic cult edicts, nothing original, it's just like Platt borrowed from several, threw a little religion in to make it seem like God's will and all that. People need something to believe in, and faith…religion gives them something to look forward to when this life is over…a purpose to the suffering."

"A religious man, Stevenson?"

"No, my parents are strict Catholics. They expected me to be a Priest or a lawyer. I didn't do either. What about you? What the hell are you doing here?"

"My wife's an officer. She wanted to be a Marine, just like all the other people in her family. We met, we had a whirlwind romance, married when I received orders that I was being shipped out. It worked for us. We loved each other. Best of friends. We were both thirty-five when an unplanned pregnancy changed all our plans. And three years ago, we decided to get divorced. We were just friends and roommates at the end. It wasn't some tragic thing, just a decision that was best for all three of us. A year ago, she earned her dream post overseas, but our daughter was twelve. She didn't want to leave her friends, change schools."

"And you did what any good dad would do?"

"Pretty much, I put in for a transfer, sold my house, and moved here to be with Savannah."

"And you got to make friends with the Cold Case Unit, the pariahs of the department."

"Y'all aren't that bad. I mean, your process gives me a damn migraine."

"Not the first time we—" Movement at the front of the building caught my attention. "Seems our boy is on the move."

"Maybe he's headed to lunch."

"Would make our job a lot easier if he is." I turned the ignition as Gerrickson appeared, and his driver was out to open the back door. I radioed Remy to let him know we were on the move and to have Vega on standby.

A few minutes later, the car pulled away from the curb and I followed at a safe distance. We didn't have cause to place a tracker on his car. And if he was the person in charge of ordering the kidnappings and murder, we couldn't take a chance a judge could throw out the case because of improper handling. This wasn't just about keeping my baby safe. This was the possible release of three falsely imprisoned women. I wanted them to have a chance at a life. A life they'd already lost decades of.

"Keep your head in the game. We work what we have, and hopefully, it leads us to what we need."

"I didn't make promises to Mary or the other mothers, but I said I'd do my best."

"Then let's get that sample. We prove that he's Platt...at the very least, we can get him for identity theft, which can lead to warrants to dig deeper."

I nodded and allowed a car to get between us and Gerrickson, but lunchtime traffic was already slow. If needed, I could turn on the siren.

"I have eyes on you two." Vega's voice filled the interior of the car.

"Could you please stop hacking into our systems?"

"What would be the fun in that, Detective? I tapped into the traffic cameras so even if you lose him, I'll have eyes on him. I want his balls, Stevenson. You don't get him, I will."

"Vega, I would appreciate not being implicated in a possible crime." Douglas warned, but I didn't miss the amusement.

"Oh, Detective Rules and Regs. Stevenson, didn't I say he couldn't join our club?"

"But the fact he annoys Graves made you happy."

"Graves has his moments. I do not confirm or deny I like the pretty boy, and if you repeat that, I'll make sure Doc has you sleeping on the couch for the next year...he's turning onto Samperson Street."

"I can see where he turned."

"Don't be snippy with me."

"And don't Mami me, save that for your babygirl."

"I need to make better life choices."

Vega and I snorted at Douglas muttering under his breath. He had no idea what he signed up for when he checked into the case for Doc and me. Traffic moved at an even pace, and he pulled off onto a street lined with boutiques and five-star restaurants. Shit, parking was going to be a nightmare.

"When he stops, just let me off down the block, and I'll backtrack."

I nodded at Douglas as I saw Gerrickson's car stop outside Calista's Bistro. "Good thing you dress all fancy, Douglas."

"I don't need to dress fancy when I have a badge. Let me out here," he said as we reached the end of the block. "I'll call you to come back for me."

"Thanks, Douglas."

"I don't like men who mistreat their partners. I'm doing this for Doc." He got out and slammed the door, and I took a right.

"Vega, how's my baby?"

"He was fine when I dropped him off at work with strict orders to go nowhere without one of us."

"But is he holding up?"

"He's fine, Stevenson. He's a survivor. But we need to get this guy and quick. Doc won't handle being on lockdown well."

"I know. We just need this sample."

"You'll get it, solve this case and settle into a nice boring life as a taken man."

"Nothing about being with Morgan will ever be boring. I just want him to be okay."

"We've got his back. He'll be protected. You just focus on taking Gerrickson down."

"That's the plan."

"Shit, I got a call coming in. Message me when I should meet you at the lab."

"Will do." I disconnected the call and pulled into an alley just wide enough for the unmarked cruiser, and waited for Douglas to contact me for a pickup. Once our suspect finished eating and left the table, getting permission from the manager or owner to take the glass or silverware was usually pretty straightforward, especially if we asked politely.

Getting a discarded sample on the street would entail a lot more recon, and may not produce a clean enough sample. I needed this to go perfectly. Yet I was well aware that nothing was ever perfect. If we could prove that Leif Gerrickson was Ezekiel Platt, requesting warrants would be an easier process. As much as I wanted to do everything within my power, legally or illegally, I needed to play this one completely by the book.

I just had to remind myself of the ladies that were counting on me. The children may be lost, but whatever I could find would allow them closure. My brain wouldn't shut off, and I kept checking my watch, an hour and then two passed.

My phone buzzed, and I tapped my Bluetooth. "Stevenson."

"I had to be charming, but I got what we needed. Circle around, and I'll be waiting outside. Gerrickson and his driver just pulled off."

"I'm parked in an alley. I'll cut through. ETA two minutes." I disconnected, quickly sent a text to Vega to meet us at the lab, and I drove to pick Douglas up. One step closer to the truth, I just hoped it was the answers we needed.

34

DOC

COLD CASE
UNIT

I'd read the email from Vega five times. Leif *was* Platt. I'd thought I was safe. Avoided all the places he'd frequented in our time together, kept myself to the strip unless my job required me to venture out. I sat at my desk with my chin cupped in my upraised hands. The panic built at a steady pace, just as it had all those years ago.

"Baby, turn on the news," Carter said as he ran through the automatic doors sideways when they wouldn't open fast enough. I clicked on the small TV on my desk, and it was a shot of the courthouse, and Gladys stood behind a podium.

I was lifted out of my chair and placed on Daddies lap as he sat down. Gladys looked professional and more than a little pissed off. We'd received a message that she was getting ready to file on the basis of incompetence.

"We'll be keeping this short. I'm Attorney Gladys Kauffman. Over two decades ago, a travesty of justice happened within the walls behind me. Three innocent women were strong-armed into admitting to guilt to crimes that were woefully investigated by the Winston Harbor Police.

The incompetence of their previous representation sickened me. Today, with new evidence in hand, I filed for retrials for Harriet Marx, Linda Farrier, and Donna Lowell for the charges of first-degree murder. There was no concrete evidence that my clients, loving mothers, had anything to do with the disappearance or deaths of their children. My team and I will not rest until these mistakes are remedied, and my clients walk free. I call on District Attorney Graves and Judge Castor to respond to my demands for new hearings. They've failed to do so, and until they do, I will be their loudest advocate. I'll take questions for a few minutes.?"

"SHE'S GOING TO DESTROY THEM." Carter's warm breath teased my ear as he spoke.

"If anyone can, she's the one to do it. What did the ladies say?"

"Gladys told them she was filing, and after the press conference, she's headed to the prison to see them in person. She wants publicity. All over the news. It works on two fronts."

"I know it puts pressure on the DAs office. What is the second?"

"As of nine AM yesterday, Leif Gerrickson disappeared. I got the report this morning from the cruiser I had following him. He failed to report to work. When the officers approached his home, they knocked on the door with the excuse of a welfare check if anyone asked. Inside was empty. Not one piece of furniture. They could only see piles of boxes. So something spooked him, and he ran. If he thinks evidence is going to come out, he messed up, or that's what we're hoping."

"What about another kinda pressure?"

"What do you mean?"

"He's waiting for his face to be plastered all over the news. He has the funds to disappear, but what if his old face showed up. Missing person flyers. We make up some stats, ask for a few favors from friends to hand them out, people go missing on the strip all the time. They won't think twice about helping. But if

Leif's paying attention…" As I turned my head, I paused, and he lifted his left hand to cup my chin.

"He might get jumpy."

"Why not? The older picture doesn't look like him anymore. The only one who'd recognize Ezekiel is Leif." If there was one thing I knew about Leif, he hated being wrong or having his mistakes called out. I'd made that mistake a time or two. I had the scars to remind me.

"I don't want to use you as bait."

"I'm not bait. I'm going to be plastered to your side. I know what he's capable of. Stitching myself up is not an experience I want to repeat. I don't have a death wish. I like to play it pretty safe."

He soothingly caressed my cheek with his thumb and softly kissed me. "I know you do, baby, but you have to promise to stay near me at all times. I can't…"

I knew what the break in his voice meant. "You won't lose me, I promise. I waited a very long time for you to notice me…I want to enjoy it for a long time to come."

"You're so smart and beautiful. I never thought I'd measure up."

"Oh, Daddy, you measure up just right." I smirked against his lips, and his deep chuckle vibrated his chest against my back.

"No foreplay in the morgue."

I laid my head back against his shoulder and suddenly realized how tired I felt. Since he'd worked almost around the clock for a week, I hadn't had my personal teddy bear to cuddle. Sleep was majorly in short supply. "Spoilsport. Pick me up when I get off, we'll head to Prof's to get a picture of Ezekiel, and after that, we'll head to the Outreach to use their office to print a small stack of flyers. We can get a few volunteers to make a fuss."

"Sounds like a plan. I was wondering when all this is over, whether that's the case goes back on the shelf or we solve it, I want to take you on a real date. You up for it?"

"A real date? I've been having a great time just hanging out on my couch with you."

"I know, but you deserve all the romance. So what do you say?"

"Just tell me when and where, and I'll get all pretty for you."

"You don't have to try too hard to be pretty. Okay, as much as I could sit here all day with you on my lap, work calls."

I reluctantly stood up from my comfortable spot on his thick thighs, and then I turned to cross my arms over my chest. "Go get the ladies out of jail."

"That'll be more Gladys than me."

"Don't sell yourself short. Come home tonight with me. As much as I love Vega, I miss my bed with you in it."

"I missed you, too. I promise it'll all be back to normal soon."

I laughed and shook my head. "There's nothing normal about us or our family."

"True enough. See you in a few hours." He leaned down to brush his lips to my forehead. I grabbed each side of his open jacket as he tried to retreat. "Tonight, I'm all yours, I promise."

"I know, it just with the Feds and their cases, this shit with Leif-Ezekiel, I'm ready for it all to be over."

"Start planning that vacation you want to take. We'll put in for time off."

"Don't tease. I'll hold you to it."

"No teasing, you and me alone for a few weeks sounds perfect to me. So get to planning."

I let him go and recrossed my arms to keep from grabbing him. I didn't want to appear too needy. Part of me didn't want to scare him off, but that portion of my brain felt guilty for automatically thinking he'd be turned off by my requirement for affection. He made it too easy to forget. He was so willing to cuddle me and pull me onto his lap—it was addictive. All I could wish was for this to end soon, and I could just focus on my Daddy and what we were building together.

THE SUN SET HOURS PREVIOUS, and the temperature dropped, and I couldn't wait for spring to arrive. The runny nose and red cheeks weren't exactly a sexy look. Davian and Cree, and a few others had taken a small stack of the missing posters. They knew what we were trying to do and were willing to help us out. Douglas had told us he was going to sit on Gerrickson's house for the evening to see if there was movement, yet so far, no one had entered or exited the property.

Carter gave my hand a gentle squeeze. "You need a coffee? It's chilly, and I don't want you to get sick."

"A few more of these…there's a coffee shop at the end of the block." I glanced around and saw Zero. He was a reclusive staple in the neighborhood. "I see someone to talk to. He's right there." I pointed to the thin younger man huddled in the doorway of an empty storefront. His shoulders slumped to disguise his height.

"Don't get too far away."

"I'll be right there. I won't go any farther."

"Okay," he said and lifted our linked hands to turn them until he could kiss the exposed skin of my wrist.

When he released me, I went straight for Zero. "Zero, what're you doing out?"

"Doc. Can only stare at code for so long before even that bores me. What about you?" He inclined his chin towards Carter. "Seems you got yourself something handsome."

"Stevenson. He's a detective in the Cold Case Unit, works with Remy. Can I ask you something?"

"Of course, don't get out much, but can't hurt to inquire." Zero pulled out his vape, and I shook my head at the fruity, sweet scent as he inhaled and exhaled.

"Heard anything odd lately?"

"Nothing that isn't unusual for our community here. There's been a new group hanging around. Throwing around some new-age bullshit. People are saying it's human trafficking. No one has taken them up on coming to their *meetings* yet. Mostly because the news was circling."

"What was the bullshit?"

"Health and wellness begins with being spiritually healthy, probably some fat-shaming thing. Want you to buy something or shove you in a shipping container. Could go either way. People are weird and not in a good way."

"Nice to see you haven't changed."

"Life's too short to be a normie."

"True enough." I pulled off one of the sheets of paper and held it out. "Do you recognize him?"

Zero studied it and shook his head. "No, he's pretty, though, not my type."

"Thanks."

"Not a problem, darlin', need to go find a little something for the night. Nice to see you so happy, Doc, even if he looks...normal."

"Not everything that looks normal is bad."

"I beg to differ, but I have no time for a debate this fine evening."

"Stay out of trouble."

"Not my style, Doc." He winked at me and slipped out of the alcove to disappear into the crowd, which wasn't easy for a man so tall.

I turned and smiled as I watched Carter talking to one of the sex workers I knew from my Saturday clinics. I pulled out my phone to check the time. I was beyond ready to go home. Our plan should've caused enough of a stir. I also wanted to tell Carter about what Zero said.

A cold, slender hand wrapped around the front of my throat, and I froze. "Hello, Morgan, if you scream, an associate of mine will make sure that young man of yours doesn't make it off this street. Do you understand?"

Fear froze my vocal cords, and all I could do was nod. I'd heard that voice in my nightmares enough. From the coldness of his tone, he'd go through with his threat.

"Drop your phone to the ground and back up nice and slow. We need to have a private chat."

I did as ordered and grimaced as my phone hit the ground with a soft thud, and even as I matched my steps to Leif's, I never took my gaze from Carter. My survival instinct cried out for him to turn, to see me, but another part of my brain that wanted to protect him prayed that he wouldn't.

The darkness of the alley swallowed us. The grind of metal on metal made me glance behind me to see the door of a van open. The interior lights dimly lit two masked men in the passenger and driver's seats. I tensed as Leif easily shoved me into the back and jumped in. I opened my mouth to scream, and the hard blow of a closed fist connected with my jaw.

"Now, Morgan, have you forgotten so easily how I'm capable of keeping you under control? I won't warn you again, behave, and maybe I'll kill you quickly."

"You won't make it quick. You like to watch me suffer too much."

"At least you didn't forget." He turned away. "Let's go before his boyfriend notices he's gone."

I scrambled towards the back of the van, reaching for the door releases for the rear door, but a brutal hand grabbed my ankle. Just as I was about to kick my way free, a hard cylinder object slammed into the back of my head. The fight ended as pain exploded and the sound of metal clanging on the floor was the last thing I remembered.

35

STEVENSON

I'd only let him out of my sight for a few minutes. He was safe on the strip, everyone had his back, and the word had gone out to be on the lookout for strangers. That was our turf. Twelve hours passed, and no one could tell us where he was. Just like with too many missing person cases, he'd disappeared without leaving anything behind except his phone, and that had been my only means of tracing him. My fist connected with the locker where they'd sent me to calm down. Yet I only grew madder at my helplessness.

A strong hand gripped my upper arm and spun me, and I almost swung until I recognized Douglas. "Stevenson!" he yelled close and grabbed my face. "Look at me, man, you need to focus. Your baby needs you to hold it together." Douglas put a few feet of distance between us but kept our gazes locked.

"I looked away for…" My voice broke as I noticed the locker room was filled with my friends, and each looked as broken as me. I'd let them down by not protecting Morgan well enough.

"We don't have time for your guilt. You were on the strip. Where was your first stop? Keep it together, man, just think.

Morgan was right beside you, maybe holding your hand. Now, tell me, what happened next?"

I inhaled deeply through my nose, exhaled through my mouth. "We'd left the Outreach just before sunset. We'd printed out flyers with old pictures of Ezekiel, missing person ones. A few trusted people volunteered to make a show of it. I think we'd been walking around and talking to people for hours. We thought…"

"What did you think, Stevenson?"

"We thought if he saw his old face, his past coming back, he'd slip up…come out of hiding. We'd matched his DNA. We just needed him to show his face."

"The hunt ain't fun if the rabbit don't run, man. We're detectives. We live for this shit. Where was Doc? Was he close enough to touch?"

"Yeah, I never let him get far. He spotted someone he knew but promised not to get out of my line of sight. Always close enough to see me."

"Now, close your eyes. I want you to picture it. Doc got a bit ahead of you, but you're too much of a Daddy to not track him even subconsciously. Where did he go?"

As I did what he asked, I leaned my head back on the locker and took calming even breaths. On the back of my lids, I saw my baby, his cheeks all pink with a big smile and his slouchy rainbow beanie covering his hair. I loved him, the sweetness and trust in his expression when I caught him watching me. "He said he had someone he wanted to talk to. Tall, painfully thin, light-skinned black guy, he was kinda hunched over."

"Zero." I shot my gaze to Vega in time to see her pulling out her phone. She was tapping at the screen and then rings echoed off the cement walls. The voicemail picked up, and she disconnected and redialed.

"Vega, is there a reason you're calling me before sunset?" An oddly gruff voice that didn't match the man I saw last night filled the room.

"You talked to Doc last night."

"Yes, our adorable Doc was asking about some normie dude, I didn't know who he was, but he asked me about uninteresting weird info."

"Did you have anything?" Vega asked. Even though her voice remained calm, I could see the anguish in her eyes. We were barely holding ourselves together.

"Some health and wellness program, screamed budding cult. I told him it could be a cult or someone looking to shove young women into crates headed overseas."

"Got names for me?"

"Why are you asking me and not our Doc?"

"He went missing twelve hours ago. His phone was found just outside the alley where he was last seen talking to you."

There were gruff curses, and then Zero cleared his throat. "Nah, I had some shit to do, so I excused myself, but when I left, he was making lovey-dovey, *wanna bang in an alley* eyes at some big blond, a little too dominant for my tastes."

"Did you see anything odd? Because Stevenson had only looked away for a few minutes."

"Exhaust. Burned oil. A cologne no one would wear on the strip. Definitely handcrafted and expensive. A shop opened up, they match or create scents by body chemistry."

"God, I forgot your sense of smell and hearing are off the charts."

"There was also an engine sound, idling, but there was a definite rattle as if the muffler was loose."

"What about the cologne smell?"

"It was pretty close during our conversation, but there were several ladies and gentlemen on the stroll last night. People were looking to get warm the old-fashioned way, so I just thought whoever it was, was checking out the wares."

"Heard anything in the last twelve hours?"

"No, but I could take a look, but I need a free pass."

"Zero, do whatever it takes, but make it look like a glitch." Remy raised his voice where he stood beside the door with Robert soothingly rubbing his belly.

"I'm on it, Remy. I have access to cameras all over the strip. And since I installed most of the security systems in the businesses, I left myself a backdoor. Give me an hour. I'll look into the feeds thirty minutes before and run them forward until I left Doc." The line went silent as Zero ended the call.

"I shouldn't have let go of his hand."

"Stevenson, if this is Gerrickson, he was going to find a way to get to Doc, whether that was last night or a few weeks from now. All we have to do is find him. If he wanted Doc dead, we would've found him in that alley. No, I think Gerrickson has a plan." Robert had that calm tone, what everyone called his Daddy voice, and tried to sound reassuring, but I wasn't buying it.

"Yeah, to pay my baby back for an old vendetta."

"You think he'd hold a grudge this long?" Douglas asked as he lowered onto one of the benches and glanced around the room.

"Remy, what do you think?" I glanced at Remy.

"He's a narcissist. He was raised in a cult environment where, as the son of the leader, he was seen as just as powerful as the supreme Elder Platt. He used the tools he honed to attract Doc. He saw the vulnerability. If he'd been doing recon for any length of time, watching from the shadows, he could've learned more about Doc than Doc anticipated."

"Morgan told me that Gerrickson wasn't his Dominant. Even as a committed couple, sex was infrequent."

"I think the sex was nothing more than a tool. I don't think Gerrickson or Platt or whoever the fuck he is was actually gay. He learned Doc required physical and sexual intimacy, and he used that knowledge to lure him in."

"I just don't understand why Doc kept him from his family?" Robert asked as he gave his husband a squeeze.

"It was something for just Doc. He believed it had nothing to do with his job as a medical examiner or his life on the strip. While Gerrickson asked about his day, he was subtle in how he pushed for details. I know Doc will bring work files home... transcribe his recordings. He usually does that while I take care of my own work. Gerrickson could've been listening to entire audio of autopsies."

"When did the relationship start to break down?" Vega slid down the wall and rested her wrists on her knees, still holding tight to her phone.

"About a year before Gerrickson carved Morgan up. He told me everything was the perfect romance until he asked Morgan to marry him. From the way Morgan explained it, it sounded to me as if Gerrickson hit a downward spiral. But unless we know the trigger for that spiral, we won't have any idea what caused it."

"I did some research on Transcendence and went to talk to Prof. Hidden within the so-called Doctrine of the group was the basis for a so-called super-soldier. Unquestioning, physically elite, and a blank slate ready to be programmed. Like a computer when you delete files, in this case, memories, empathy, free will, the core information still exists just now it's free to be overwritten."

As Vega spoke, I once again imagined what the boys' lives were like. How much they'd seen? How much emotional damage existed and wondered if it was kinder if they'd perished before whoever used them for whatever purpose they were taken.

"You're telling us that he created blanks slates with the intention to reprogram them?" Graves asked from the corner where he'd stood quietly.

"Exactly. Think about it. In some ways, the military does it by way of basic training. You sign up. They put you through physical exertion and turn you into a powerhouse. Then you learn the edicts, the laws the recruits must follow. The women had very few roles within the group. They all had children previously, and when they joined, they were expected to produce more. You get a recruit from birth...they know no different." Vega wasn't being very comforting.

"So when they get the older children, they have to work harder to break them?" Graves shook his head and went to join Vega where she was seated on the floor, and as he sat beside her, she titled her head to rest on his shoulder.

"But also when you get a kid between the ages of eight and ten, they're pretty self-sufficient. In the nineties, you had an entire generation of latchkey kids that would come home and take care of themselves for a few hours until the parents got home. Within the cult, you had the women as caretakers, they handled the care of the children, but if Gerrickson found a different use for his father's program, he may not want to deal with the changing of diapers, feeding."

"As much as I hate to agree with Vega on the batshit craziness right now, but I watched good men make horrible decisions based on orders from commanding officers. We're taught our higher-ranking commanders have the best intentions of the unit in mind. How much would a completely subservient bodyguard go for? An assassin with absolutely no moral code. A sociopath perfectly designed to his buyer's specs. Certain organizations would pay whatever for that, and they'd be expendable. One goes down...they just send out another attack dog."

"Do you think they could still be alive, Remy?" I asked.

"Possible, depending on how well they were trained and the medical attention they received if they were wounded. They could also be used as sleeper cells. Hell, they could be out there living completely ordinary lives awaiting orders. They've had decades to perfect the process. Yet part of me hopes they didn't survive. Even if we got them back, the children they were aren't the men they've become."

"Stevenson, we'll bring Doc home, but I need you to hold it together. All of us need to. They took an important part of our family, but we also have to remember that there are three women locked up. Gerrickson and his accomplices maybe the only means to get them out. We need them alive." Robert was being the voice of reason as if he hadn't been around us before.

"What about damage?" Graves asked.

"They threw the first sucker punch. We make them pay for that."

"I am not listening to this." Douglas shook his head at Remy.

"We handle this our way. I need everyone on the phone to whatever contacts on the strip that we have. I want a call-out for any information leading to the recovery of Doc. Daddy?" Remy's voice dropped.

"Oh shit, yes, baby, what do you want?"

"We need a tactical team for possible breach, um, do you know anyone?"

"Sharp's going to regret making my acquaintance at that lecture six months ago."

"Thanks, Daddy. Everyone, let's get to work."

Remy herded Douglas and Robert from the room, and I slid to my butt to the cement floor. I closed my eyes as I regretted every decision that I'd made in the last twenty-four hours. My eyes opened as I felt a body on either side of me. Graves and Vega pushed in to share comfort and warmth.

"I didn't tell him I loved him. I planned this big, romantic event, our first real date. He said he'd get pretty for me, and I told him he was always beautiful. What if…" Vega's fingers lacing through mine cut me off.

"We don't play the *what-if* game here. You'll find your baby. We can't know the future, Stevenson. All we can do is tear this fucking city down brick by brick, steel beam by steel beam until we bring our Doc home. And no matter what you think, you didn't fail him. He was only several feet away on a busy street."

"She's right, and when we bring him home, you can make all the romantic declarations you want. Tell him you love him every minute of every day. He survived Gerrickson once, and he'll do it again. We'll sit here a few more minutes while you wallow in guilt, but after that, you're getting your ass up."

"You're not a very good motivational speaker, Graves."

"Good thing that wasn't my career path. Instead, I thought it was a great idea to transfer to the basement with the ever-present stench of possible black mold, bitterness, and questionable choices, while everyone wonders *is he or ain't he*."

"You should just come out. You know we won't judge you." Vega leaned forward and peeked around me at Graves.

"You forced me to go to Xanadu's, and I was a hostage negotiator to a pissed-off, drunk-crying twink with a cheating boyfriend who said the stall was his home now. Which reminds me, I have to call and check on him. He got a new boyfriend."

"Why do you complain? We made your life so much more interesting."

"I could do with a little less interesting."

"My baby was right. We do have weird friends." I announced and then stood with my friends gasping at my insult behind me, but I knew what they were doing. "Thanks."

"It's what family's for." Graves whispered with a hint of hurt in his voice.

I left the room to get to work, to distract myself until Zero hopefully called back with a lead, and I could bring my baby home. All I could think about was he warm enough, was he unharmed, was he scared, and I wasn't there to pull him onto my lap and make everything okay. I wouldn't survive if something happened to him.

36

DOC

COLD CASE
UNIT

My arms were stretched wide where the shackles and chains secured me to the walls. The collar around my neck kept me bent at an odd angle where it was attached with a ring through a metal plate welded to the floor. There was the constant buzz piped into the tiny box with frost on the walls. Occasionally a mist would hit my naked skin and instantly freeze. It wouldn't last forever. They waited until I almost passed out and then would slowly heat the box. Spotlights didn't allow for sleep.

I read the literature, I knew what they were trying to do, but I'd long lost track of time once they'd thrown me into the metal crate. I'd noticed the room was filled with them in neat rows, ten across, but the darkness didn't allow me to see how many were hidden beyond the dim light shining down in the cavernous space.

That never-ending droning sound was driving me crazy, and I wanted to cover my ears. Blood and snot dried to my face. I lowered my head enough that maybe my hair would block out the light and squeezed my eyes closed. As much as I wanted to formulate a plan of escape, I wasn't Remy, Robert, or Graves—or even Daddy. They had the strength to fight. My survival instinct would kick in, but I couldn't take on the at least five men and Leif who were between me and safety.

I shivered so hard my body seized, and metal cut into my throat and wrists. My toes and fingers were painful, and I tried to calculate how long I had before frostbite set in. I flinched as I heard the click as warm air filled the box, but that had its own dangers. Dehydration from sweating, and I hadn't had anything to drink since I walked out of the Outreach. The overload to my temperature regulation, the almost constant switching between hot and cold, meant I had maybe a few days if that.

I didn't tell Stevenson I loved him. I assumed I'd have time. I should've said it. I'd whispered it in my mind so many times as I took in his handsome face and that adoring smile he'd give me as soon as he awakened.

"Morning, baby." Mental Daddy tucked my hair behind my ear, which was a habit of his I loved. I'd waited too long, took too much for granted.

I jerked my head up at the sound of metal grinding on metal as the lock disengaged. The door opened, and crouched on the other side was Leif. Years of cosmetic surgery and Botox had his face virtually the same as when I'd seen it last. His hair was unnaturally dark—a fresh dye job to hide his ash-blond hair.

"Morgan, still alive, I see."

"What do you want?" My voice croaked as I spoke.

"That's easy. I want to make you suffer. I didn't complete my task as I should have the night I tried to rid myself of my problem. You only survived this long for the simple fact that law enforcement would've searched high and low for your killer. Your friend, Remy, and the rest have an extraordinary amount of determination and loyalty. I've never let you out of my sight, though. I knew there'd come a time when my past would reveal itself."

"You took those boys and killed Angie."

"The girl was a casualty. My men were informed to leave the blood to a minimum. She attacked, and they responded. If she'd just let us have him, she'd still be alive today. The boys, though, they were the point."

"Why?"

"My father was far too shortsighted to see what he had...the limitless power. I had no use for the sycophants. The exhaustion from pretending to care about their useless lives. To Isiah, they were just a crop of victims. He became lazy, spoiled by an endless supply of flesh to use, and that's why he's spending the rest of his life in prison. Although, sex does have its purpose, it worked quite well on you even as I suffered through having to reduce myself to cater to those unnatural urges of yours."

Tears burned my eyes, but I refused to let them form. I wouldn't give him the satisfaction.

"You do understand that you look ridiculous with that much younger man of yours. I will admit I enjoyed your oral fixation immensely, so I can see why he keeps you around."

"Fuck you." My voice shook from a combination of fear, rage, and the lingering effects of the cold.

He tsked at me. "Morgan, Morgan, Morgan, such vulgarity. I wasn't hurting anyone here. I was just providing a service, a profitable one at that. I treated the boys well. Rewarded them when they performed as ordered. I gave them a prosperous life. What was the harm in that?"

"What did you do to them? Where are they?"

"They're...around. And to answer your first question, I made them better. I stripped them of their baser instincts, the uncertainty of free will. I morphed them into superior beings. Ones without that pesky humanity. What would they have become if they remained with their broken mothers? I gave them...everything, and you want to punish me for that. It's very judgmental of you, Morgan."

"They're mothers loved them. They went to prison for something you did, and you want gratitude," I yelled as I tried to get a reaction of some kind out of him, but his features remained unchained. This was the true Leif Gerrickson or Ezekiel Platt, the man I knew had masked the monster behind the façade so well.

"You see, my father wanted to be rich. He wanted to be worshipped. He used his followers for the adoration and love he didn't get as a child from his parents, but he liked perfect things, too. So he devised a way to make everything...perfect. But I saw the bigger picture, Morgan. I saw what it could become, and I manifested. I made it real. I designed the most flawless human. I stripped away all of society's rules. It's survival of the fittest, kill or be killed, and it was beautiful."

"You're insane."

"Such a nasty word to throw around. You have a world obsessed with the latest products. The most followers. We're a world in love with anti-intellectualism. I gave those boys and more like them a world where they had the best in education and training. And all I asked was for them to do one thing...rid this planet of those that don't deserve to be here. I'm clearing the landscape of the pests. The mistakes of nurture. Isn't everything better with less inferior beings?"

"You...it's not up to you. They were children. You didn't know what they would've become."

"The world is here for the taking. My creations are all over the planet. Free to move as they want and well-financed, they want for nothing."

"They're not free. You control them."

"There is always a master, Morgan. It's the way the hierarchy works. I simply expect their loyalty. A small price to pay for what I offer."

"You tortured them until they broke."

"It was too much to ask that you were smart enough to see the big picture. I respected your intelligence, but I loved your submission more."

"You tried to kill me."

He waved his hand as if dismissing the fact that he tried to murder me. "You were getting out of my control. You were worth a wealth of information. My creations sent a lot of people to your table. I had to know the inside variables, the forensics, the progress of cases. The trick was to make sure you never figured it out, but once I realized that your friends had more of a hold on you, I had to make other plans. There are plenty of lonely people in the world who would fall for a bit of caring...some romance. And it cost me nothing but time. You weren't the first and definitely not the last."

"But why? It doesn't make sense."

"It makes perfect sense. There's groups all over the world who pay exceptionally well for the perfect soldier. One who can blend into whatever environment. Seduce, assassinate, blackmail, I give them the tool they need. Occasionally ones made to order with their own product. A very long-term investment, so to speak. I provide a service. Should I be ashamed of that? Supply and demand. My supply just happens to be people."

"Are you going to kill me?"

"No, not right away, but I do have something special planned for you. We're working on interrogation techniques at the moment, and we need a volunteer. As you seem to be here with us for a while, you can earn your keep." He pushed up with his hands on his knees, and then all I saw were the legs of his expensive trousers.

A man in black tactical gear crouched down, and I gasped at the face. I knew it from the aged phots of the boys. "Aiden," I whispered, but he didn't even acknowledge me. He roughly removed the shackles and then unclipped the hook from my collar.

He grabbed my arm and dragged me from the crate. My legs

wobbled, but my slight weight didn't deter him from hauling me beside him. The air smelled stale, and all I could hear was countless fans whirring in the other crates, and the horror hit me that there could be children in each one.

"Aiden, your mother never stopped looking for you." There was still no reaction. He didn't even acknowledge me as I tried to pull away. His eyes were dead, it showed no expression, and he made no sounds.

His boots muffled on the cement floors as he led me through a series of hallways, electronic locks on each door. When we stopped at one at the end of the hall, he typed in a code and the keypad beeped. He threw me into a room where another man dressed exactly like him waited. My fear increased as I saw the instruments on a stainless-steel tray beside a table—very much like the ones I used in the morgue—and the drain for easy cleanup.

I fought, tried to reason with them but still nothing was there. They were blank, as if nothing existed except the task. They strapped me to the table, and the chill of the metal sent a shiver up my body.

"I see you're about ready. Joshua needs to learn subtly. He's best for jobs that require someone to learn a lesson. All brute strength and maximum damage. Today he will learn the best interrogation techniques. How to inflict pain for extended periods without causing death. As I said, my creations need a well-rounded education. As much as I would love to stick around and observe, I have plans to make. Aiden, please instruct Joshua and keep him on task. Our guest needs to prepare for an extended stay, no accidents."

"Yes, sir."

Suddenly, I was left alone with Aiden and Joshua. They didn't speak as they positioned themselves on either side of the table. They both slipped on gloves, and Joshua picked up a scalpel, and I prepared. I braced myself for the first slice. It would be shallow with minimum blood, but it would hurt, and that was the point. Leif wanted my pain, and he'd have it by any means necessary.

STEVENSON

COLD CASE
UNIT

I stared at the screen of Zero's laptop. We'd smuggled him in through the basement because he didn't want anyone to see him. Zero was even taller than Remy and Douglas's six-four. I couldn't tell what age he was. He had that eternal babyface that most people who never see the sun usually had.

"At nine-thirteen, a van entered the alley but didn't exit the other side. There's nothing in that alley. It was barely wide enough for the van. I zoomed in, and there were two people in the front seats. I couldn't get clear images. The tinted windows obscured the view. Twenty minutes later, Doc approaches me with the flyer."

I didn't take my eyes off Morgan. He was smiling and animated. In his element, I jerked my gaze to my right as I felt Vega give my hand a small squeeze.

"You make him happy, Stevenson. Just remember that," she whispered and released my fingers.

I watched as Zero said bye and disappeared off-camera, and then a shadow appeared right behind Morgan. A hand wrapped around the front of his throat, the screen flashed, and the camera angle changed and showed my baby's fear and a clear image of Gerrickson.

"I contacted a friend who lip-reads. He told Doc if he screamed, he'd make sure Stevenson didn't make it off the street and then ordered Doc to drop his phone. They needed to have a private talk."

"Did you see where the van went after that?" I asked.

"It pulled out on the opposite side about three minutes after Doc disappeared off the street. I followed them on cameras, lost them a few times but picked them up in the financial district. From there, they entered an underground parking garage, and then they just went poof, gone. I think they parked a second vehicle elsewhere. I couldn't tap into the building and garage's security system in time. Financial district takes a bit more time to pass their encryption programs. Sorry, but I went a little further for you."

"Find something?"

"I ran his financials, personal and business, in the past week he's had a fire sale, everything had to go, his pharma company is shuttered. He has three remaining properties. All under Transcendence Corporation, two storefronts that are listed as rental properties, but the electric hasn't been connected to those for around three years. And a derelict factory that's been abandoned for about thirty years. But a friend...we will not name names because he's useful...he checked satellite imaging, and for a factory that hasn't been in use and condemned for safety reasons, there's a lot of movement. Also, their electric usage is off the charts. If I had to say, that's his main operation hub. There's no digital blueprints for it."

"I got this," Graves said as he pulled out his phone and connected a call. "Flo, my beautiful cougar, what would I have to do to get some blueprints...now, now, I'm at work..." He read off the address and waited. "Thanks, I'll be over in twenty." He disconnected the call.

"We need to hook him up with the pansexual Dominatrix. She'll eat him alive, and he will love it." Vega had an almost maniacal glee in her voice.

"Still not taking the bait on setting me up. I'll be back within the hour. Someone needs to call Sharp."

"That's all on Daddy. Sharp hates everyone, and I'm not butting heads with him. I'm gonna get us a warrant." Remy walked away from the table and exited the room.

Robert crossed the room to his desk and took a seat on his chair.

"I'm headed out. Let me know what's going on so I can patch into communications and listen in." Vega picked up her messenger back and left the room.

Zero and I were the only ones left at my desk, and I backed up the video just before Gerrickson took him. "He looked happy."

"He was. I've known Doc a long time. There's always been a little something broken about him. I mean, fuck, he hides it well behind his sassy attitude, but you pay close enough attention you can see when the mask drops. Don't blame yourself. Men like this Gerrickson? He would've gotten Doc one way or another. And Doc would rather deal with the unknown than lose you. That's gotta mean something. Vega and Remy have my number. Let me know."

"Thanks, man, for…all of this."

"No thanks needed. Family has each others' backs. If you need anything else, Vega can track me down."

I nodded as he gathered up his things and left, but I looked around before I pulled out my phone. I unlocked it and swiped up to get to my apps, tapped on gallery, and opened the last picture I took of Morgan and I. He was cuddled back against my chest, his doll hugged tightly to his bare chest, and he was shyly smiling at the camera. We'd slept in.

"Stevenson?" Robert called my name, and I glanced to my right to find him smiling at my phone. "You did good."

"It was Sunday, we were being lazy, and he wanted Daddy cuddles with his doll. That was one of his birthday presents. I wanted him to know I respected his Little. He acted like I'd given him the world."

"For him, you probably did. You may not have thought you could make him happy, but look at that smile. I live for Remy's. Sharp is putting together a small unit to come with us to the factory. If I know Remy, within the hour, he'll have a warrant sent over."

"What if my baby's already…"

"We're not going to think about that. Doc is fine. If they'd wanted him dead, they would've killed him where he stood. If something does go down, I don't want to know what Remy and his people are going to do. I need plausible deniability."

"They do take care of their own."

"They do. You see how quickly we got answers from Remy and Vega's people. Between Vega and Zero, those two could bankrupt countries with a few keystrokes. It's good to have friends that sometimes don't have a lot of respect for authority."

"I'm going to take a short walk. Text me when everyone is here."

"You got it."

I slipped my phone into my back pocket and grabbed my jacket. I needed some air. But I wouldn't breathe free again until Morgan was back with me. When I got him back, he'd be lucky if I didn't move my office into the morgue.

"MY TEAM IS SET up to breach at the rear and front. We're going in heavy. We don't know what's waiting for us," Sharp said where he stood at the back of the SWAT van. "You and your team stay behind us. You can search as we clear rooms."

"You're the professionals," Robert said as he adjusted Remy's vest like he always did.

"We don't know if there are any friendlies in the mix, so try to maim." Douglas was dressed similarly to the SWAT team and seemed ready for anything. With his past military experience, they'd approved him to enter first.

"When we go, we're going to go fast, blitz attack. I don't want them prepared."

We all stood back. I could see all of us were dreading what we'd find. All of us tried to be positive, that Morgan was fine, but Gerrickson had tried to kill Morgan before. I barely heard Sharp ordering three of his men to circle the building. There were no lights, and as far as the scan of the building showed, there were no exterior cameras. Yet that didn't mean they weren't there.

The next ten minutes were a blur as we jogged towards the front of the building, Sharp had the ram ready, and one of his men counted down from three. The door flew open, and shots rang out as we all identified ourselves. One man after another went down as we cleared the front rooms and then entered a large room filled with metal crates. I stayed behind Sharp as men were taken down and cuffed.

Each room we passed, we stared through the window to find them empty, and that pit in my stomach became filled with despair. Morgan wasn't anywhere to be found, and by the time we reached the last door, this one was wooden with no lock. Sharp and I positioned ourselves on either side. Once more, he counted down from three. I stood in front of the door and kicked, and as the door opened, I entered with Sharp behind me.

"Ah, you arrived quicker than I anticipated." Gerrickson sat behind his desk, his reading glasses perched on the end of his nose, and he looked very much normal. You couldn't see any of the monster we knew he was.

"Where's Morgan?" I demanded as Sharp dragged him out of his chair and cuffed him.

"Did you lose something, Detective?"

"I don't have time for your games. We have you on video taking him. We have a warrant to search this entire building and seize any and all records and computers."

"Your Remy has very powerful friends, I hear. I heard he earned those favors on his back."

My trigger finger flexed, and the only thing keeping me from squeezing was the fact I may need him to find my baby.

"It seems you've got me, but my lawyer will have me out in no time. Please, inform Joseph that I'm being arrested. But since we've already established my guilt, why don't I show you to Morgan. He's been waiting for you."

Gerrickson's smile never fell, self-satisfied, and I wanted to wipe the arrogance away. I wanted him lying in a pool of blood, a single shot between his eyes to make sure people were safe from his cruelty.

"Please, follow me," Gerrickson said as he left the room with Sharp holding onto his hands that were cuffed behind his back.

He led us back out to the main room.

"Stevenson," Graves whispered as I passed. "We have a huge problem."

"What's wrong?"

"Aiden Maxwell, he's over there with a shoulder wound. He's the only one I recognize, but if he's alive..." He didn't have to finish that statement.

I was bringing Aiden home. But who was I giving back to Mary? Remy and Robert, as well as Graves and Douglas, joined us at a crate. Gerrickson chuckled as he recited the code for the electronic lock. I opened it and lowered to my knees. A blast of freezing air hit my face. And if I wasn't already knelt down, the sight in front of me would've dropped me to the floor.

"Baby," I whispered, and my voice cracked as I crawled inside. Morgan was covered in blood and too many cuts to count. My hand shook as I touched him, and his skin was frozen with a hint of frost as if he was wet. "Medic, I need a paramedic now! Baby, hey, look at me." I cupped his chin and lifted his head to find his face just as bloody as the rest of his bare body.

I frantically slipped the pin from the shackles to release his wrists, and he fell forward against my body. I quickly unclipped the chain from his collar. I wrapped one arm around him and eased him from the box. I cradled him against my chest as tears streamed down my cheeks. I combed his hair back from his face, and his head fell backwards.

"What the fuck did you do?"

"He held out so much longer than I thought. If I could've kept him a little longer, I would have repeated the process."

"Remy, take him," I ordered as Remy appeared with a blanket and wrapped it around Morgan.

I stood, grabbed my weapon, and approached Gerrickson. I leveled the barrel right between his eyes. My finger caressed the trigger as I looked into cold dead eyes. I waited for weapons to be drawn on me, but everyone, even Sharp, stepped back.

"What are you going to do, Detective? Would shooting me bring your boy back? With all these witnesses, a violation of my rights, I'll make sure to inform my attorney of your actions."

I flinched as arms wrapped around me, hands gripping my wrists. "Carter, listen to me," Graves whispered in my ear. "He's not worth your career, your freedom, the years you'll miss with Morgan. You want to be free when you tell that beautiful boy that you love him. Look at Gerrickson. This was a good bust. We have evidence. Carter, put it down. What would your baby want?"

"But he needs…" My voice broke, and I felt no embarrassment for that.

"And he will, one way or another, he'll get sentenced by judge or jury, or he learns Strip justice. One way, he'll pay. Your baby needs you right now. Give me the weapon, Carter." He slipped around me, curling his hand under the barrel. "Let it go and go keep your baby warm."

I reluctantly surrendered my weapon.

"You disappoint me, Detective."

Sharp told him to shut up and jerked him away, leading him out of the building. I turned and dropped, taking Morgan out of Remy's arms. His body started to shake, and his eyes opened as they rolled back.

"Get him on his side," Remy said, and I rolled him. I stretched out behind him, and I held him firm to keep him from injuring himself.

"Baby, you just gotta hold on, the paramedics will be here in a few minutes, and they'll fix you right up."

Time seemed to stop as we waited for his shivering to stop, but it didn't, not when the EMTs took him, accessed him to make sure he was stable, and I was on the move behind them. I was riding along. I didn't care what they said. I left my friends behind to deal with the chaos and whatever horror Gerrickson had hidden away.

STEVENSON

The room was eerily quiet, and the only sound was my baby's deep, even breaths. They'd taken him off the ventilator the day before and stopped the meds keeping him in the medically induced coma. His body temperature had dipped so low he'd gone into hypothermia, and his other wounds had weakened him. When he'd arrived, they pushed two bags of fluids.

I hadn't slept peacefully in days. All I could see was that box with Morgan secured to the floor by a chain attached to the collar around his neck. We'd found videos of what Aiden and another man had done to him—the slow torture as he'd thrashed on the metal table. Aiden and his accomplice had discussed technique as if a teacher were instructing a student. There had been no emotion at all and no hesitation.

A knock sounded on the door, and I glanced over my shoulder to find Robert. "Hey."

"Hey, you okay for a visitor? It's just me. Remy's trying to keep Vega from going to jail or kicked out. Doc's doctor called security on Vega because she told him he was incompetent and demanded to know where he got his medical degree." He entered, and the door whooshed closed. "We called Cash to distract her Mami."

"Sounds like Vega." I leaned forward and stretched out my arm to sweep Morgan's pretty silver hair away from his forehead. My thumb traced along the perfect arch of a brow.

"How are you? Have you tried to sleep?" Robert asked as he took a seat on a chair in the corner of the room.

"I just lay my head on his bed and hold his hand, power naps."

"You need more sleep than that. You'll need your energy when our Doc wakes up."

"I don't want to miss him waking up. I want to see his pretty eyes. The way he smiles when he first wakes up and sees me."

"What did they say?"

I sighed heavily as I held his limp hand in both of mine. "Hypothermia and blood loss, he went into shock. The reports said that Gerrickson and his people alternated between freezing and trying to cook them. He has some blisters from the metal getting too hot. His fingers and toes will be fine. They were worried about frostbite. Only a few of the cuts actually needed stitches. It was the first step in the conditioning process. I think they were using him as a teaching aide. Have you seen Mary?"

"Remy called her. Aiden has been taken to a facility. Gladys said that she was working on a deal that Aiden and the other men were to be assessed for a recommendation to a long-term facility to see if they could work to reintegrate them into society. It's special circumstances. Mary wants to see you and Doc when he gets out of here."

"What about the other boys?"

"We found records of them. Marx died at the age of eighteen. He was a failed experiment. Apparently, a target he was sent to take out, well, he developed feelings. Gerrickson had him euthanized...his words. Lowell is in Brazil somewhere, and they're still looking for him. Farrier, he was shot and killed when the team breached the back exit. He wounded one of the SWAT guys. Gladys sent a request for the records to have the ladies released."

"I wanted to bring them all home."

"I know, but look at what you did accomplish. You gave them answers...fuck, man, you gave them their freedom and redemption. Gladys told me the other children were informed and were coming here."

"Intellectually, I understand that. I feel closure that I could mark the case as solved, but look at all the damage Gerrickson has done."

"We can't change what he did. I heard Joseph dropped him as a client when he learned why Gerrickson hired him."

"Joseph is a cut-throat in the courtroom, but he does respect the law. But more than that, he worries about his image. Gerrickson is talking too much."

"Gerrickson was denied bail. With his resources and the nature of his crimes, the judge considered Gerrickson a danger to society and a flight risk. We found several IDs and passports under different names."

There was another knock, and Graves walked in and approached the bed. "How's our sleeping beauty?"

"It's just a waiting game now. When his body and brain are ready, they said he'd wake up. Where have you been?"

"I was helping go through the records. He documented everything. Day one of conditioning until they graduated to active status. He's definitely a mad scientist, but those records are going to sink him." Graves lifted onto the ledge in front of the window. "It showed his process of choosing his candidates."

"What was that?"

"Medical records. He had an operative that was a pediatrician. He tested them. Knew their family situation. He chose boys between eight and ten with no genetic conditions and were in perfect health. Having the excuse of exams, they took blood samples, and because the doctor suggested it, no one questioned them."

"What about the other crates?"

"There were ten boys. Only two were local. They're on the Peds floor being treated for dehydration, pretty much the same as Doc. Parents were called. You did good, Stevenson."

"I almost shot him."

"I would've shot him, but I don't have anyone to stay out of jail for. You, on the other hand, have someone you love."

"Thanks, Graves."

"As I said before, family takes care of family. And as weird as it is, I'm rather fond of all of you...on most days."

"We finally corrupted him," Robert said with a smile, and Graves flipped him off. "We're getting out of here. Roo called to make sure I was going to be home for storytime. Is there anything you need or something for Morgan? We'll bring it or have someone drop it off."

"Bring his doll. She's on his pillow. My overnight bag is in front of the dresser. A change of clothes would be good."

"I'll have th—"

"Daddy." My baby whimpered, and I was out of the chair with my arms braced on the pillow on either side of his head. He looked at me and covered his mouth as an anguished sob slipped past his lips.

"Look at my beautiful baby, finally awake."

"Are you real?" He placed his hands on my cheeks and stroked my beard, and tears flowed heavy from the corners of his eyes to fall into the hair at his temples.

"I'm very real, baby." I gently pressed my lips to his repeatedly. That feeling of coming home was back. Morgan was safe. "I missed you."

"I pictured you in the box. You made everything okay."

"You know how much I love being your safe place."

"Did I lose my toes? My feet hurt."

"No, you're going to be just fine. Nothing that won't heal in time. God, baby, I love you so much," I whispered as I fisted my hands in his soft hair. "All I could think was that I was never going to be able to tell you. That you'd never know." I hushed him as he sobbed and shook on the bed, snot bubbles in his nose and his face red from crying.

"I-I love you, too. I want to go home."

"You're here for a little bit, but soon we can go home to our little cottage."

"I really want that."

"Hi, Doc, Vega and Remy are going out of their minds. They're going to give you shit for scaring them like that. Graves is off to inform everyone you're awake. Be prepared. Vega is going to Mami you so hard."

"She does it anyway. Aiden, Aiden was—" He shook his head.

"Yes, he was booked and then sent to a facility to have a psychological evaluation, along with all the other men found. Gerrickson was booked and was denied bail at his arraignment. So, no looking over your shoulder. I'm going to do crowd control so you can have a few minutes with your Daddy." Robert stroked the backs of his fingers across Morgan's cheek and then left so we could reconnect without a crowd.

"Is this real? I'm not still in the box, right?"

"No, you're right here with me, in my arms right where you belong. I'm going to keep you so close from now on you'll get sick of me."

"I'd never be sick of you."

"Doctor Warner, I'm your nurse Felicia. I need to check on you. Stevenson has to move a bit for me, but he can stay close."

I reluctantly straightened but grabbed my baby's hands and held them tight as the nurse checked his vitals.

"So glad you're awake, Doctor Warner. Your husband was worried." I caught her wink and smile as she finished examining the cuts and pulled his gown back down. "Your vitals are good. A doctor will be by to check on you soon. Your friend...Vega, I think...has a dislike for him, but I assure you he's an amazing doctor. We enjoyed the show when she asked was his medical license in crayon."

Morgan snorted and then giggled. I mouthed a thank you to her, and she smirked at me as she left us alone.

"Daddy, I need a cuddle."

"What my baby wants, he gets." I helped him ease over, and then I stretched out beside him, drawing him into my arms, and he buried his face against my chest. I heard the deep inhale, and the tension eased from his body as he took in my scent. I'd been here two days, I probably wasn't all that fresh, but he didn't seem to mind.

"I was so scared...all I could think was I'd never see you again."

"That didn't happen. No matter what, I would've never stopped looking." I buried my face in his hair and closed my eyes. "My only regret when you were taken was that I didn't tell you how I felt...that I'd never get the chance."

"I'm still sleepy."

"I am, too. Why don't we take a nap until the doctor comes? I haven't slept right not being able to hold you."

He nodded and burrowed closer, and we both relaxed, my head on the thin pillow as I felt the stress disappear and exhaustion take over. He was safe and in my arms, so I could let my guard down. We'd worry about everything else later.

EPILOGUE

DOC & STEVENSON

Doc

The party was bittersweet. Months had passed, but we wanted to check up on the ladies. Stevenson still felt guilty he couldn't bring them all home, but they kept telling him to knock it off. They had long mourned their children. Boss had set them up in apartments so they could settle into their freedom.

"Doc." Mary's voice made me smile as I turned to find her standing beside the table.

"Hey, Mary. You okay?"

"Yeah, maybe I'm getting there. Aiden still won't acknowledge me. It's like looking at a stranger."

"I'm sorry."

She waved off my apology and took a seat at the table. We'd rented out a pub near the precinct for our reunion of sorts. Mary looked lighter, the deep lines on her face softer.

"Me and the others have been hanging out, going to the groups at the Outreach. We're our own little club that no one wants to be in, but it's good. At least we know. I know I don't have to, but I'm sorry for what Aiden did."

At first, I couldn't separate the Aiden I'd learned about in the files and home videos with the man who instructed someone to torture me. I reminded myself that he was brainwashed.

"That's not your responsibility. I experienced some of what he went through, and I'm a grown man. I have no idea how a child would've survived it." I couldn't restrain my smile as Carter sat beside me and slipped his arm around me to hug me close to his side.

"Are you hungry, baby? Are you ready to order?"

"I'm okay right now. You made me a snack this afternoon." In the months since he found me, his internal Daddy intensified. He catered to my every need without question. Presents, clothes for my doll, and a few friends for her. He'd bought an oversized rocking chair when I mentioned I liked being rocked to sleep. Read me stories. I loved it all, and I loved him.

"Where are the other ladies?" Stevenson asked.

"Boss got them phones, and they have no idea how to function. We're working on reintegrating them, but after almost thirty years, they were released to a strange, new world. They're institutionalized. Boss and me are easing them into it. Linda still feels as if she has to ask permission for everything. Also, she spent a lot of time in closed management. She was labeled a suicide risk. She'd tried it a few times early on."

"They've only been out a month. There's a lot to take in. I thought Farrier was going to live with her daughter."

"I think a move would be too much too soon. She needs to do this on her own. Donna's kids are staying with her to reconnect. Sometimes I don't think they feel it's real. I did my time, got out, and I did a short bid. I can't imagine decades locked in a cell for something they didn't do."

"It's great you became friends, though."

"We're the only ones who understand what the others went

through."

"A club no one wants to belong to." I repeated her words from earlier.

"Stevenson, I want to thank you. Every other cop just brushed it off. Didn't give a shit, but you went above and beyond for a dusty old box in storage. I'll never be able to thank you for that."

"No thanks needed, Mary. I didn't promise you anything. I just did my job."

"You gave a shit, and me and the others, well, you restored our faith a little and gave three women their freedom. That's extraordinary."

I glanced at Carter, and his eyes were glassy with unshed tears. He should be proud of himself; I knew I was. He'd shown compassion and never gave up even when he ran out of leads. He was a good man and an amazing partner.

"I'll leave you two to cuddle and go gather up the ladies. Vega wants to shoot pool. Cash is going to play here shortly. We're going to celebrate with several rounds of shots. It'll be a learning opportunity to order a car in an app." Mary winked, and we chuckled as she stood, easing into the crowd.

"Could we sneak out early, Daddy?"

"Just a little longer at the celebration, and then you and me are going home to our nice warm bed. We have a vacation to plan. Mountains with no cell reception."

"I can't wait."

Stevenson

As Doc reclined against my chest in our bed, I traced the faded scars on my baby's chest and stomach. The newest ones were finally losing that hint of red, and he caught my hand, bringing it to his mouth. I still bore the guilt of not being able to protect him the way he needed me to. He'd been on the edge of death by the time I'd found him. I'd nearly lost my freedom. If Graves hadn't stepped in to keep me from taking the kill shot, I wouldn't have stopped until the bastard was dead. As I relived that moment, I'd have had no regrets about killing Gerrickson.

"Quit, I know what's going on in your head. You came for me. I knew you would."

"I almost didn't get there in time."

"You got there, and that's all I care about, Daddy." I tried to tighten my arms as he turned over and lifted to his knees to stare at me. "I love you, and I don't want your guilt."

I never got tired of hearing him say he loved me, several pounds heavier and several more grays in my hair. He still looked at me like he did the first night we fucked. My baby had made everything better. Stripped away decades of self-loathing with three simple words.

I gripped his hips and pulled him up until he straddled my thighs and sat down. "What do you think of marriage?"

"A lovely institution but not one I need. What about you?"

"I did it once, and I wasn't happy. I'd be lucky to have you say I do, but it's not a requirement to prove how much I love you." His cheeks turned the prettiest shade of pink. "And no kids."

"That is a definite. I love being Uncle Doc, but it wouldn't be fair to a child with our schedules. With Roo and Robert and Remy's big brood of kids and grandkids, we spoil them and send them home."

"Complete agreement. Also, I'm selfish and don't want to share." I stroked his cheeks up to the sexy crinkles beside his eyes. "You're absolutely perfect, baby." I straightened as I cupped his face and brought his mouth to mine, and I met him halfway.

"No, it's the other way around. My Daddy is the sexiest man I've ever seen." He rubbed the curve of my hairy belly and tugged at the hair. My cock started to harden and he rubbed his to mine. "Daddy, your baby needs some loving."

"And as always, what does Daddy say."

"What your baby wants, he gets. You know you're going to spoil me."

"Just like my baby should be, spoiled and safe." His back arched as I stroked my hands around to the small of his back and then down to palm the lush curves of his ass.

"Daddy, can I play with my favorite toy? I'll treat it so good."

"It's all yours." My voice dipped until it was a guttural rumble. I didn't take my attention from him as he scooted back, and I shifted my legs to make room for him. "If you treat Daddy good, I'll give my baby a reward. Now suck it."

His gaze never left mine as I groaned when his small hand circled the base and lifted my cock, the head still covered with the loose foreskin. He opened wide, and I barely prepared myself before he swallowed me to the back of his throat.

"Fuck, baby, get my cock nice and wet." He eased off my dick, sucking the skin over the head. "That's right, play with it." My chest heaved as he sucked and buried his nose in my thick pubes. He opened wide to get me deeper. He sucked me off sloppy, moaning and humming. I fisted my hands in his longer hair. His eyes were closed, his little ass moving as he humped the bed.

Sweat misted my hairy skin, my breathing harsh as pleasure arched my back and curled my toes. He liked it dirty and nasty. I nearly growled as he tapped my hip, our signal that he wanted me to use him.

"Open wide for Daddy. I'm going to fill that throat until you're gagging on my cum." I roughly took his head in my hands and let go of all my control, my compulsion to treat him gently. The way I loved on him—no, that's not what my baby needed. I shifted until I moved a bit down the bed, bent my knees, and I held his head still as I fucked his beautiful, greedy mouth. Forced his throat to loosen and take the head.

I watched my length appear and disappear, spit soaking my cock and pubes. His cheeks, red and wet with tears. The more debauched he looked, the harder I took his throat. I grunted as my cock and balls ached for release. I clenched my teeth as he started letting out choked, high-pitched whines as he began to jerk himself off.

"You better swallow every fucking drop, Daddy's slutty baby." I deep stroked his mouth at an increasing pace until my hips stuttered, my rhythm changed, and I had no chance to warn him as heat infused every aching muscle. I slammed him down until I held him to take every bit of my release. His throat worked, and his back bowed upward as he choked while reaching his own pleasure.

I collapsed and released his head. Then I laid there to let him clean my cock like he always did. He said he didn't want to miss even a small taste of me. I laid there completely relaxed as I waited for my heart to slow, and I smirked as my baby licked up my belly, over my chest, and when he reached my mouth, I cupped the back of his head. I groaned at the taste of myself on his tongue.

"I love you so much, Daddy."

"I love you more than anything in the world, Morgan. You're everything I've wanted and never thought I deserved."

"But, Carter, that's where you're wrong. You deserve the world, and I'm so lucky to have a man who loves and keeps me safe."

I'd waited forty-three years to hold a man in my arms who got me. Who I didn't have to hide myself with. And to think, he'd been right in front of me all these years. I'd never take him for granted. Whatever he wanted, it was his. All my love and devotion belonged to a beautiful silver-haired man who was selfless and intelligent. I kissed him until he laid on my chest, felt his smile against my lips, and nothing in the world could be better than this.

COLD CASES AND BITTER ENEMIES

An unknown enemy wanted to take everything from us.

Graves

I'd spent all of my forty-plus years paying for mistakes when I'd simply been human. Living my life in the shadow of the happiness my friends from the Cold Case Unit found grew harder every day. I didn't mind being the odd one out; didn't mind being considered the unloveable straight-laced-ish one to their mayhem. Acceptance after a lifetime of not measuring up was nice. I'd found my rhythm and my place among the weirdness of my unit. That was until Marcel Douglas the new ego-manic in Homicide decided he had to pick apart every case I'd left behind.

Douglas

Leaving Chicago hadn't been in my plans, but my daughter needed me. I'd do about anything to make her happy. When her mother was transferred out of the States I'd moved so my daughter could stay with her friends—the place she'd come to love. Being at the bottom of the hierarchy and earning respect didn't sit right with my pride. I wasn't afraid to admit that. And

I'd made one hell of an enemy. Graves and his Cold Case Unit frustrated me and I didn't understand their method. A series of body dumps brought me back to Graves for help, but he wasn't feeling charitable.

We'd thought we were our biggest and bitterest enemies until the threats came, could we work together before the man gunning for us could finish the job?

ABOUT THE AUTHOR

Two time USA Today Bestselling author J.M. Dabney is a multi-genre published writer of Body and Fat Positive Romance & Fiction. They live with a constant diverse cast of diverse characters in their head. They live for one purpose alone, and that's to make sure everyone gets the happily ever after they deserve. There is nothing more they want from telling their stories than to show that no matter the package the characters come in or the damage their pasts have done, that love is love. That normal is never normal and sometimes the so-called broken can still be beautiful.

The author is Non-Binary and uses the pronouns They/Them.

ALSO BY J.M. DABNEY

Cold Cases Unit

Cold Cases and Second Chances

Cold Cases and Dark Secrets

Cold Cases and Bitter Enemies

Cold Cases and Bruised Hearts

Sappho's Kiss Series

When All Else Fails

More Than What They See

Dysfunction it its Finest Series

Club Revenge

Soul Collector Prophecy

Twirled World Ink Series

Berzerker

Trouble

Scary

Lucky

Brawlers Series

Crave

Psycho

Bull

Hunter

Adoring Beast

A Yuri Sorenson Mystery

Not Another Statistic

Permanent Freebies

Has the Honeymoon Ended? (Brawlers Short Valentine's Story)

Once Upon a Bear Claw

The Scars She Bears (Executioners Short)

WRITING AS SIOBHAN SMILE

Little Love

His to Own, Hers to Claim

Shug's Daddy

Mama Didn't Sign Up for This

Butcher's Babygirl

Printed in Great Britain
by Amazon

86584016R00183